PUFFIN BOOKS

Sufiya Ahmed was born in India and arrived in the UK as a baby. She lived in Bolton, Lancashire, before moving to London where she still lives. Sufiya has worked in advertising and in the House of Commons, but is now a full-time author. In 2010 Sufiya set up the BIBI Foundation, a non-profit organization, to arrange visits to the Houses of Parliament for diverse and underprivileged schoolchildren.

For further information about Sufiya and her books, the BIBI Foundation, or to arrange an event at your school, visit her online at www.bibipublishing.co.uk

spinebreakers.co.uk

Secrets
OF THE
HENNA GIRL

SUFIYA AHMED

PUFFIN

PUFFIN BOOKS

Published by the Penguin Group
Penguin Books Ltd, 80 Strand, London WC2R ORL, England
Penguin Group (USA) Inc., 375 Hudson Street, New York, New York 10014, USA
Penguin Group (Canada), 90 Eglinton Avenue East, Suite 700, Toronto, Ontario, Canada M4P 2Y3
(a division of Pearson Penguin Canada Inc.)
Penguin Ireland, 25 St Stephen's Green, Dublin 2, Ireland (a division of Penguin Books Ltd)
Penguin Group (Australia), 250 Camberwell Road, Camberwell, Victoria 3124, Australia
(a division of Pearson Australia Group Pty Ltd)
Penguin Books India Pvt Ltd, 11 Community Centre, Panchsheel Park, New Delhi – 110 017, India
Penguin Group (NZ), 67 Apollo Drive, Rosedale, Auckland 0632, New Zealand
(a division of Pearson New Zealand Ltd)
Penguin Books (South Africa) (Pty) Ltd, 24 Sturdee Avenue, Rosebank, Johannesburg 2196, South Africa

Penguin Books Ltd, Registered Offices:
80 Strand, London WC2R ORL, England

puffinbooks.com

First published 2012
004

Text copyright © Sufiya Ahmed, 2012
Map copyright © Puffin Books, 2012
All rights reserved

The moral right of the author has been asserted

Set in Sabon Mt by Palimpsest Book Production Limited, Falkirk, Stirlingshire
Printed in Great Britain by Clays Ltd, St Ives plc

Except in the United States of America, this book is sold subject to the condition that it shall not, by way
of trade or otherwise, be lent, re-sold, hired out, or otherwise circulated without the publisher's prior
consent in any form of binding or cover other than that in which it is published and without a similar
condition including this condition being imposed on the subsequent purchaser

British Library Cataloguing in Publication Data
A CIP catalogue record for this book is available from the British Library

ISBN: 978-0-141-33980-1

www.greenpenguin.co.uk

MIX
Paper from
responsible sources
FSC® C018179
www.fsc.org

Penguin Books is committed to a sustainable
future for our business, our readers and our planet.
This book is made from Forest Stewardship
Council™ certified paper.

In memory of my nannyma, Fatima Yaqub Manjra,
who wanted the world for me

United Kingdom

Pakistan

'*Obtain the virgin's consent before you marry her*'
Prophet Mohammad (pbuh)

Chapter 1

The rain was beating hard against the window. It was the typical English rain of the summer – fast and furious as it attempted to wash away the dusty, dry heat of the unbearably hot days. We had been looking forward to the predicted heat wave for weeks, but when it came it proved too much for Britain. 'It's too hot,' were the cries emanating from a people designed for the cold rather than the sun's unforgiving glare. I, too, had become frustrated, trying to find relief from the humid, sticky atmosphere that hung in every classroom and corridor of my school building. At least the teachers had arranged fans in the halls where we sat our final-year exams.

I still could not believe it; my school years were over. I was sixteen and the world was my oyster. I still had no idea what I wanted to do with my life, but my teachers anticipated a great future for me. My English teacher said my writing was exceptional and a world of opportunities lay ahead. Of course I knew education wasn't all over yet; I still had to do my A levels at college and then do a degree. It was the twenty-first century and I, Zeba Khan, would get an education just like everybody else when we returned from our summer holiday in Pakistan.

While all my friends prepared for days lazing by a pool in France, Italy or Cornwall, I was destined for my parents' homeland.

I had only ever visited Pakistan once, when I was eight. I remembered vaguely my cousin – an older boy by eight years who smiled a lot and ruffled my hair sometimes, but never had much to say to me – my dad's older brother whom I addressed by the traditional name of Taya-ji, my sweet grandmother on my mum's side and many, many servants. I did not have good memories; it had been hot, full of mosquitoes and little else.

'But it will be different this time,' my mum insisted. 'Taya-ji has installed air-conditioning and the windows are closed to the mosquitoes.'

But I had a nervous feeling about this holiday, and it had nothing to do with the temperature. I was a little afraid of Taya-ji. Known as Mustaq Khan to the world, he was a very stern man who made people quake with fear, including my dad. Whenever he visited us from Pakistan, I ceased to be my dad's little girl. Dad even stopped calling me *Rani*, the Urdu for queen. Instead he gave everyone the impression I was a responsibility, a burden because I had been born a girl. There was no doubt in my mind that Dad would revert to type in the company of his older brother and I would become a stranger to him . . . again.

'You're so lucky', my best friend Susan said, her blonde hair half covering her impish face as she peered into the suitcase of *salwar kameezes* – traditional trouser suits. 'The weatherman said we've had all the sun and from now on it will only rain. Typical English weather. At least you'll be able to come back with a tan.'

I gave Susan a small smile, but said nothing. My best friend since our first day at nursery and yet she still didn't understand some things about me. Get a tan? I was an Asian girl with creamy, fair skin that my mum was extremely proud of. It was what got me noticed at weddings and parties by the buxom aunties peering at the new stock of teenage girls who would one day become the wives of their sons. I glanced in the mirror and a brown-haired teenager with dark eyes, a straight nose and prominent chin stared back at me. Many aunties had already commented on my lack of fragile beauty, instead placing me in the 'will do' category: good strong bones, child-bearing hips and sparkling skin. It had been made clear to me a very long time ago that my outer dermis was my saving grace, and so like every insecure girl possessive of her one good quality, I tried to avoid the sun as much as Susan tried to bask in it.

The rain suddenly died down. The clouds disappeared as quickly as they had gathered and the sun's shy beams began to peep through. I scrambled to my feet and urged Susan up by grabbing both her hands.

'Let's go for a walk,' I said, suddenly desperate to get out and feel the clean air before I was forced to endure Pakistan's engulfing heat.

Susan pulled a face but followed me anyway, and as we passed the kitchen my mum emerged.

'Where are you going?' she demanded, pushing a strand of black hair off her forehead with hands covered in chapatti flour.

'Just for a walk,' I replied, surprised. What was the big deal? It was only after three in the afternoon.

'Zeba, we are leaving tonight for Pakistan. I don't want you disappearing.'

'I'm going around the block,' I protested. 'We'll be back in about fifteen minutes.'

A range of expressions crossed Mum's face. She was only twenty-two years older than me and we were often mistaken for sisters, but there was nothing friendly about our relationship. She was my mother, fully in charge of me, and she never let me forget it.

'I'm not sure. Eh . . . Zeba's daddy,' Mum called out to my dad, who was in the living room.

Susan giggled next to me. She had always thought it was hilarious how my mum could never bring herself to call her own husband by his name, Kamran. I had tried to explain to Susan that this was our culture. Women respected their husbands and it was disrespectful to say their names aloud. I tried to justify it by adding that it wasn't just the Pakistanis like us who did it. The Arabs did it too by using the word 'Abu' in front of the eldest child's name. So if your child was called Adam then the father would be known as Abu Adam. It was such a common practice that I had noticed Middle Eastern leaders being referred to as Abu this and Abu that by journalists on the news.

My dad stuck his head out of the living-room door, a look of annoyance on his normally happy, smiling face. 'What does a man have to do for some peace and quiet, eh?' he barked, shattering the tranquillity himself.

Susan and I stared at him, a little shocked by his aggressive manner. Normally, my dad would invite us both into the living room and entertain us with amusing stories about his customers. It was a set routine from as far back as I can remember. Dad owned a small grocery store on the high street and he always had funny stories about his regulars – from the man who insisted on buying identically sized carrots to the woman who bored him with exaggerated tales of her doctor son. Then he would switch the conversation to us, mocking and teasing us about our taste in music, or the latest Saturday-night programme we were addicted to. He would compare the 'dumb-down culture' as he liked to call it, to the wondrous words of Muhammad Iqbal, Pakistan's national poet who was long dead.

Susan and I would laugh and reply 'whatever' and he would point at me and tell Susan that I was his favourite *Rani*. I would respond that I was his only *Rani* as he had no other children. Then Dad would tut at me and say that Susan was like his daughter too. Susan would grin and say 'whatever' again, but really she would be secretly pleased. Her father had left a long time ago, unable to cope with the demands of a wife and two daughters under the age of five.

'Nighat?' Dad barked out Mum's name.

That was another thing Susan found strange. How was it that the men were allowed to call out their wives' names? Did the women not deserve the same respect? I didn't know the answer and had to satisfy her with my usual blanket response to all her questions: it was our culture.

'Zeba wants to go out,' Mum sniffed.

'So let her have her last moments of freedom!' Dad snapped, slamming the door shut and causing the three of us to jump.

'Very well,' Mum conceded, her features pulled together tightly in a pinched look. 'Be back in fifteen minutes.'

'What's up with them?' Susan asked, as I closed the front door behind us.

I shrugged my shoulders. I had no idea. Both my parents

had been acting very strangely since they had announced the trip two weeks ago. Their conversations were all about Pakistan, and from the little bits that I caught they were either about our relatives, or about the endless suicide bombs that were going off in the cities and at the army barracks. More disturbing, however, was Dad's behaviour. A black cloud seemed to have descended on him and he was short-tempered with everyone, including his beloved customers. Just the other day I'd seen him shout at an Asian lady for the crime of rummaging through a box of coriander for the freshest bundle.

Susan and I walked along the road in silence. We were good like that. We could spend hours in each other's company without feeling the need to say anything. We turned a corner at the end of the road and came across a group of girls from our year. Our school year was over, but they had returned to wait with bags of flour for the Year Eleven boys from the nearby academy. It was all so predictable. Both sides would egg and flour each other until the neighbourhood elderly would emerge, outraged at the mess on their street. They would then call the police and everyone would flee.

Susan and I thought the girls were just desperate for some attention from the boys. It was as though their lives had no purpose unless they were being harassed. Susan and I were going to wait for our true love. Of course, we would find the boy of our dreams when we were travelling the world or working in our top professional jobs. We were special and we were going to wait for someone better than a spotty boy from Norland Boys' Academy.

'So you going to email me, Zee?' Susan asked.

'I'll try,' I answered, not sure if there was a computer in my taya'ji's house. 'But it's not a very advanced village. It's in a really remote part of western Pakistan.'

Susan shot me an envious look. 'It sounds really adventurous. I might travel across Pakistan in my gap year. You know, see the authentic Pakistan, the real people.'

I shrugged. It always amazed me how indigenous English people thought everything foreign was exotic, with an air of glamour. I knew that Pakistan was far from exotic. I couldn't see what was glamorous for the millions of poor people who lived in mud huts, or pulled water from a well, or were denied an education and free healthcare.

We continued walking to the small park at the end of the road and, finding it empty, I grabbed a swing. The seat felt wet through my jeans, not yet dry from the rainstorm. Susan chose to stand by the side, her expression making it clear that she was not going to join me. I didn't care and pushed my feet against the ground so that I could soar in the air. To some people perhaps the view from the highest point of the swing might have appeared dull. Row upon row of brown brick houses with black slate roofs, and then sprawling far, far into the distance England's hills. Yorkshire hills. This was my home; this small English town was where I belonged, tucked away in the valleys of my country, and the thought of leaving it, even for four weeks, filled me with dread. Unfortunately I had no alternative.

Chapter 2

The giant wheels of the Boeing 747 screeched to a halt on Karachi's runway.

Letting out a sigh of relief that we were back on the ground after the eight-hour flight, I rested my head against the seat to watch the commotion around me. Half the passengers had jumped to their feet in a clamour to get to the luggage stored in the overhead compartments. The pilot had not yet turned off the seatbelt sign, but people didn't seem to care. I wondered if it was because they couldn't wait to see loved ones in the terminal, or if some were just anxious to get home. Suddenly I felt sick at the thought of home. I did not want to be here. I wanted to be in my house with Susan, listening to our favourite music and dancing around the bedroom pretending we were at a live gig.

As a Muslim I was not allowed to go to pop concerts, and I was always so jealous of Susan, who had been given the freedom to do pretty much whatever she wanted since she had turned fourteen. The funny thing was, apart from the odd concert she went to with her older sister, Susan was happiest hanging out with me in my bedroom. We would spend hours surfing the internet, watching DVDs, reading books or just talking about how successful we were going to be when we grew up. I realized I was going to be bored on this holiday. How was I going to pass the time in a tiny village in the middle of nowhere? I was quite sure that I would be brain-dead by the time we boarded a flight for home.

'Zeba.'

I turned in the direction of Mum's voice. She was indicating to me to follow her example and, aware of what was expected of me in Pakistani society, I raised the shawl hanging loosely on my shoulders to hide my hair from view.

I wondered how long we would have to remain in what now seemed to be an overcrowded cabin as people stood in the aisle, avoiding eye contact so they would have no qualms about shoving each other out of the way. Suddenly a dry, overwhelming heat blasted us and I knew the cabin doors had opened.

About forty minutes later, as my parents and I emerged from the Jinnah International airport's glass doors, Taya-ji and countless other men rushed forward to hug my dad. In a manner that can only be described as dutiful, Mum and I stood to the side and watched this male bonding, which centred on the two brothers. Physically they could not be more different. My dad has a slight build and a friendly demeanour, whereas Taya-ji is a big man, well over six feet tall and with a huge pot belly. He looks fierce with his scowling face and air of impatience, and I did not think there would be many who would cross him willingly, not in this country anyway.

Two years ago Taya-ji had visited us in London and Susan had caught a glimpse of him one morning when she had knocked for me on the way to school. She had laughed hysterically outside my front door at the man who was feared in the twenty villages of his local district. The reason had been his moustache – the thick patch of black hair on his upper lip styled against gravity into an uplifted curl at the corners of his mouth. Susan had found it comical, but I knew from what my dad had told me that Taya-ji's moustache was a sign of his masculinity, wealth and status in Pakistan's rural society.

At that point I had wondered what the Pakistani people thought of my dad with his clean-shaven face. Perhaps their view was similar to Taya-ji's, which erred on the side of disappointment. Taya-ji made no secret of the fact that he thought Dad 'wasn't man enough' – whatever that meant – and not because of the absence of whiskers on his upper lip, but because Dad had chosen a simple life as a grocer, rejecting what Taya-ji regarded as the reasons for existence: power and influence.

On his last visit, I'd heard Taya-ji mock my dad in front of other relatives at a wedding. 'My brother spends his day selling vegetables to women,' he'd said. Dad had joined in the nervous laughter, but I was convinced there was hurt in his eyes. Even back then I could see my father possessed something Taya-ji could never have – dignity.

'Zeba!'

My taya-ji's voice boomed loudly as his attention finally moved away from his younger brother to focus on me.

'Come here!'

I took a hesitant step forward, my eyes darting nervously towards my dad who gave me an encouraging smile. I expected Taya-ji to grab me in a crushing hug, but he stopped two steps short to beam down at me, his fierce scowl momentarily disappearing. I stared up at him with a weak smile. On my last visit

I had been eight years old and Taya-ji had swung me up into his arms. I still remember bursting into tears and pleading to be put down by this scary giant, all of which had been to no avail. He might not be swinging me in his arms this time, but I was still intimidated.

Suddenly, a skinny man appeared with a garland of lilies. Snatching the flowers, Taya-ji placed them around my neck.

'Welcome, *beti*.'

My smile widened at Taya-ji as the fresh fragrant smell of the lilies invaded my nostrils. He had just called me 'daughter' in Urdu.

Taya-ji's attention then turned to Mum who had been standing to the side, a stiff, awkward smile on her lips. A second garland of lilies magically appeared to be placed around her neck.

'Nighat!' Taya-ji declared, still beaming. '*Mubarak!*'

Mum repeated the Urdu word of congratulation back to her brother-in-law, her expression more relaxed now. I watched the exchange with puzzlement. Why were Mum and Taya-ji congratulating each other? What was that all about? However, before I had a chance to ask, Mum and I were bundled into one of five Land Rovers pulled up outside the terminal and Taya-ji began to talk loudly to Dad about the latest numbers of soldiers killed in gunfire. Sitting there listening to his frightening talk, I felt glad to be cocooned in the bullet-proof vehicle that would take us across the smooth highways, and then along the rough, rocky roads to the distant rural village in the province of Sindh.

I stared out of the window at this country, which had been created just over sixty years ago. My dad had made sure I knew its history well. The great, big subcontinent that lies in the Indian Ocean had been divided into two when the British Empire had come to an end in 1945. Mahatma Gandhi, the pacifist, had been the leader of the Indians, later assassinated by his own countrymen, and Mohammad Ali Jinnah, known as Quaid-e-Azam, meaning 'great leader', was the father of Pakistan. My father had explained how both men had been educated in England. Gandhi was a graduate of University College London and Jinnah a student of law at Lincoln's Inn.

'It was in this free, progressive country that these two prominent statesmen of the twentieth century learned about the everlasting principles of freedom and justice – ironically, the very motivators for their campaign to end the British occupation of India.'

I'd just nodded my head, preferring not to get roped into one of my father's educational lectures. In junior school we were once taught about the British Empire and its evils by a temporary teacher. Mr Parker was a scruffy, middle-aged man who told us that money was the root of all evil. He'd also kept going on about how awful imperialism was and how we should never be allowed to forget it. Staring gloomily at the Afro-Caribbean and Asian students, he'd kept saying: 'And your people suffered. You were torn from your roots.'

We had just stared at him blankly until Krishna, an extremely clever Hindu boy, had put his hand up to say, 'Uh, sir, but we were born here.'

Suffice it to say that Mr Parker did not return to our school, not after Krishna's mum had met with the headteacher anyway. And that was all I knew about the British Empire: that it had not been very nice, its collapse was the reason why Pakistan was now the second biggest homeland to Muslims after Indonesia, and that India was the homeland to just under a billion Hindus.

But I didn't think the religious divide was as clear-cut as that, which was confirmed to me on a visit from one of my dad's uncles. Imran-chacha was a retired Pakistani army officer, funny and charming, who had moved to Dubai with his new wife. He had lots of adventure stories to share about his past, including the one about when he'd been a bomber pilot in the 1971 India-Pakistan war.

'I stared down at this enemy territory and I knew I had to annihilate them before they did it to us,' Imran-chacha had said, smoking a cigar in our living room. 'But as I looked down, you know what I saw? I saw the domes and minarets of mosques in northern India. I had been sent to bomb a Muslim neighbourhood.'

'What did you do, Imran-chacha,' I'd asked eagerly, convinced he had turned his plane around and saved hundreds of lives.

'I released the bombs, of course,' he'd replied forcefully. 'I was a soldier. My job was to follow orders.'

'But they were Muslims,' I'd gasped. 'You killed Muslims?'

Imran-chacha had eyed me pityingly from behind the veil of smoke.

'Zeba,' he'd explained patiently, 'I know there are as many Muslims residing in India as there are in our pure land. But these people are the citizens of an enemy nation. In war you do not look at a person's religious beliefs, you look at whether they are siding with the enemy.'

I had wanted to reply that I didn't think those poor people would have had much influence on whether their country entered a war or not, but I had said nothing, noting my mum's stern expression warning me not to question an elder.

Now, gazing out of the comfortable, air-conditioned vehicle, I was fascinated to see that the further we travelled, the less developed our surroundings became. Townships of brick houses began to be replaced by huddled mud huts and cars were parked side by side with animal-drawn carts. At one point we were reduced to a snail's pace as grazing cows wandered on to the road. Women and young girls walked alongside the car, carrying bales of hay or clay water-pots on their heads. They were dressed in loose-fitting *salwar kameez*es and their *ajrak* shawls covered them from head to waist.

Seeing the elaborately patterned shawls reminded me of home again. The *ajrak* cloth with its distinctive printed designs was a symbol of the Sindh region, and we had an indigo-coloured shawl displayed proudly on the wall above the TV in our living room. In England you could tell a Sindhi wedding because the male guests wore *ajrak* caps and the women *ajrak* shawls. My father once explained to me that it was one of the things that distinguished us, the Sindhis, from the people of the other three regions of Pakistan: the Punjab, Balochistan and the North-West Frontier Province. There was a lot that separated the people of Pakistan. The first was language. Although Urdu was spoken nationally, each region had its own local language. Ours was Sindhi and I spoke it as well as I did Urdu, but I couldn't read either of them; the beautiful shapes and squiggles of the written language were just patterns to me. My dad had thought it was important for me to be able to recite the poetry of Muhammad Iqbal as well as the language of his ancestors so I had learned to speak them both. Hindi came more naturally to me because Bollywood films were always watched in our house.

The second thing that separated the people of the different regions was our facial features, which we had inherited from invading ancestors ranging from the Mongols to the Arabs and the Turks. I wasn't quite sure who my forefathers had been and quite frankly I didn't care. I was happy to be British.

Despite the differences, I was beginning to see that there was one thing that was common in the rural parts of the entire country – and that was guns.

The deadly items were a feature that became more and more visible the further we travelled into the landscape. They were openly displayed: shotguns slung over shoulders or handguns tucked into the waistbands of trousers. It was like venturing into a Wild West movie, except the guns were not props and the men were no actors. I turned my head to stare behind at the four other vehicles following us. They were filled with the men who had greeted my dad at the airport. I had no doubt that more than a few, if not all, were in possession of handguns.

Five hours later, when our convoy finally drove into my ancestral village, the fascination with what Susan would have termed 'authenticity' had somewhat worn off. Tired and hungry, I decided that when I got home I would explain to Susan that poverty was not something to be admired.

Chapter 3

My taya-ji's house stood on its own in the middle of a field. The white structure was big and modern, and very different from the handful of modest houses located about a quarter of a mile away, where small traders like the grocer, the baker and other shopkeepers lived. The five small shops were lined up in the lane behind their houses and provided the basic needs of the villagers. I suppose their main customers were the peasants who lived in a huddle of mud huts about five minutes away.

Another feature that separated Taya-ji's house from the traders was that he had not built a compound wall around the building. It was another of his status symbols; no imposter would dare breach the invisible boundary surrounding the house if he valued his life. My dad had once explained to me that Taya-ji's wealth and high status came from his role as a fixer for the landlord; he enforced the landlord's will, just as his father and his father before him had done so. I think my business studies teacher would have described it as executive management of the property-owning class.

Taya-ji's house would have been the biggest in the village had it not been for the local landlord's residence. The *haveli*, which could only be described as a mini-palace, was a dusky rose colour – a monstrosity lying in the middle of the green fields on the other side of the village. The tacky structure loomed over the nearby mud huts where the peasants lived. Setting foot here was like stepping back five hundred years. Susan would have loved it.

When Taya-ji had pointed out the landlord's house, I had let out an involuntary giggle. The man was Taya-ji's best friend and his name was Sher Shah – 'Sher' meaning tiger in Urdu and 'Shah' the Persian for king. I found it ridiculous that a man would allow himself to be called 'Tiger King'. I mean what were his parents thinking when they named him? A tiger was a hunter – a selfish killer that inspired fear. Why would anyone curse their child with a name like that?

As we walked up to Taya-ji's house, a welcoming party of relatives and village residents rushed forward to greet us. My dad was led away by the men and Mum and I were left to be met by Taya-ji's wife, Mariam-chachi. A short, round woman dressed in crimson, she was standing at the centre of a crowd of women and girls from the village, who had been waiting to receive us in the traditional manner. The wives and daughters of the village's grocer, butcher, tailor and others took turns to place garlands made up of lilies, jasmine and roses around our necks. Within minutes our chins disappeared from view behind the layers of flowers and I smiled shyly at everyone around me. It was actually really nice to be made to feel so welcome and, in the hustle and bustle of the villagers trying to touch me, I felt like a Bollywood star being greeted by fans.

Moments later, a pathway was cleared from the mass of bodies and Mum and I were led through the house into the open courtyard at its centre. There, waiting for us, was my maternal grandmother, Nannyma, who had been invited to the house to welcome us.

'*As salaam alaikum*,' she greeted us, using the Islamic words of welcome.

'*Wa alaikum salaam*,' Mum and I responded together.

My only living grandparent was a tiny woman with silver hair scraped back into a bun at the nape of her neck. Nannyma's actual name was Fatima and she had an air about her that defined dignity, charm and kindness, a combination that set her apart from all the other women in the courtyard, particularly my mother. Perhaps it was because she was regarded as an elderly maternal figure of the village that Nannyma carried herself with such confidence. Or maybe it was because she was also a landowner. Nannyma owned a small plot of land which she had inherited from her husband on his death. The land was independent of that which was owned by the main landlord, and she didn't control any livelihoods, but it still gave her status in the village; they all paid attention when she spoke, including the men. I had warmed to her immediately on my previous visit, and the same was true now.

When we had freshened up and eaten lunch, Nannyma invited me to sit next to her on a traditional wooden swing. Silver rods poked out of the ceiling to hold in place the smooth wooden seat that was three feet in length. Three people could sit comfortably on it all day long if they wanted to. Other women and girls were gathered around her chatting.

I sat down next to Nannyma and immediately began to enjoy the gentle swaying.

'Tell me, Zeba,' she asked, 'how are your studies?'

I looked up in surprise at the question. The only interest my other relatives had shown in me so far was centred on my physical appearance, and the fact that I had grown so much since my last visit.

'I've sat my exams and I'm waiting for the results,' I said clearly in Urdu.

A girl who looked about my age giggled. What had I said that was so amusing?

'Oh, English girl,' she explained as I looked at her, perplexed. 'It doesn't matter what your results will be. You need to be more concerned about passing other exams.'

'What?' I stared at the girl as she began to giggle again, an irritating noise, which was so contagious that three other girls joined in. I glanced around the room and it seemed all the women were in on the joke too. I managed a weak smile and turned back to Nannyma, who was studying me with a concerned look.

'They have not yet told you, have they, child?'

'Told me what?'

Nannyma reached forward and let the palm of her old hand smooth my forehead. It was an act of love, I knew that from the emotion that shone in her eyes, but I also knew the reason behind it was sympathy. This old lady felt sorry for me. But why?

Suddenly, a commotion broke out in the room. The women and girls all straightened their shawls and flicked away imaginary specks of dust from their clothes. It seemed they were standing to attention like soldiers ready for inspection: eager, nervous and a little in awe.

When the object of their excitement walked in, I wanted to

laugh out loud. I had been spot-on with my perception of them as eager soldiers because the man who walked in was an officer in the Pakistan army. It was Asif, my cousin and Taya-ji's only son.

Dressed in his country's uniform, twenty-four-year-old Asif cut a stern figure as he marched into the room. Some of the girls giggled, but the nervous laughter stopped immediately when he glanced their way in irritation. My cousin was a younger, slimmer version of his father, without the gravity-defying moustache, but with the same air of impatience.

'We have been waiting for you, Asif,' Mariam-chachi cried, hurrying towards her son. 'Come and meet Nighat-chachi.'

Asif approached my mum and she reached up to pat him awkwardly on the shoulder.

'Now meet Zeba,' Mariam-chachi said.

Asif turned towards the swing and stared down at me. His gaze was direct, unflinching, and then a small curl of a smile appeared on his face. It seemed to transform him from a hard army man to the boy I had known on my last visit here – the teenager who was always smiling and laughing.

I smiled back, happy at a vague memory of him ruffling my hair.

The giggling started again and Asif's stern face reappeared. Excusing himself, he left to rejoin the men in the front of the house.

'You are so lucky, Zeba-ji,' said one of the girls. 'Asif-ji will one day become a general in our army.'

I looked at the girl who had spoken. She was still staring at the door through which Asif has disappeared, and I sensed that she had a crush on the village's very own hero. I wondered at her comment about how lucky I was. I supposed that for the villagers, anyone in Asif's family would be seen to benefit from his status.

The guests stayed for another hour and then left in small groups as the sun began to set. The welcome party was coming to an end and I was glad because I was exhausted. I sat back and watched the room empty until only Mariam-chachi and Nannyma remained with Mum and me. The four of us sat, me and my mother facing Nannyma and Mariam-chachi on opposite sofas, each waiting for another to break the silence.

I looked at my relatives, each one seemingly lost in her own thoughts. I found it strange that my mum was not sitting next to Nannyma, chatting away about this and that after their years of being apart. The atmosphere between them seemed strained. Earlier in the evening I'd seen them exchanging heated words in another room as I'd passed on my way to the loo. But I hadn't been able to hear what they were saying and I didn't want to get caught eavesdropping. By the time I came back they were back in the main gathering talking to different people.

Now my mum was doing her best to avoid Nannyma's eyes, as was Mariam-chachi, while the old lady sat there with an uncharacteristically grim expression on her face.

We continued to sit silently for another five minutes and then Asif walked in. He sat down beside his mum, who leaned over and began to stroke his hair. It was a bit odd and I didn't know where to look. Mariam-chachi was treating her son as if he were a five-year-old.

'My *beta*, why do you spend so much time away from your mother?' Mariam-chachi asked dotingly.

Asif smiled. 'You know I have to, Mummy-ji. Our country needs me.'

Mariam-chachi's mouth set in a firm line and she didn't say anything.

'Mummy-ji, don't sulk,' Asif teased, grabbing his mother's hands to kiss them.

I couldn't help staring at the pair of them. I'd never seen a mother and son act so affectionately towards each other. Perhaps I found it strange because my own mum was so aloof with me most of the time. But even so, they were acting like something out of the Bollywood movies Susan and I watched and danced along to, where a son was always the centre of a mother's life.

'*Beta*,' Mariam-chachi said, stroking Asif's hair again. 'You know I worry about you every minute of every hour when you are away with the army. I can't help it. It is a mother's love.'

'Mummy-ji,' Asif said quietly. 'You know as a soldier I am not just your son. All the nation's women are my mothers. I have to protect them all.'

'Asif, you are *my* son!' Mariam-chachi insisted.

Something seemed to snap in Asif and he leaned forward, away from his mother's hands. 'How many times will you do this?' he spat. 'You burden me with all this worry. I need to think clearly when I am away!'

Mariam-chachi's lips trembled, but she didn't say anything.

'Asif,' my nannyma said firmly. 'Your mother was merely expressing her worries. It does not befit a soldier to be so disrespectful to elders, let alone a parent.'

Asif immediately looked sheepish and grabbed his mum's hands again to kiss them over and over in apology. All I could do was stare at the spectacle in front of me and shift uncomfortably in my seat. There was clearly an ongoing battle of wills between Asif and his mum – she obviously didn't approve of his career, whereas he seemed to relish it.

I looked at my mum to find her staring at Mariam-chachi and her son. Perhaps it was my imagination, but I was sure I saw envy in her eyes. I wondered if my mum regretted not having a son of her own, one who would kiss her hands to apologize for his shortness instead of a daughter who stormed out of the room as I had been known to do.

Asif seemed to notice my mum's wide-eyed stare because he turned to her. 'You must be tired, Nighat-chachi,' he said. 'Perhaps you should rest. It's been a long day.'

My mum smiled slightly as if in agreement, but made no effort to get up.

'What about you?' Asif said to me.

I nodded my head. 'Yes, I'm very tired actually. Perhaps I can be shown to my room.'

Asif moved forward as if to get up, but he was held back by his mum.

'No!' she declared. 'You stay here. No need for you to accompany Zeba. I will take her.'

Asif blushed a deep crimson and flopped back on to the sofa just as Mariam-chachi got up. For a man who was used to giving orders in the army, it must have been humiliating to have been put in his place by his mother not once, but twice. I gave him what I hoped was a reassuring smile.

Half an hour later I lay down on the low, wide bed in the guest room. The deafening silence of the village rang in my ears, reminding me just how far I was from the constant noise that came with living in a town. Going over the day's events in my mind as I drifted off, I couldn't help wondering what my mother and Nannyma had been arguing about and what was the cause of the obvious tension between the women in Taya-ji's house.

Chapter 4

Taya-ji's house had a large rooftop garden containing a range of expensive plants, ornaments and garden furniture. It was empty during the day because the sun was so hot, but the evenings were very different. With the sun's beams shining on the opposite side of the world, the rooftop was usually a place of cool calm and tranquillity . . . but the day after we arrived, it became the place where my world was shattered.

After a day of unpacking and reading my book in the shade, I was now perched on a wooden swing at the garden's centre, pushing with my feet so that I could feel the cool breeze. My parents were sitting opposite me on a bench, their faces grim. I gazed at my dad, noting the new lines that had appeared almost overnight on his forehead. What was he so stressed about? This was a holiday!

'The engagement with Asif will take place next week.'

It was my dad who spoke the words, calmly and firmly, in contrast to his tortured expression.

A butterfly started to flutter in my stomach. 'What engagement?' I whispered.

My parents exchanged a brief look.

'Your engagement,' my mum said casually.

'My engagement?' I echoed blankly, halting the swing's movements with my feet.

'Zeba, don't act dumb!' my dad snapped harshly, his voice finally giving up the pretence that everything was fine.

Dumb? Huh? Engagement?

'Zeba,' my mum said quietly. 'We have arranged for you to be married to Asif. Taya-ji wants it and so do we.'

For a few seconds I stared at Mum and then I opened my mouth, but no words came out. My throat was suddenly dry and my tongue felt numb. *Find your voice*, my head screamed. *Find your voice!*

'I don't want to marry Asif,' I finally managed to blurt out.

My dad rose to his feet slowly and glared down at me. 'Do not make this more difficult than it has to be,' he rasped through gritted teeth. 'In our family, girls do what they are told. Marriages are arranged by fathers. I have given my brother my word. It is my honour and your honour to accept.'

Honour?

'You're playing a trick on me, right?' I pleaded, trying in vain to search his face for a sign of my real father, the funny, relaxed man who doted on me, his *Rani*. Who was this imposter? 'This is a joke,' I said. 'Not a nice one, or a funny one, but a joke, right?'

My dad's furious kick sent a small table flying. I flinched and stared at him in shock, my mind yelling at me to flee the roof-top, but my body was unable to move. So this was how a rabbit felt when it froze in the glare of an approaching car's headlights.

'You will marry Asif!' my father shouted. 'That is my wish. Final!' Then he stormed off.

I sprang up and ran to my mum, burying my head in her lap. This was all crazy. My dad was like a man possessed. So what if Taya-ji wanted this marriage. It should not be his will that mattered, but mine. Why was Dad doing this? Why didn't he stand up to Taya-ji and put my wishes first? Surely my mother would understand.

My mum lifted my face off her lap and wiped my tears. 'Zeba,' she said quietly. 'We are women. We carry the honour of our fathers and husbands. We must do as they say. It has always been the way. Don't fight it.'

Accept it? 'No!' I cried.

'Look at me and your dad,' she persisted. 'Our marriage was arranged. We are happy. You will be too.'

'But I don't *want* to marry Asif,' I sobbed. 'I don't like him.'

'Love will grow after the wedding,' my mum explained, an impatient edge in her voice now.

'But I'm too young to get married!' I insisted. 'I'm sixteen. I want to go to college and university, not get married and have babies!'

My mum pushed me away and stood up. 'You have been spoiled!' she snapped, taking her turn as a parent to glare down at me. 'We have given you everything you have ever wanted. Now it is your turn to honour us.'

'No!' I cried loudly.

'Yours was a difficult birth, Zeba,' she spat out icily. 'You spoilt my chances of having any more children. You have to do this for me and Daddy.'

I stared at Mum horrified. I couldn't believe she was throwing that at me now. All my life my mum had placed emphasis on my duty and it all stemmed from the fact that I had not had an easy birth. It was a cultural thing: you owed the woman who pushed you out, and that debt would be collected one day. She often described it as a stormy night: lightning, thunder, rain and contractions that were crippling her. In the end they'd had to grab my little head with those things that look like giant salad spoons to pull me out. I was always sure my mum had confused it with the births that took place in Bollywood movies where an abandoned woman was giving birth in the opening scene. I mean how many storms did England have in June?

'Mum!' I cried, appalled at her use of emotional blackmail for doing the most natural thing in the world. 'How could you blame me for that?'

But I had no effect on her. The expression on her face was as hard as nails as she too turned and walked out.

Alone, the tears started and they did not stop. I could not believe this was happening to me.

I wasn't Pakistani . . . not in the real sense. I didn't live here. I wasn't born here. Why me? I did not love Asif. I barely even knew him. Not to mention the fact he was eight years older than me. I was going to be somebody important one day. I was supposed to be getting an education . . . Tears of frustration and rage flowed freely.

I remained on the rooftop by myself for hours. Nobody came to see if I was all right. It seemed they had left me to cry by myself. I could just imagine my mum explaining to Mariam-chachi to leave me be until I came to my senses. But I did not come to my senses. Far from it. Once the shock of the situation had eased, I threw the most vicious tantrum, kicking and smashing everything in sight as a red mist descended, causing me to act completely deranged. In no time Mariam-chachi's precious plants were turned over, the expensive furniture kicked and dented and the glass vases smashed.

I hated them!

I hated Pakistan!

At some point in the night I fell asleep from exhaustion and the next thing I knew, I was jolted awake at the sound of the muezzin's *adhan*. It was the call for prayer just before dawn. The voice was clear and crisp, the loudspeaker of the mosque succeeding in its task to wake anyone who was not shielded by steel walls. I raised my shawl, which had fallen off in my sleep, to my head, and listened quietly to the Arabic words that are used by Muslims all over the world.

Allahu Akbar, Allahu Akbar
Allahu Akbar, Allahu Akbar

Ash-had al-la ilaha illallah
Ash-had al-la ilaha illallah
Ash-hadu anna Muhammadan rasulullah
Ash-hadu anna Muhammadan rasulullah
Hayyal ala salahh, Hayya ala salahh
Hayya ala l'falah, Hayya ala l'falah
Allahu Akbar, Allahu Akbar
La ilaha illallah

I knew the translation in English. It meant:

God is Great, God is Great
God is Great, God is Great
I bear witness that there is no God except the One God

I bear witness that there is no God except the One
    God
I bear witness that Mohammad is God's messenger
I bear witness that Mohammad is God's messenger
Come to prayer, come to prayer
Come to success, come to success
God is Great, God is Great
There is no God except the One God.

When the muezzin's final words died away, it was eerily quiet again. It was still dark and I raised my head a little to peer out over the empty space surrounding Taya-ji's house. There was nothing out there but darkness and I suddenly felt scared as childhood stories of demons and ghosts sprang into my mind.

Jumping to my feet, I ran across the rooftop to the stairs, avoiding the broken shards of glass on the floor. Taking two steps at a time, I almost fell down the narrow stairwell and into the deserted hallway of the top floor. Using my hands to guide me in the dark, I managed to find my way to my bedroom. I climbed under the sheets and pulled them up to my chin. Keeping my eyes wide open, I counted the seconds until they drifted into long minutes and then finally the sun came up, and a cock began to crow somewhere nearby. With the rays of light beaming into my room, I finally relaxed and my mind fell through darkened tunnels into a deep and exhausted sleep.

It didn't last long. I was jolted awake again, but this time by the shrieking voice of Mariam-chachi, who had discovered my handiwork on her rooftop.

Calmer now than I had been last night, I felt a little ashamed of my behaviour. *Perhaps I should make my way to the rooftop and apologize*, I thought, but that idea didn't last very long when she stormed into my room like a raging bull.

Mariam-chachi was a round woman with a podgy face to match. When I had greeted her yesterday, I had marvelled at how the folds of her cheeks were so fleshy that they almost succeeded in hiding her small eyes. Today, however, her brown eyes had lasered through the flesh to flash angrily at me.

'What did you think you were doing?' she screamed at me.

I stared at her, trembling slightly. I had known even in my rage last night that I would have to pay for my actions, but I had expected the fury to come from my parents, not Taya-ji's equally scary wife.

'Answer me! You have broken the Mughal table. It was an antique item from Shah Jahan's time, the emperor who built the Taj Mahal. Do you know how expensive that was? I bought it from an old aristocratic woman selling her family's fortune to survive. Shipped from Agra . . .'

She halted in her tirade at the sight of my grinning face. I couldn't help it. Her reference to the table made me want to laugh hysterically. I wanted to tell her that Dad was actually the one responsible for that bit of vandalism. But I didn't get the chance because my parents rushed into the room, followed by Taya-ji.

'Mariam-bhabi, I'm so sorry, let us handle this,' my dad hurriedly apologized, respectfully adding the Urdu word for elder sister-in-law to her name.

'What kind of children do you raise in the UK?' she spat.

My dad visibly winced and I felt a touch of regret at what

I had done; I had not been raised to rampage around other people's houses.

'Come, Mariam,' Taya-ji said firmly.

Taya-ji and Mariam-chachi left the room and I sucked in my breath, ready for the onslaught of parental rage. But it never came.

Instead my dad said quietly, 'We have decided that you will live with Nannyma until the wedding. The engagement is put off for now as Asif has been called for emergency army duty. You also need the time and space to get used to the idea.'

I stared up at him, aghast.

'My word is final,' he added, and left the room, leaving me alone with Mum.

'You know, Zeba,' she said icily, 'that Mariam-bhabi has always thought of herself as a better daughter-in-law than me. It is sad that this is how you repay my gift of bringing you into the world, by showing me up in front of her.'

'Mum,' I pleaded, wanting her to stop.

'No, Zeba,' she continued, ruthless in her condemnation. 'Today has confirmed to her that she is better because you are my daughter. And, for once, I agree with her.' And without another word she left the room.

Chapter 5

I left later that day for Nannyma's house. Taya-ji and my dad had gone into the city for some business while Mariam-chachi exacted her revenge for the precious vases and plants.

The house servant Feroz-baba, an old stooped man, heaved my suitcase downstairs and I smiled gratefully at him, wishing I had dragged the case down myself. In Pakistan the male servants have 'baba' added to their names and the females the word 'bhaji', as a mark of respect to people who are older. Urdu is a language that commands respect between its speakers, but I found it strange that the very same people thought it was acceptable for an elderly person to lift heavy luggage when he could barely hold himself upright. Noting my embarrassment and my gratitude, the corners of Feroz-baba's mouth lifted slightly in acknowledgment before he began to walk away.

'Where are you going?' Mariam-chachi's shrill voice sounded behind me.

'To Nannyma's,' I said quietly, still feeling a little ashamed.

'Not you! Him!' Mariam-chachi declared, glaring at Feroz-baba. 'You need to put her luggage in the cart. Hurry up.'

Cart? I turned around and walked through the front door

into the evening warmth to find an ox cart parked outside. As I had witnessed on my journey to the village less than two days ago, it was not unusual to find transport pulled by animals in the poorer, rural parts of Pakistan. The ox – a sturdy, white, field-labour animal – pulled a cart made entirely of entwined wood, held up on four big wheels.

My mum emerged, ready to accompany me to her mother's house. 'Shall we go?'

I nodded and swung my handbag on to the cart, and jumped on the back. Feroz-baba had already lifted my suitcase with the help of the driver, another elderly man.

'Zeba, what are you doing?' Mum snapped.

'I thought this was our transport to Nannyma's house.'

Mum's eyes widened in shock and she stepped up to the cart, noting my luggage. With her lips pursed in a thin line, she turned sharply to face Mariam-chachi, who was standing by the doorway.

'You want us to ride in *this* to my mother's house?' she asked incredulously.

Mariam-chachi avoided her sister-in-law's eyes, preferring to look into the distance as if she were searching for someone. 'There is no other vehicle free at the moment,' she said vaguely.

Mum snorted in disbelief. 'I can see a Land Rover parked right there,' she said through gritted teeth, pointing to the big black vehicle with its tinted windows, luxurious leather seating and cool air-conditioning.

'Yes, but there is no driver,' Mariam-chachi insisted. 'Who will drive it? The cart is the only thing available and your mother's house is only ten minutes away. Come now, Nighat, the cart is not beneath you even if you are from the UK.'

Mum inhaled sharply and I could tell from her expression that she was fighting the urge to scream something obscene at Mariam-chachi. But I knew she would not. Mariam-chachi was the older bhabi and, in our culture, my mother was obliged to offer respect even if it killed her.

'Very well,' Mum said, clambering up into the back of the cart. 'If it is the only means available, then so be it. I shall see you tomorrow on my return.'

Mariam-chachi took a hesitant step forward, clearly surprised that my mum hadn't put up more of a fight. By accepting that we would travel in the ox cart, Mum had effectively turned the tables. It was unacceptable for a host to provide such basic transport for guests, and by doing so Mariam-chachi had proved herself to be ungracious and petty.

'Let's go,' Mum said to the cart driver.

'Wait!' Mariam-chachi called out, rushing forward. 'Let me see if Feroz-baba's son is available. He can drive the Land Rover.'

Mum was about to protest, seemingly enjoying my aunt's discomfort, when the ox decided at that precise moment to release a pungent brown solid from its backside. The smell was disgusting.

'Oohh,' Mum cried, scrambling off the cart and holding her shawl over her nose. 'Couldn't you have made it wait?'

The cart driver stared bewildered at the figure of my mother rushing indoors away from the stench. *Make the ox wait?*

Mariam-chachi was also holding her shawl to her nose. 'Get that animal off my driveway,' she shrieked. 'Making dirty mess on my clean white stones. Go!'

The driver whacked a thin bamboo stick on the ox's rump and the animal moved slowly off the driveway, pulling the cart away.

'Zeba!' Mariam-chachi called out in alarm at the sight of me still perched at the back of the cart, my legs dangling over the side.

'Don't worry,' I cried. 'I can get dropped off at Nannyma's.'

Mariam-chachi ran up behind the slow-moving cart, obviously in two minds about what to do. I could tell a big part of her wanted me and the ox off her land, but the combined roles of being my aunt and future mother-in-law demanded that she should not let me leave like this.

'I'm fine,' I called. 'The fresh air will be good for me.'

Mariam-chachi finally gave up and halted in her tracks to watch the ox cart slowly grind away, the small bell round the animal's neck chiming with its every step. *Tinkle, tinkle, tinkle* it rang all the way through the village, past the five small bricked houses, which were Taya-ji's nearest neighbours, and then down a muddy path scattered with rocks and stones that led to a collection of mud huts. As we passed the homes of the poorest people, small children dressed in clean but tattered clothes came out to gape at me. They pointed at me and giggled, revealing white teeth set against sun-bronzed skin. I knew why they were amused. I was the foreign girl, the England *guri*, and yet I was travelling in an ox cart, the vehicle of the peasants. As the cart wheels creaked and the bell rang, apologetic-looking mothers came out of their huts to usher the children away. I smiled at them, hoping to reassure them that I wasn't offended.

Nannyma's house was smaller than Taya-ji's, but much prettier, with colourful flowerpots lining the edges of the veranda. Nannyma was waiting for me, sitting serenely on a wooden swing on the deck. As the ox cart arrived at her house, Nannyma stood up and walked slowly to the edge of her veranda and reached over to stroke the animal's neck. It reminded me of when she had stroked my forehead only two days earlier, and I wondered if she was one of those people who instinctively reached out to those who suffered.

'Kareem-baba,' she called over her shoulder. 'See that the ox is watered and fed, and give Mariam's servant some refreshment.'

A middle-aged man materialized as I jumped off the cart and walked tentatively up to Nannyma. Smiling, she reached out and pulled me into an embrace and I relaxed against her, suddenly feeling better and calmer. Her unique scent drifted into my nostrils – a combination of Lily of the Valley talcum powder (which my mum displayed on her dresser, but never used) and something else. What was it? Cloves? Yes, that was it. I remembered the dried flower buds swimming in her tea when I had sat with her in Taya-ji's courtyard.

Nannyma stepped back and led me into her house. 'This is your home for now,' she said gently.

I was grateful to be inside and off the cart. The ride had started out well, but by the end my body had felt the impact of every rut and rock the wheels had rolled over. Grateful to spot a soft-looking sofa under a whirring ceiling fan, I hurried over and flopped down.

Nannyma's house did not have air-conditioning and to another westerner it would not have been so comfortable, but after the last forty-eight hours I felt like I had come home. I felt I could finally breathe a little more easily again.

'I spoke to your mother on the phone,' my grandmother said, as Kareem-baba placed a cool glass of lemonade in front of me.

'I hope you don't think I am imposing,' I muttered politely.

Nannyma let out a whoop of laughter. 'No, my dear Zeba. You are not imposing. How can you? You are my only grand-child. I welcome this opportunity to get to know you better. However, I have one rule which you must abide by.'

I nodded.

'You shall not worry about your upcoming wedding. You shall put it out of your mind and instead spend your thoughts and time with me. This time is for us. After three weeks, we will discuss the situation of your marriage and whether it is to be or not.'

I stared at Nannyma. 'I don't want to get married, though and . . .'

'What did I say?' she interrupted.

I swallowed hard, trying to erase the lump in my throat, but it was no good and the dam broke. Wailing as if the world was crashing in on me, I allowed Nannyma to place her thin, frag-ile arms around me and rock me tenderly until there was nothing left but exhaustion.

'There, there, feel better now?' she said, and to my surprise I did. The hug was everything I'd wanted from my own mother. A reassurance that everything was going to be OK, and that I wasn't the only person in the village who didn't believe in this marriage. It felt good to know there was someone who might be on my side.

Over the next two days, the tears of frustration dried up and I spent my time sitting with Nannyma on the veranda swing talking about everything and anything. She told me how she had arrived in this village as a bride nearly fifty years ago from

Karachi. An educated daughter of a moderately successful businessman, she had moved to the village in order to be with her husband – a college friend of her brother's. My nanapapa had hated the city and only tolerated it to get an education. Nannyma had agreed to return with him, and so began a life in which she shared her space with cows and chickens, and kept her mind active through subscriptions to newspapers and magazines.

Decades after she had arrived in a bride's wooden chariot, Nannyma was now loved in this village as an arbiter of justice. Her sense of fairness was so well respected that villagers sought her out to resolve their disputes. There was an unofficial understanding that whatever Nannyma decided would be the final outcome. In my first few days with her, many people came to her with their differences and she helped resolve them, which I found completely inspiring. I couldn't imagine it working quite so well back home, or even in my school, where so many 'procedures' seemed to get in the way of common sense.

My nannyma also told me about her other daughter, Nusrat, who I addressed as *kala*, meaning 'mother's sister'. Nusrat-kala had emigrated to America about ten years ago – the proud possessor of a green card, allowed in by a nation that valued the brightest in the world. Unlike my mum, who had chosen not to attend college despite being the daughter of educated parents, Nusrat had demanded an education, leaving home to live with Nannyma's relatives in Karachi while she attended a leading college for women. It was in Karachi where she had met her husband-to-be, Tahir. Once their studies were over, he secured a job as an engineer in America and then asked her to join him as his wife. Nusrat had been reluctant to leave her widowed mother, but my nannyma said she had been adamant that her younger daughter should follow her fate, her *kismet*.

'As she left I remember I whispered to her, "Go, I want the world for you,"' Nannyma recalled. 'And so she did.'

I'd met Nusrat-kala and Uncle Tahir on their one and only visit to England two years ago. Nusrat-kala and my mum were like chalk and cheese. Mum was quiet and liked to sit in the shadow of my dad – literally – whereas Nusrat-kala was a confident woman who, despite being the same height, appeared to be a foot taller just by the force of her personality. She laughed loudly and was unreserved with her opinions of the world. (Susan said it was an American thing and my mum moaned it was not a feminine thing.) Within minutes of meeting her, I had come to adore my aunt and I think she liked me too.

If my mum could have had her way, she would have kept Nusrat-kala hidden from her world. I remember while she was in England we all attended a wedding of a distant relative and the auntie-jis were eyeing Nusrat-kala with interest. To them she was a rare breed, one who did not look like she would cower in the face of their sharp tongues.

'So what is America like?' one auntie-ji asked.

'Great,' said Nusrat-kala. 'It's truly the land of opportunity. You know you are an American if you believe in the American Dream.'

'Then you must be a twenty-four-carat American,' the auntie-ji joked.

'And what *is* the American Dream, huh?' another auntie-ji asked. 'To be like men?'

'No,' Nusrat-kala replied clearly. 'It is to achieve your full potential and not to hide behind your men. Honestly, ladies, you remind me of the villagers I grew up with, who deny women their potential. The whole point of emigration is to escape to new opportunities.'

'You sound like a politician!' the first auntie-ji accused.

'Well, back in Chicago, Tahir and some of our friends think that I might have a good chance of running for political office.'

A shocked silence followed. Not at the possibility of Nusrat-kala having a political career – that was something that hadn't even been digested. No, the shocked horror had been at Nusrat-kala's reference to her husband by his name. To the auntie-jis this was the ultimate disrespect to the man she was married to. Husbands could only be referred to as 'ji' or 'him' or something equally . . . well . . . dumb.

My mum's reaction had been to close her eyes for a moment and then make an apologetic face to the auntie-jis before leading Nusrat-kala away to a quiet corner.

I have to say I think Mum was relieved when Nusrat-kala's holiday came to an end, although I was devastated to see her leave. She was so full of joy and laughter that everyone missed her, including our neighbours and even Susan's mum.

Looking around Nannyma's quiet house now I wondered how she'd coped without her children around, especially after the death of my grandfather twenty years ago. Thankfully she'd always lived with a housekeeper couple, Kareem-baba and his wife, Ambreen-bhaji, whose three daughters were now happily married and settled in surrounding villages. Nannyma had been instrumental in finding good suitors for the girls, who had grown up in her house.

Kareem-baba was a thin, bony man, but his wife was the complete opposite of him. She was round from her face to her feet, with a warm smile that revealed slightly buck teeth. Since my arrival we'd formed a mutual adoration society and I became her little project to fatten up. Ambreen-bhaji's two magic ingredients for eternal happiness and peace were ghee and sugar. She said I was far too thin, much like those Karachi *guris*, and believed that all girls should have big breasts and rounded hips. After all, a woman's role was to make her husband happy and to have his babies, wasn't it? Much as I wanted to protest, I decided that Ambreen-bhaji was in fact very happy with her husband, and it was probably best not to burden her with my predicament just to make a point.

Ambreen-bhaji was also in charge of the two cows and dozen or so chickens, which were kept in the backyard. When she watered the cattle, she would lovingly stroke the animals' heads and murmur reassuring words. She also had the same one-way conversations with the poultry that ran around her feet gobbling up the seeds she dropped. It was due to this devotion that I initially thought Ambreen-bhaji was an animal lover. This impression, however, was brought to an end on my third day when Ambreen-bhaji invited me to join her in the preparation of my favourite dish.

'Today I will show you how I make chicken tikka from scratch,' she announced.

I smiled and parked myself on a chair in the backyard. Maybe if I learned to cook this, I could impress Susan with my 'authentic' chicken tikka when I got home. Looking forward to lunch, I settled back, my mouth already watering.

'First,' Ambreen-bhaji began, running after a chicken and grabbing it by its neck, 'we have to catch the chicken.'

I sat bolt upright. What exactly had she meant by 'starting from scratch'?

'Then I get a knife and cut its throat and say . . .'

I was on my feet now, my hands covering my mouth in horror. The chicken was flapping its wings and desperately trying to escape Ambreen-bhaji's lethal hold round its throat. It was as if it knew what was coming . . . that death was inevitable.

'. . . *Allahu Akbar.*' God is Great.

The shiny steel slashed the chicken's scrawny neck and unleashed a stream of scarlet blood all over the ground. The chicken jerked for a few seconds in Ambreen-bhaji's grip as the life seeped out of it and then it went quite still. I stared down at the lifeless bird, which had been running around the yard only seconds ago, and I felt the bile rise in my throat.

'It is very important to do it quickly so the chicken does not suffer,' Ambreen-bhaji continued, oblivious to my revulsion. 'Now I will pluck the chicken . . . see, like this . . . feathers are coming off and . . .'

I ran to the side of the yard and vomited.

Suffice it to say that I did not eat the chicken that afternoon. I could not.

Nannyma tried to hide her amusement as I nibbled on the chapatti bread.

Ambreen-bhaji, on the other hand, was like a broken record. She kept repeating: 'And I thought the England people were educated. So how do they think the chicken tikka appears on their plate? Huh? Do they think it falls from the sky?'

'I thought she was an animal lover,' I mumbled to Nannyma miserably, trying to get the image of the scarlet blood splashed on the ground out of my mind.

'She is,' Nannyma said, tucking into the chicken breast on her plate. 'She looks after the animals lovingly when they are alive and ensures their death is quick. She is a rural villager and she has a practical attitude towards domestic animals. You, my sweet child, are proving to be quite the squeamish westerner.'

Chapter 6

Three more days slowly passed and my parents kept in touch by phone to check on my progress. I think they were under the impression that Nannyma was slowly talking me around to the idea of marrying Asif, but this could not have been further from the truth. Asif's name had only been mentioned once, and that was to inform me that he had to stay longer in Lahore, a city on the other side of the country. Nannyma did not bother to give me the reason and I didn't want to know anyway. Frankly it was a relief to know he was not even in the province of Sindh, let alone the village. However, the happiness I originally felt at the news soon seeped away to be replaced by depression and panic.

Sometimes I felt these emotions would choke me and, when I was not raging at my parents in my own mind, I found other targets for my frustration. One such moment was on a bright hot morning as I stared angrily at the village women who walked past the veranda to gather water from the well in Nannyma's grounds. They came every day in a group, huddled together, laughing as one of them entertained the others with some tale or gossip about a mother-in-law or a neighbour. They were dressed from head to toe in flowing bright robes in shades of red, pink, turquoise, purple and blue. Nobody wore white and nobody wore black. The colours of their clothes hinted at happiness, but I knew appearances could be deceiving. It was not the dye in their clothes but rather the sunburned faces, fatigued and prematurely old, peeping out through their shawls which really told their fate. There was no denying that their lives were full of hardship.

Or perhaps I was judging too much. Was I spoilt in my Western life where everything was about choice? I thought of my teachers, always emphasizing that I should give thought to my future – what A levels, what degree, what career. Or even the afternoons that Susan and I spent in Boots agonizing between two shades of nail varnish. But surely it was a right to have choice where it existed, not a luxury?

Choice, choice, choice. Something that I had now been robbed of.

Was I just another version of them, bound by the decisions of my male relatives to control me? But I knew I was luckier than them. There was running water in the two houses I had visited, so why were they forced to collect theirs from a hole in the ground?

My wise nannyma noticed the bubble of rage brimming just under the surface. 'You do not approve, Zeba?' she asked me.

I flashed angry eyes at her. 'They should have running water! Why don't they have it?'

'Because, my dear,' she said patiently, 'the villages are all owned by the landlord, Sher Shah. They are his tenants. They work the land for him and he lets them live there.'

Ah, yes, the Tiger King. 'You mean they are his slaves?' I spat.

My nannyma grimaced. 'That is not a term we like to use, but yes . . . I suppose your description applies. They are bound to him.'

'But that doesn't explain why they have no running water,' I rasped. 'Why won't this landlord arrange the plumbing?'

'Because Sher Shah chooses to keep things this way,' Nannyma explained. 'He chooses not to progress with the times. Keeping other people down makes him feel like a big man. Remember this, my dear: if a man feels inadequate with his own peers, he needs to surround himself by others, more disadvantaged, more unfortunate and more deprived to feel superiority.

'They could be poorer people; they could be women or even another country's people. It is why some men have invaded other countries and why some women are treated as inferior. It is why caste systems exist so a person is made to believe he or she deserves nothing better than the poverty they have been born into.'

'But that's awful!' I cried. 'How does he sleep at night?'

'Very easily, Zeba. You see, he has convinced himself that these people are sub-human because they are poor and uneducated. If he gives them their rights: basic education for the children, a sustainable wage and the opportunity to progress and climb out of the underclass they occupy, then all they will do is bite him. They would not be afraid of him any more. They might decide to no longer humbly accept the crumbs he throws their way and challenge his authority. By convincing himself that they will act like mad dogs if he releases his hold on them, he keeps them tied up like animals.'

A shiver ran down my spine, even though the afternoon sun was beating down on us.

'It's not like that in England,' I declared proudly. 'This village is feudal . . . it's backward.'

My nannyma gave a small smile. 'Perhaps you no longer have slaves in England, but you have men who try to keep women down through domestic abuse. And isn't it true that in many cases women are paid less than a man for doing the same job?'

Was that true? I didn't know that.

'It is about control,' Nannyma continued in a wise tone. 'The desire to feel better about oneself by keeping another person down. Power is about control, Zeba. Don't ever forget it.'

I nibbled at my lower lip, the village women forgotten as I mulled over Nannyma's words. Power was about control. Was my planned marriage about power in the family? Was Taya-ji trying to control my dad? Was my father trying to prove his masculinity to other men by controlling me? And, if that was the case, what chance did I have of escaping it?

My parents came to see me after a week. I think they thought it was sufficient time for me to have calmed down and accepted their plans.

I watched them climb the veranda steps together and I hardened my resolve. It occurred to me how natural it had felt to be apart from them, despite the fact that I had never even spent a night away from them before. In fact, ever since the night on the rooftop I'd found it hard to believe they were the same parents I'd left home with. It was as if they'd been brainwashed.

Mum came up to me and hugged me, but I was half-hearted in my response. She started fiddling nervously with a silk handkerchief and her face was taut with tension as her eyes darted nervously between her husband, her mother and me, her only child. I stared at my mum. This was the home in which she'd been born. She had taken her first steps, bloomed into a teenager and married my dad here, yet she seemed a stranger to the surroundings. Living with Nannyma had made me realize how different a mother could be from her daughter; my mum was nothing like Nannyma and I was nothing like Mum. Nannyma was the wisest woman in the village, greatly respected, independent and articulate. Mum was in the shadow of Dad, never speaking up, always siding with him, forever looking for the easy way out. I couldn't believe that she was a child of Nannyma's, and suddenly I wondered if in fact she was not to blame. Perhaps in married life my father had eroded the principles that I knew Nannyma would have tried to instil. Although this image of Dad didn't fit with the loving father I knew from my childhood, neither did the figure standing before me now. I eyed my dad from across the veranda and his hateful words rushed back at me. Unlike Mum, he hadn't approached me. He kept his distance, and I could see the reflection in his eyes of something that I had felt: hurt.

Did he feel I had let him down by not agreeing to his demands immediately?

Did he feel I had failed him? Embarrassed him? Dishonoured him?

'I hope she's been behaving,' Mum said with a nervous laugh, breaking the silence.

'Yes, she has,' Nannyma answered, looking directly at Mum. 'You know you could have stayed here with her. This is your home too.'

Mum shot a helpless look at Dad.

'She is my wife. Her role is to remain by my side,' he said quietly, as if he were reciting the words from a script. 'Zeba, my *beti*,' he added, turning to me as he used the Urdu for daughter. 'I need to talk to you.'

My heart gave a flutter. Had he finally come to his senses? Was he going to side with me now?

My mum and Nannyma retreated into the house as my father sat down heavily on the swing. He patted the empty space beside him, inviting me to join him. I did. We sat there for a few minutes, neither saying anything. I knew my dad was looking for the right words, but as the seconds passed my heart grew heavier as I realized from the grim expression on his face that he was not going to tell me what I wanted to hear.

'Tell me, Dad,' I finally said, unable to take the silence.

'*Beti*,' he repeated, his voice wracked with emotion. 'It is my wish that you marry Asif.'

'Dad, I'm not going to –'

'Just please listen to me,' he said, turning to face me. 'I realize that perhaps your mother and I should have been straight with you from the start. We should have been honest. You see it would not have been my first choice to arrange your marriage in this way. I had planned that you would finish your education and then we would think about arranging your marriage . . . to someone of your choice.'

He paused and I stared at him. So what had changed?

He continued: 'You see, my *beti*, family is everything for

people like us. There is nothing above it. Without respect within a family a man is nothing. Without a family he has no honour. It is like wandering the earth without a soul, like a ghost. No respect, no meaning, no position. A man may as well not exist.'

'But I don't –'

'Let me finish!' he snapped.

I closed my mouth. I wasn't sure where this was going. I didn't know why he was going on about honour. I knew every-thing there was to know about family honour. My dad had always talked about it. When I was a child he would sit me on his knee and tell me that wives, sisters and daughters were like precious glass vases within which a man's honour was contained. These glass vases must never be broken. If the female did not behave accordingly then a man's honour was compromised. His friends would laugh at him, his brothers would jeer at him and – even more shamefully – other women would ridicule him.

I had grown up listening to these words and I knew that I would never intentionally dishonour my dad. In our community there was one way to do it at my age and that was to have a boyfriend. I frowned slightly and the words escaped my mouth even though my dad had asked me to be quiet.

'But I haven't dishonoured you. I've never had a boyfriend.'

My dad patted my head awkwardly.

'I know, *beti*,' he said softly. 'Your mother and I raised you well . . . but . . . it is your taya-ji's wish to see Asif and you married. It is his wish for Asif to leave the army and to join us in England. Taya-ji is worried about Asif's safety. These are dangerous times. Asif is his only son and it is not safe for him to remain here in Pakistan. The only way Asif will leave the army is if he marries you and lives with us.'

The creaking of the swing's metal rods was the only sound for a while. My dad stared into the distance while I sat motionless trying to absorb his words. I couldn't quite get my head around it. I was expected to marry Asif so that he could leave the army? What was I? His get-out-of-the-army-free card?

The true reason for the marriage was almost an anticlimax. For days I'd assumed that, at best, the marriage had been arranged in order to strengthen family ties. The truth was far from it. Taya-ji saw me only as a passport for his son. That's all I was to him. It explained why Asif's mum, even after the rooftop incident, still wanted me as a daughter-in-law. This was all about saving their son.

But what about me? Why should I be sacrificed to save Asif? Surely there was another way he could come to the UK?

'Dad,' I ventured.

'Yes?'

I knew what I was about to say were not the words he wanted to hear, but I said them anyway. 'I don't want to sacrifice my happiness just so Asif can leave the army.'

There was a long pause and then my dad said softly, 'That is a very selfish thing to say, Zeba.'

I noticed I was back to being Zeba rather than *beti*, so I decided not to hold back.

'Why should I give up my life?'

My dad had clearly assumed that confiding in me the true reason for the marriage would convince me to follow his orders. He sprang up from the swing and glared down at me. I stared back, defiant.

'You will marry Asif!' he shouted. 'I will not have it on my conscience that I failed to protect him. You are my daughter and you will do as I say!'

I glared at my father, hatred in my eyes. 'I'm your daughter,' I yelled. 'And so you should protect *me*. Can you live with *that* on your conscience?'

'How dare you speak to me like that, Zeba!' he barked. 'I will put my honour first! I did not raise you to disobey me. My brother has asked this one thing from me and I will not fail him.'

'What about me?' I screamed, sudden tears streaming down my face.

My mum and Nannyma ran out on to the veranda, anxiety all over their faces.

'We are leaving!' Dad snapped at my mum and then he turned to Nannyma. 'She will marry Asif. Final. I will not let my brother down and I will not be held responsible for his son's death.'

With those words he stormed off the veranda and into the waiting Land Rover. My mum followed closely behind him without saying a word to me.

'Zeba.' My nannyma's hand came to rest on my shoulder.

I turned towards her and buried my face in her neck. 'I bet they regret raising me in England,' I mumbled.

'I can see how it must be difficult for you,' Nannyma responded. 'To have been given a Western life with all its opportunities, but then be expected to remain constrained by our culture.'

'I am British. Not Pakistani,' I agreed.

'But your parents are Pakistani at heart, despite their pride in owning those red passports.'

'Yeah, but it doesn't mean I am,' I said heatedly. 'And just because I'm their daughter doesn't mean they own me, that they can force me to do things that I don't want to! Why didn't they tell me about this before?'

'Would that have made it any easier, Zeba? Your father told you the reasons for his agreement to the marriage just now, did he not?'

I bit my lip. 'He did.'

'And how do you feel about the reason?'

'I don't care about Asif. Sure, he's my cousin and I don't want anything bad to happen to him, but there's got to be another way for him to leave the army other than by marrying me!'

'There isn't,' my nannyma said simply.

'But how can that be?'

Nannyma eyed me warily for a few seconds and then said: 'Zeba, my dear, do you think your taya-ji has not tried already to remove Asif from the army? He has tried everything to persuade his son to leave. But Asif refuses. It is honourable I suppose – a man's dedication to his country . . . but try telling that to his parents. He is their only son. Scores of soldiers die every day in their own land, at the hands of the enemy within. It is the heart of a parent that is ploughed with worry. They don't care about the shame of deserting the army. They just want him alive and safe.'

I mulled over Nannyma's words, resentment growing in my own heart. So Taya-ji and Mariam-chachi loved their son and were prepared to do anything to save him, but what about my parents? Why weren't they prepared to do as much for me? And then something occurred to me. I remembered Asif's sharpness with Mariam-chachi when she had complained about the army on our first day here.

'Asif doesn't know he is expected to move to England, does he?'

Nannyma did not reply.

'Does he?' I pressed.

'Everybody is hoping that he will come round to the idea. After all, a man with responsibility for a wife and children will put them ahead of everything else.'

I couldn't believe it. Nannyma had just admitted that Asif did not want to move to England. The thought sent my head spinning. What if he refused?

And even if he agreed, would he be able to live in our little English town? Here was a man who used guns against men whom he regarded as enemies of his beloved country. His life was probably both exciting and dangerous as he fought to save his Pakistan . . . so then would he really be able to spend his days serving middle-aged Asian women their groceries in my dad's shop? What would he think of the small terraced houses that made up so many of our narrow, grimy streets? The small playgrounds with baby swings and slides dotted around these estates. Our stone-paved backyard, and then the posh parts of town with the bigger houses where mostly white people lived. How would it all seem to him after the spacious surroundings of his parents' home and the servants at his beck and call?

And what would he make of the weather? The grey clouds and rain that fell on our heads for more months than there was sunshine. Would he like it? Could he stay? All the questions brought me back to the same point: what if he refused?

Did he really think I would remain in this village as an obedient wife?

Stuff my father's honour. If he was taking my freedom, it was a price too high to pay.

Chapter 7

The following day I ventured out alone for a walk by the river behind Nannyma's house. The sun was beating down and my *kameez* was clinging to my back as the sweat trickled down my spine. It was the siesta and everybody was asleep. It was tradition. It was culture. I think that's why I felt so rebellious against it. It was the one thing I could easily reject as my British body naturally found it alien to settle down for a nap in the middle of the day.

I first saw Sehar sitting by the riverbank under a giant tree, splashing the water with her feet. She was beautiful: long limbs, fair skin and with an air about her that made you feel quite intimidated. I couldn't work out whether it was arrogance or confidence, but I approached slowly anyway. When I did, she turned to look directly at me with a raised eyebrow over one of her large brown eyes.

'So are you the new *bakri*?'

I winced at her description of me in Urdu as a sacrificial lamb. Did everyone know about my forced engagement with Asif?

'I don't know what you mean,' I lied.

'Never mind,' she said. 'I'm Sehar, the original *bakri*. Come and sit down . . . the water is cool.'

And that's how we, the two *bakris*, bonded.

Sehar was from Birmingham and she had already been forced into a marriage with her cousin. She also had a seven-month bump, which tied her well and truly to her husband, who was the youngest son of the village landlord I'd condemned, Sher Shah. Sehar had been told to visit Pakistan to see relatives by her father. But, unlike gullible old me, eighteen-year-old Sehar had had her suspicions about the purpose of the trip. She had seen young girls she had grown up with go on family visits to Pakistan only to return as married women after a few months. Sehar said some seemed genuinely happy with their arrangements and others not so happy. The one thing all the girls had in common was accepting the will of their parents, but it was not in Sehar's personality to go quietly.

When Sehar's father had informed her of her impending trip, she had immediately contacted the government's Forced Marriage Unit. Sehar had first got to know about it when leaflets had been distributed at her school. We'd never seen any such leaflets at our school, but it didn't stop me feeling more and more naive as she told me her story. I too knew of girls who had returned from trips abroad happily married, or at least that's how it had seemed to my young eyes. But I had no reason to doubt it – in the films I'd watched love at first sight was something to believe in, and I was never close enough to the girls to see anything other than their public display of happiness.

Sehar explained how the Foreign Office had put her in touch with one of the charities they worked with. The charity worker who had picked up the phone was a woman called Tara who had immediately tried to help her. She had assured her that if she needed to leave the family home, then she would help her with accommodation and money. All she needed to do was leave.

Sehar had thought about it.

All she needed to do was leave.

Was it that simple?

All she had to do was get to the main railway station. She needn't worry about money for a train ticket to Euston; Tara would meet her at the station and take her to London herself. Sehar would be safe and nobody could force her to go to Pakistan.

'I was sorely tempted to escape, to run away and meet this woman, Tara, who had promised to help me,' Sehar told me quietly. 'But a big part of me thought this was the coward's option. The questions kept hammering around in my head. Did I really need to break ties with my family to avoid the marriage? No I didn't. I wanted my family and I wanted to avoid this marriage. I felt at the time that this would be possible. All I had to do was hold my ground.'

Sehar paused and tears welled up in her eyes. 'This belief in myself proved to be my biggest downfall. It would have been more courageous to leave than to stay, then at least my life would have been my own.'

Sehar's 'marriage' had taken place four days after she had arrived at Sher Shah's house. Apparently it was the wish of Sehar's dead grandmother that her British granddaughter marry within the family. Sher Shah and Sehar's mum were brother and sister and the marriage had been arranged by both families years ago to strengthen family ties. Sehar told me that this was usually the practice of less wealthy people in order to keep the land and property within families. Sher Shah's family was wealthy and didn't have this tradition, but the dead grandmother's wishes had to be obeyed.

Sehar had tried to escape in the first few days. The first time she had got as far as the fields on foot before they caught her. Her tormentors decided to lock her up in a room, but she still managed to climb on to a tree outside her window before skidding down it like a cat. This time she managed to get to the front gates, and this time the response of her captors was to beat her – though they were the family of her own mother. Brushing her tears away roughly and looking more defiant, Sehar said, 'I don't believe I'm married. For an Islamic marriage contract, a *nikaah*, to be valid, the bride has to give her consent freely. I never gave mine and the imam announced the marriage as complete without my consent. This man was complicit in selling me to another man. In our religion, sex before marriage is one of the worst sins that can be committed, and yet my entire family has contributed to this sin by announcing my part in a marriage that is not valid.'

I listened quietly, fear gripping me as I realized all of this was to come my way. I wasn't, however, prepared for what she said next with a bitter laugh and hatred in her eyes.

'I'm like those single teenage mums back home who get knocked up except . . . those single mums haven't been beaten night after night "until they've got pregnant".'

Sehar's husband thought she was far too outspoken and that as his wife she should be subdued and in thrall to him. It literally drove him mad that he could not break her defiance – so he tried to break her bones instead. Recently, however, he had stopped throwing her violently across the room. Apparently it was his mother's advice that pregnant women should be hit across the legs and arms only – so as not to harm the baby.

But Sehar had a plan. She told me that as soon as the baby was born the two of them were going to leave for England. Her husband and his family believed that the baby would tie her to them. Sehar laughed hysterically. 'They're crazy. They haven't got a clue about home. They think I will be just as alone and skint and desperate as I am here. But I'll be the one in control in England. I will be the one who can speak the language. Women are free in Britain. As soon as I land at Heathrow, I'm reporting him to the immigration police. They'll put him straight back on a plane to this place when I tell them what's happened. I can't wait.'

'What will your parents say?' I asked tentatively, thinking of my own situation.

'Who throws their own daughter into the lion's den?' she raged. 'When I get back to England, I'm getting on with my own life, without them! And I won't forget you, Zeba. As soon as I'm back I'll send the cavalry for you too.'

We bonded quickly because of our common circumstances, and then spent many an afternoon lazing in the shade of the giant tree on the riverbank, imagining our great escape. There was no denying that it was the thought of England, of home – of freedom – that kept us both going. We just had to hold on a little while longer. In the meantime we were waited on hand and foot by another young girl.

Farhat was Sehar's maid and shadow – a tiny little thing, but nevertheless a determined ball and chain. She was dark-skinned with jet-black hair that was immaculately oiled and braided into a plait, which began at the nape of her neck and ended as a swinging tail by her hips. Every day a different brightly coloured ribbon was woven into the thick, long braid. Farhat always made sure her ribbons matched the colour of her shawl, and I was sure that the strips of fabric were her pride and joy.

Farhat's mother was one of the many servants in Sher Shah's household, and at sixteen Farhat had been the natural choice for Sehar's maid, having worked in the *haveli* since she was ten. She was a sweet girl and insisted on speaking to us in broken English with the amusing singing lilt accent of the South Asians. The peasant girl had picked up the English language from the cable channels that were religiously watched in Sher Shah's *haveli*. As a result she said 'naa' and 'yaah' a lot, both of which were just sounds to demonstrate her mood rather than words to communicate yes or no.

Sometimes when Sehar and I were in full conversation, she would stare at us, her mouth wide open as her mind grappled to catch the words. Sehar's Brummie accent and my Yorkshire vowels were too much for her and she would grumble that we did not know how to speak the Queen's English and the Pakistanis pronounced the words better. Sehar and I would laugh at her, but in different ways. I grew quite affectionate towards Farhat, but Sehar treated her like she was the plague.

'She's not my mate,' Sehar once insisted when I'd invited Farhat inside Nannyma's house. 'She is a maid in the employment of Sher Shah. Her loyalty is with him. She can wait outside your nan's house.'

It was noon and the sun unrelenting in its scorching heat, but Sehar was insistent, justifying her action by naming Farhat as the one who had raised the alarm when Sehar had once tried to escape.

Everything about Farhat seemed to annoy Sehar – from the maid's fascination with her baby bump to her chatter about her own upcoming nuptials. Farhat's wedding to her second cousin Abdullah had been arranged by her father. Abdullah was one of the younger men who was always in the background guarding Sehar. He was a tall boy, a year older than Farhat, who watched over the *haveli's* daughter-in-law like a hawk.

Farhat was very excited about marrying Abdullah and giggled uncontrollably whenever he was within five yards of her. I also noticed how she would sometimes loudly rattle on in broken English in a bid to impress her fiancé. And she did – Abdullah would gaze at his clever girl and marvel as she demonstrated her ability to speak another language.

Farhat never seemed to take offence at Sehar's rudeness. I guess it never occurred to her that she was allowed to be offended. In fact, people of Farhat's status took it as an honour to be addressed by the *haveli* dwellers at all, and I was reminded of Nannyma's words: power and control. I didn't think I would ever get used to this way of life, which made me even more determined that Sehar's future would not be mine.

Chapter 8

Sehar invited me to the *haveli* a few days after we met. It was raining and, resigned to a quiet afternoon, I was planning to fill the time waiting until it was time to go by listening to Nusrat-kala's old music collection. Nannyma had kept her daughter's ancient record player on display in the living room and I fiddled with it, unsure how to work it. Where was the play button?

Standing by the doorway, an amused Ambreen-bhaji watched me for a few minutes before offering to help. She placed my chosen Bollywood record on the turntable, set it spinning and dragged the needle on to it. A high-pitched gabbling sound filled the room and I instinctively covered my ears with my hands.

'It's just at the wrong speed,' Ambreen-bhaji said dismissively, flicking a switch next to the turntable. Now a normal voice blared out and as I listened to the beat of the music I was struck by its similarity to the music Susan's mum played. Mrs Taworth still loved the sounds of ancient groups like Duran Duran and Spandau Ballet, and every time she blasted out their songs Susan and I would make a hasty exit.

Looking at the big hairstyles and shoulder pads of the men and woman on the record covers, it was obvious that the same type of music had been globally popular, even if the accompanying singing had been in different languages. It was funny that Nusrat-kala and Mrs Taworth had similar taste in music despite the thousands of miles between them.

Enjoying the infectious beat of the music, I grabbed Ambreen-bhaji's hands and urged her to dance with me. Laughing, she shooed me away and I whirled round and round until I banged head-on into a smiling Farhat, who had come to collect me. I hurriedly yanked the needle off the record and yelled a goodbye.

Farhat and I huddled under a big, black umbrella to set out on the muddy path towards the *haveli*. The umbrella was doing little to protect us from the fat drops falling from the murky grey clouds above, and we were half drenched within minutes. Suddenly I was reminded of the times when Susan and I had danced in the rain back home. If ever we were caught in a downpour on our way home from school, we would laugh, twirling and skipping about, and raise our faces to soak up the fresh water. I wondered if I would feel the same sense of liberation here if I gave in to the skies. I could only try. I ran out from under the umbrella and whirled around and around, just like I had moments ago to the beat of the Bollywood tune. For those few moments I forgot that I was a prisoner in this village. The rain made me feel free . . . for a moment anyway.

Farhat stared at me with bewildered eyes, her confusion at the antics of the foreign girl evident on her face. 'You will be getting sick,' she scolded like a mother hen.

'The rain makes me feel good,' I breathed, running back to her. 'It reminds me of home.'

Farhat nodded vaguely and increased her pace to get us inside as quickly as possible. By the time we walked through the heavy mahogany doors of the *haveli*, our *salwars* were splattered with mud and our *kameezes* were soaked through.

'Stop! Stop!' A woman ran forward, her hands held up to stop us. She was thin with wrinkled skin, but her eyes shone brightly, expressing her warmth.

'This is Zeba-ji from England,' Farhat said in Sindhi. 'Zeba-ji, this is my mother, Rachida-bhaji.'

I smiled at Rachida-bhaji and she responded shyly before turning her attention to her daughter, tutting at Farhat's drenched appearance.

'Memsahib will get angry,' Rachida-bhaji warned. 'You will mark her clean floor. The other maids and I have already wiped it twice today.'

I leaned a little to my left to peer at the white marble floor. Pillars rose from it to form a circle within which plush creamy leather sofas formed a sitting area. High above, an enormous crystal chandelier hung from the ceiling. It was easily large enough to crush anyone unfortunate enough to find themselves beneath if it fell. At the far end stood a majestic staircase. Outside the circle of pillars, shiny white doors with gold knobs hid other parts of the house, and on two of the walls hung huge portraits of a middle-aged man with a gravity-defying moustache. He was wearing a purple *ajrak* turban on his head. I guessed he must be Sher Shah, the landlord. His *haveli* reminded me of the mansion homes of American celebrities that were featured in the MTV show *Cribs*.

'Rachida!'

A shrill, high voice startled me out of out of my daydream and I looked up to stare into the eyes of a tall, statuesque woman in her mid fifties. She was draped in an expensive silk sari, the colour of sunflowers, and her face was heavily made up in bright colours that had been applied far too harshly. Green eye-shadow stained the lids above eyes that were completely circled in black kohl, and her thin lips were a hot bubblegum colour, which I thought only succeeded in making her mouth appear like a pink slash across her face.

Was this Sehar's mother-in-law, the woman fearfully known as Memsahib? Sehar had told me that the landlady preferred to be addressed as 'memsahib', like the English women of the British Raj, rather than the accepted Urdu term, 'sahiba'. This was the one who ordered her son to carry on beating his wife?

'Memsahib,' Rachida-bhaji gasped, confirming my suspicions.

'What is happening here?' Memsahib snapped. 'Why are your family all coming to my house?'

Rachida-bhaji and her daughter giggled nervously and then Farhat said, 'This is Zeba-ji from England. She is Mustaq Khan Sahib's niece.'

Memsahib's eyes travelled from my flattened wet hair, down my clinging *kameez* and all the way to my feet, which were hidden from view under a cake of mud. Her disdainful expression revealed her thoughts: she was not impressed with me at all.

'I see,' she said slowly. 'So you are Sehar's new friend. Well, Farhat, perhaps you should take her to Sehar's room and give her a towel.'

Farhat nodded.

'But first please remove your shoes, Zeba; my maids have more important tasks than to constantly wipe up after all who pop in and out.'

Farhat and I removed our footwear, hoisted up our *salwars* and trod carefully over the marble floor to the stairs. We reached a door at the end of the first-floor landing and Farhat knocked.

'Come in.'

We walked in to the sight of Sehar sprawled on a king-size bed watching MTV.

'Look at you two,' she remarked, eyeing us both up and down. 'What did you do? Dance in the rain?'

'Something like that,' I answered, standing by the door awkwardly as I looked around the luxurious bedroom with its wall-to-wall wardrobes, plush cream carpet and expensive furniture.

'So you want a bath?' Sehar asked.

I nodded and minutes later I found myself in a bathroom bigger than many of the village huts that housed whole families. Sitting in the giant tub I was reminded of home and wondered when I would be able to return.

Sehar supplied me with an outfit she could no longer fit into. It was a lavender colour and the *salwar* trailed on the floor no matter how high I raised it on my waist. The *kameez* too ended below my knees. Sehar burst out laughing when I emerged, scrubbed and clean, smelling of her delicious bath foam.

'Where's Farhat?' I asked, looking around.

'She has gone to clean up in the servants' bathroom down-stairs,' Sehar explained. 'She'll be back. Don't worry. That one is never far away.'

I settled down on the bed and Sehar put on a Bollywood DVD. 'We haven't got any Hollywood stuff,' Sehar explained. 'You don't mind, do you?'

'Of course not,' I reassured her. 'I like them.'

The film was a typical love story – a boy and a girl forbidden to be together by family differences eventually overcoming the odds to live happily ever after. We spent the three hours of the film supplied with savoury snacks brought up by Farhat; samosas and onion bhajis washed down with masala tea. The film's happy ending left me in a much better mood.

Somebody knocked on the door just as Sehar began to flick through the satellite channels.

'Come in,' she called.

A pretty, petite woman in her late twenties walked in. Dressed in an expensive *salwar kameez* with gold jewellery sparkling at her throat and ears, she greeted us, '*As salaam alaikum.*'

'*Wa alaikum salaam,*' Farhat and I replied together. Sehar ignored her.

'I heard you were here,' the woman said to me in English, and in an accent much like Sehar's. 'I wanted to come and greet you.'

'Oh,' I said, wondering who she was.

The woman gave a small tinkling laugh. 'My name is Shabana,' she explained. 'I am married to the eldest of Sher Shah's sons.'

'You're from England as well?' I asked.

'Yes, I've lived here for nearly seven years, and as you can hear I still haven't lost my Brummie accent.' She turned to Sehar. 'Perhaps you'd like to join the rest of us in the lounge with your friend? It's always nice for us women to get together.'

Sehar refused to avert her eyes from the Michael Jackson video playing on MTV. 'No,' she said rudely.

Shabana sighed heavily. 'Sehar, you can't stay cooped up in here all the time. You must learn to mingle. It will make things so much easier for you!'

Sehar pretended not to hear.

'Very well,' Shabana said and turned to me. 'It was very nice to meet you, Zeba. Please come again.'

'Yes, I'd like that,' I said awkwardly, and watched Shabana leave before turning to Sehar. 'You never told me about her,' I almost accused.

'What's to tell?' Sehar said flippantly. 'She's just a busybody. Just because she's happily married to her husband doesn't give her the right to tell me what to do.'

'She's from home,' I said. 'Was she forced to marry her husband too?'

Sehar snorted. 'As if! That one couldn't wait to be the eldest daughter-in-law of Sher Shah. She loves it here; no housework to do, no money worries. Life of Riley for her.'

'Seriously?' I couldn't believe it.

'Yeah,' Sehar continued. 'She actually wanted to marry and live here. She returns to Birmingham once a year to visit her parents and then she's back lording it over everyone here.'

'But she seems nice,' I said.

'Yeah, well appearances can be deceptive,' Sehar declared with an air of finality. 'Now let's watch another DVD.'

Chapter 9

Afternoons spent lazing in the *haveli* became the norm if it rained, or if it was too hot to even sit in the shade of a tree. We also spent time on Nannyma's veranda; Farhat would sit on the floor by the steps, Sehar on a deckchair and I on the swing.

Farhat always had Sehar and me in stitches of laughter. It was not that she was even trying to be amusing – only voicing her views and questions, which were limited by her experience of the world. Once Sehar and I were staring at a jet in the distance, dreaming that we were on board on our way home. Farhat, too, was gazing at the speck in the sky, but her face was a picture of puzzlement.

'Zeba-ji,' Farhat began, 'how can you fitting into plane? I mean the plane is so small. Look, it could be fitting in palm of my hand; it is so tiny in the sky. How then can you be sitting in it?'

Sehar and I stared at Farhat in bewilderment and then burst out laughing.

'Fatty, you are so silly,' Sehar howled.

Farhat looked at us wide-eyed, unable to understand the reason for our laughter. As far as she was concerned, fully grown people on a tiny plane in the sky was one of the great mysteries of the world. In between the laughter, Sehar and I explained that distance made an object look smaller, and I even demonstrated it by running out into a field so that she could fathom it. Finally, the penny dropped and Farhat clapped her hands in glee.

'You are both so clever,' she gushed. 'I wishing I was more like you.'

'You know all you had to do was go to school,' Sehar said sarcastically. I shot Sehar a sharp look. There was no need to put the maid down. It wasn't exactly her fault that she had been denied an education. I immediately felt ashamed of my own laughter.

'No, no,' Farhat said happily, oblivious to the put-down. 'I am girl. Girls not going to school.'

Nannyma would sometimes join us after a short siesta, claiming that she was too old now to need much sleep. Our afternoons were spent musing about the world and to an observer it would have seemed that a gentle old lady was subtly teaching the values of equality and justice to her three students. Of course, it had to be said that although Sehar and I lapped up whatever came out of Nannyma's mouth Farhat always looked a little doubtful. She just could not get past the village patriarchy, which dictated that men always knew best and that women were put on this earth to serve them.

One of Sehar's favourite topics of conversation was Bolly-wood films featuring Muslim courtesans. Her favourite was the 1972 film *Pakeezah*, a tale of forbidden love between a rich man and a dancer. After much strife, tears and murder, the besotted pair get their happy ending. Her second favourite was *Umrao*

Jaan, a 1981 film whose ending she insisted she would change.

It was about a courtesan, Umrao, who was kidnapped and sold as a child to a dance house, known as a *kota*. In the story she grew up to be a very famous singer and lost her heart to a man she could not marry because of her profession. Tired and disillusioned with her life, she tried to escape, but tragedy forced her to return to the *kota* she had abandoned. The moral of the story was that the world would not accept a courtesan in their midst; she could exist, but only within the four walls of her *kota*.

I was always amused at Sehar's obsession with the heroine's fate. She would always insist that Umrao, played by the beautiful Bollywood star Rekha, should have had a happy ending. I did try to point out that the film was set over a hundred and fifty years ago, but that did not change her mind. That was one of Sehar's basic beliefs: everybody deserved a happy ending.

It was also in one of these conversations that Sehar let slip that she would love to be a Bollywood actress, and in time, when she got her life back, she would head for Mumbai.

'Sehar, it is a shame that a bright girl like you cannot think of an alternative way to use your brain to contribute to the world,' Nannyma commented.

Sehar did not respond.

'Yes, Sehar-ji,' Farhat chimed in. 'You know my mum and aunties say when actresses revealing their bodies, the men watching imagining doing lots of naughty things to them.'

'Yeah, all right, no need to go on, Fatty,' Sehar snapped.

'You are an intelligent girl,' Nannyma repeated. 'You should use the mind God has given you.'

Nannyma always succeeded in challenging our beliefs and our prejudices. Sometimes I was struck by the irony of the situation. Sehar and I had both been raised in a country where women's liberation and rights had been fought for decades – that's what I had learned in my GCSE history class anyway. And yet it was this elderly woman, hidden from the world in a remote village, who taught us to treat our own gender with fairness and empathy.

One afternoon we were sitting in our usual positions on the veranda, crunching on homemade pickle mix when Farhat began to tut loudly.

'What's up with you?' Sehar asked through a mouthful of mix.

'That woman,' Farhat spat, a look of dislike on her face.

I straightened on the swing to follow Farhat's gaze, intrigued to know who could have caused such a reaction. My eyes fell on a woman walking by herself to the communal well, a plain brown water-pot under her arm. She appeared to be in her mid twenties and was dressed in a black gown, the Arabic *burka*, with her shawl tied tightly around her head.

'Who is she?' Sehar asked, also craning her neck to get a better look at the lone figure.

'She is a loose woman,' Farhat revealed in a voice dripping with disgust. 'All good people staying away from her because she tainting them. Not good reputation.'

Sehar and I stared at the back of the woman as she approached the well. Throwing the tied bucket down the long shaft of the well, she jiggled the rope to ensure that the container was submerged in the water before pulling the long rope slowly up the shaft. Reaching out, the woman grabbed the bucket and emptied its contents into the simple water-pot. I wondered who this woman was as she slowly began to make her way back with the pot cradled into the curve of her waist.

Nannyma, who had silently observed the scene with us, stood up and walked to the edge of the veranda. When the woman was just a few feet away she called out, 'Husna, come here.'

The woman looked up, startled, having seemingly been oblivious to the four pairs of eyes watching her every move. As she approached, Farhat jumped to her feet, scowling.

'Husna, will you join us for tea?' Nannyma asked.

The invitation took us all by surprise, including Husna-bhaji. She gazed up at Nannyma with round eyes that were as green as the surrounding fertile fields.

I stared at Husna-bhaji. I couldn't help it. I don't think I had ever seen such a beautiful face before. She looked like a fragile doll. Her skin was the colour of toffee, her cheeks were apples and her mouth was a pink pout that needed no lipstick to enhance it. Even Sehar was staring at her, wide-eyed.

'Come, Husna, join us,' Nannyma said again, holding out her hand.

Husna-bhaji placed her water-pot next to one of the flower plants, removed her plain sandals and climbed the two steps on to the veranda. As she did she passed Farhat, who stepped back as if scorched.

'Sehar,' Nannyma said. 'Make room for our guest, please.'

Sehar blinked, looking puzzled. She had no idea what was being asked of her.

Nannyma smiled patiently. 'Offer your seat, dear.'

'Oh,' Sehar gasped, jumping up as fast as her baby bump would allow her. Down by the steps, Farhat's disapproval of Nannyma's instruction was clear for all to see.

Husna-bhaji perched on the edge of the deckchair, her hands clasped together on her lap. Sehar, who was hovering undecidedly, caught my eye and I beckoned her to take my place on the swing. I moved to lean against the wall behind it.

'Ambreen, bring tea,' Nannyma called as she settled back on the swing next to Sehar. 'Now, my Husna, how are you?'

'Well as can be,' Husna-bhaji answered in a low, soft voice that added to her fragility.

'And your sewing, how is it coming along?'

The corners of Husna-bhaji's lips rose in a slight curve. In school we had read stories that referred to a type of beauty that could turn men into warmongers. Husna-bhaji's face fitted into this category, and I think many men would've happily launched a thousand ships in her name, just as in the myth of Helen of Troy.

'The work is steady,' Husna-bhaji was saying. 'I have a lot of work put my way. I am so grateful to Nusrat-ji for her gift of the sewing machine.'

'Good,' Nannyma said. 'I shall be sure to let Nusrat know that her gift has made you self-sufficient, but I shall not pass on your gratitude because there is no need for it. Nusrat did it because it was the right thing to do, not because she needs you to worship her.'

Sehar and Farhat looked puzzled at the words, but I knew why Nannyma had spoken them. She once told me that people should give to the poor out of the compassion of their own hearts, and to please God. Applause and gratitude should not be the factors determining generosity.

Husna-bhaji stared at her hands again.

'If you would like to do something in return, then please remember my Nusrat and her family in your prayers.'

Husna-bhaji met Nannyma's eyes and nodded vigorously. 'I do,' she said. 'I do so every day. Five times a day.'

The conversation halted as Ambreen-bhaji came out on to the veranda. She was holding a large tray laden with an expensive china tea set and two very ordinary tin mugs. I cringed inwardly when I saw the crockery, knowing that the tin mugs were going to be used to serve Husna-bhaji and Farhat. It seemed I was not the only one who was unhappy.

'Ambreen,' Nannyma scolded gently. 'You are missing two china cups. There are five people on this veranda, not three.'

Ambreen-bhaji's eyes widened to saucers and her stiff body language as she retreated into the house illustrated what she thought of the violation of village etiquette. She returned nonetheless with the appropriate china and poured the steaming hot masala tea into five cups. Typically, both Husna-bhaji and Farhat tried to object to the fine china when it was offered to them, but Nannyma insisted they drink as they were her guests. She also insisted Ambreen-bhaji join us, which she did – but with a tin mug of tea.

Later that evening when Nannyma and I were alone, she told me Husna-bhaji's life story. Her husband had been a field hand who had died five years ago following an accident with a tractor. He had had little money to pay for medical care and a lot of pride, so the simple wound he had sustained in the accident had been allowed to fester until it had become so septic that it poisoned him. Husna-bhaji had been childless when her husband died and her in-laws wanted nothing more to do with her, fearing that any compassion towards the new widow would mean an extra mouth to feed.

Husna-bhaji was thrown out of the extended family home

and it was Nannyma who had ordered a simple mud hut to be erected for her, not far from the field in which her husband had been injured. Nannyma had also arranged for Husna-bhaji to learn the craft of sewing clothes from a teacher in a neighbouring village, and then Nusrat-kala had sent money from America for a sewing machine. Husna-bhaji spent her days sewing for the teacher, who kept her supplied with orders, and her nights alone with the door bolted against the world.

But her in-laws could not stand to see her live and prosper when their son was dead. They had thought that throwing her out of the house would result in her leaving the village, but Nannyma's intervention had put paid to those ideas. Husna-bhaji's continued presence only exposed the family as the mean-spirited lot they were, and even the poor knew that the gates of heaven would not open for those who ill-treated widows and orphans.

Wanting an excuse for their heartlessness, her in-laws began to spread rumours that Husna-bhaji was a green-eyed witch who lured men. In a feudal village where women have no status without their husbands, the women began to believe the rumours and feared that this beautiful woman would steal their men away. The men began to fear Husna-bhaji too, believing their wives' tales that she could ruin a man if he did not satisfy her.

I found the whole thing quite bizarre and would not have believed it had I not seen Farhat's behaviour towards the widow. Farhat was an honest and simple girl, and I could never imagine her being unjust with anyone.

'Do you think,' I wondered aloud to Nannyma, 'that there may be some truth in the rumours? After all, there is no smoke without fire.' As soon as I spoke the words I regretted them, for a dull disappointment took hold in Nannyma's eyes.

'Zeba,' she said quietly. 'I want you to remember these words. In our holy book, the Qur'an, it states clearly that you need four witnesses before you can accuse a woman of adultery, except when a woman has been raped. There does not need to be witnesses for such a crime. However, in the case of Husna and the rumours about her, not a single soul has witnessed anything untoward against her, and believe me when I tell you that many jealous beings have spent days and nights spying on her to gather evidence.

'In my eyes Husna is innocent until four witnesses can stand up, put their hand on the Qur'an and swear that they have seen her in the company of strange men. "No smoke without fire" is a phrase used to accuse and wrongly convict the innocent of the imaginings of perverted minds. The Qur'an protects women. I suggest you read it properly.'

Put in my place by Nannyma's stern reply, I said nothing, but my cheeks burned with embarrassment. For all my education – both in England and on this very veranda – it seemed that even I had temporarily fallen victim to the village gossip.

Chapter 10

The days continued to pass slowly at Nannyma's house, and I did not hear a word from my parents. I knew they were in touch because they phoned my grandmother every morning, but not once did they ask to speak to me. I preferred it this way. It meant that I didn't have to think of the reality of my situation, I could block out all thoughts of Asif and instead pretend that I was just enjoying a holiday at my nannyma's and spending time with my new friends.

It would not be an overstatement to say that Sehar and Farhat had become my world. I began to love the two girls like best friends. I wasn't sure if they felt the same about me, but I knew Farhat loved Sehar dearly, although their relationship was complicated by Farhat's equal devotion to Sher Shah's family. They would often argue, or rather Sehar would shout and Farhat would patiently try to explain that men knew best. They were like a broken record, circling and repeating the same views against each other.

One afternoon the three of us were lounging under a mango tree away from our usual spot.

'I want that fruit,' Sehar said, gazing up. 'Go get it, Fatty.'

Farhat stood up immediately, her head falling back to reveal the arch of her neck as she looked up. She seemed to be considering her words and cleared her throat before speaking.

'Sehar-ji, is really high,' she eventually volunteered. 'I'm thinking, I'm not reaching.'

'You are my maid and I want that fruit . . . Actually . . .' Sehar said slowly so that Farhat could understand, a glint suddenly in her eye. 'The baby wants it. It's a craving. Yes, the baby wants it, and the baby boy is your lord and master, remember? You are bound to the men of this family. Get the mangos.'

Farhat swallowed. 'I . . . if baby wanting it, I is getting it,' she said, but her voice was trembling.

I shot Sehar a look. 'Don't be so mean; you know she won't be able to reach.'

'Fatty's job is to make me and the baby happy,' Sehar insisted stubbornly.

'Sehar . . .' I tried again.

'I would have escaped had it not been for that little witch!' Sehar suddenly erupted.

Farhat dragged her gaze away from the fruit hanging temptingly from the branches. Her eyes settled on Sehar nervously. She had heard the change of tone in Sehar's voice, although she had not fully grasped what her mistress had said. Farhat showed her nervousness by hopping from one foot to the other, seemingly unaware that she was doing it at all.

'Farhat!' Sehar was suddenly like a cold empress, heartless and bitter as she ordered her maid about.

The peasant girl stopped hopping and began to jump up on both legs, the thick rope of her plait, twined with a lime-green ribbon today, swinging violently. Her arms waved frantically in the air as she attempted to grab the lowest branch, which was still three feet above her head. It was a useless attempt.

'Fatty, leave it,' I ordered, feeling sorry for the girl.

Instead of obeying my instruction, Farhat ignored me and jumped up a few more times. Then she paused, rested her little face in the cradle of her palm before throwing her hands gleefully in the air.

Sehar and I stared at her, bemused.

'I is knowing how to getting the fruit,' Farhat declared. 'I seen the boys do it, isn't it. Zeba-ji, let me on your shoulders.'

I glanced down at Farhat's grubby red flip-flops that shielded her dry, coarse feet with their chipped toenails from the hard earth.

Sehar followed my gaze and snorted. 'What's up, girl? Don't want her dirty feet on your shoulders?'

'Don't be daft!' I snapped, immediately feeling ashamed of my snobbish instinct.

'So let her do it . . . eh. Fatty, get on Zeba's shoulders now.'

I wanted to object. Farhat was tiny, but I still doubted whether I would be able to hold her weight on my shoulders.

'Why can't she climb on you?' I demanded. 'I mean you're a lot taller.'

'Cause I've got a baby in here,' Sehar said, stroking her stomach. 'Eh, Fatty, get on with it. It's the best idea you have ever had.'

Farhat's face beamed with the compliment and she strode purposefully towards me. Gazing into her determined face, I was in no doubt that the tiny girl would wrestle me to the ground in order to serve her mistress.

Seeing no escape, I lowered myself to my knees and shot Sehar a dirty look.

'This is going to be so much fun,' Sehar declared, ignoring my venomous glare.

I rested my hands against the tree trunk for balance and readied myself for Farhat's weight. I thought of Asif's mother, Mariam-chachi. She would have been horrified to see me behaving in this way. After all, girls did not do this kind of thing, any more than they refused their father's orders.

Farhat placed her right foot on my shoulder and using the trunk to steady herself, lifted her left foot on to me. She was even lighter than I had imagined, but a weight nonetheless.

'Hurry up!' I rasped.

'It's not high enough,' Sehar drawled to the side of us. 'You're going to have to stand, Zee.'

Muttering under my breath, I managed to raise myself slowly to a standing position, my legs wobbling with the weight. I sensed Farhat reach up and stretch her body before she suddenly lunged off. With the girl suddenly off my shoulders, I fell back on the ground and found myself staring up at the sight of her swinging like a monkey off a branch. Farhat was trying to gain momentum so that she could swing her entire body on to the tree. She managed it within seconds and I was impressed at how agile she was. Sehar too had a grudging look of admiration on her face.

Farhat moved along the branch until she could get to a thicker, stronger one and climbed on to that. The mangos were now within plucking distance.

'Eh,' Sehar called up. 'The fruit at the top of the tree is meant to be the sweetest. Reach up to the highest branch.'

'Stop it!' I cried, knowing the foolish maid would do anything to please Sehar. 'How is she going to get down if she goes higher? It's dangerous.'

Sehar ignored me and jabbed a finger in the air. 'Up . . . up . . . baby wants the sweetest fruit.'

We both watched as Farhat climbed another two branches. She did look like she was dangerously high and she was gripping the branch tightly with one hand as she plucked the fruit with the other.

'Sehar-ji,' Farhat called from high above. 'I throw fruit down? You catch, isn't it?'

'Don't bother,' Sehar drawled. 'Baby has decided that it doesn't want the fruit now. But it wants you to stay up in the tree.'

The voice was uncertain. 'Sehar-ji?'

'Baby has decided that you are not a girl. You are, in fact, a monkey and you deserve to remain in the tree.'

'Hey, stop it!' I objected, but Sehar ignored me.

'Baby thinks that you are the monkey of Sher Shah's family, therefore you should live like one.'

'You're out of order, Sehar!' I said, shaking my head in disgust.

Sehar turned icy eyes on me. The mischievous look was gone and in its place was a cold anger.

'She needs to understand that I would be free if it wasn't for her ratting on me the day I escaped.'

'She was only doing her job,' I defended. 'It would have been worse for her if she had remained quiet.'

'What about me?' Sehar demanded furiously. 'She betrayed me!'

I thought about it and then said, 'She was never yours to trust.'

Sehar's breathing became faster suddenly and she staggered back. Pushing my outstretched hand away, she lowered herself to the ground and placed her hand protectively on her bump.

'Are you all right?' I asked, concerned.

Sehar nodded and looked up. 'Farhat!' she called.

It was the first time I had heard Sehar use her maid's name.

'Sehar-ji?' The voice was small and frightened.

'I need you to understand something. I hate you because you betrayed me. Do you understand that?'

'Yes, Sehar-ji.'

'I want you to know that you are a betrayer of women. Of sisters. Do you understand that?'

'No, Sehar-ji.'

I closed my eyes. We were going to be here all day at this rate. Sehar was unrelenting.

'You should have chosen to side with me. I am your sister. I am a girl like you. We needed to stick together, but you chose to side with the men.'

'But men know best,' came the reply.

Sehar let out a high-pitched scream, clearly frustrated at this girl who worshipped her, but demonstrated no loyalty at all.

'Sehar-ji, please forgive me saying this. It is not being my place.'

'Say it then!' Sehar snapped.

'You is a woman. You not know what good for you.'

'I'm going to kill her,' Sehar gritted out. 'That is if I let her down.'

'Enough now,' I muttered wearily.

'Farhat, if I tell you to remain in that tree until tomorrow morning, will you?'

'For you Sehar-ji, yes.'

'So you love me?'

'Yes, Sehar-ji.'

'So if I run away tomorrow will you tell anyone that I have gone missing?'

'Yes, Sehar-ji.'

'Yes what?'

'Yes, I will tell Sher Shah. I having to tell him, isn't it? You is woman. You shouldn't be . . . uh . . . is word . . . umm . . . right . . . I know . . . displeasing him.'

'She really is a monkey,' Sehar breathed.

'She is a product of this system,' I said quietly. 'Forget it, Sehar. When that gang of boys isn't following us around keeping an eye on you then she's your ball and chain. You won't escape her.'

Sehar stared moodily into space, not replying, and I knew that something had happened to her.

'Why don't you tell me what's wrong?'

Sehar's lower lip trembled. 'He hit me again last night,' she said in a small voice. 'He's supposed to leave me alone now that I am pregnant, but he came to my room last night and called me a lot of names before punching my arm.'

'Why?' I whispered.

'I don't know. I think his family laugh at him because he can't control me. That he can't get me to accept that I am married . . . That I can't be trusted to appear in front of guests without swearing at him. I think his dad calls him weak and so he hits me to prove that he is strong.'

'I'm so sorry, Sehar,' I said, close to tears.

'You know I should've left home when that Tara offered to help me,' Sehar said miserably. 'I should've got to the railway station and met Tara. I know she would've helped me.'

We sat in gloomy silence for a few minutes. I could not think of the words to make my friend feel better.

'You know I'm being a cow to Fatty because I can take my rage out on her,' Sehar said quietly. 'But that means I'm not really any better than him. I'm picking on her because I can.'

'So be better than him,' I advised.

Sehar nodded. 'Let's get her down.'

Not surprisingly we couldn't get Farhat down easily. She managed to get on to the lower branches, but short of a ladder, there was no way of getting her to the ground without her jumping and risking breaking a bone.

Sehar and I decided that we would go back to the *haveli* and get one of the men to arrange a ladder.

'Wait here,' Sehar called and we both turned to walk away. Unfortunately we had not moved five paces when we heard a thud behind us.

Farhat had jumped.

We ran back in astonishment to the small crumpled figure lying on the ground. She was crying softly, her face twisted with pain.

'Why did you jump?' Sehar cried, leaning over Farhat with worry.

'Because you leaving me in tree and my job is staying with you,' Farhat sobbed.

'Oh for crying out loud!' Sehar shouted. 'We were going to get a ladder for you.'

We both helped her to her feet and Farhat was able to hobble, albeit painfully, all the way back to the village. Back at the *haveli* her mother diagnosed a sprained ankle.

'I twist it running along path,' Farhat lied. 'I stupid girl.'

Sehar shot me a look to see if I was going to tell the truth. I bit my lip and said nothing.

In the days that followed I noticed that Sehar's hatred of Farhat almost disappeared. Farhat's willingness to lie for her was about as much loyalty as she could expect in a culture where the whole idea of sisterhood was an alien concept and unquestioning duty to the landlord prevailed. And above all that, she'd realized that she wasn't making herself feel any better by being horrid to a person more vulnerable than herself.

Chapter 11

I watched from the floor as Nannyma swayed back and forth on her swing. Behind me on a low stool sat Ambreen-bhaji as she emptied a handful of coconut oil on my hair.

She had seen me kick a stool this morning when a bout of frustration had overtaken me at the news that my parents were planning to return to England the day after tomorrow. And without me!

I knew why they were going home. Dad's shop couldn't run itself and he was losing money every day that he remained in Pakistan. But I still couldn't believe they were actually leaving without me. I winced as a searing pain took hold in my big toe where I'd kicked the stool.

'Too much tension in your head,' Ambreen-bhaji had announced, rushing over to push me down on the couch before taking my foot in her hands. 'Too, too much,' she repeated, squeezing my injured toes. I yelped with pain.

A few hours later when Nannyma and I had settled on the veranda after a lunch of rice and vegetables, Ambreen-bhaji had stepped out brandishing a large jar of solid white coconut oil.

'This will help you relax,' she declared. 'We need to ease tension from your head.'

'She is very good,' Nannyma offered, indicating with her eyes for me to follow Ambreen-bhaji's silent instruction to sit down.

'And you are next,' Ambreen-bhaji warned Nannyma, who in turn held her hands up in mock defeat.

I had imagined that I would be receiving one of those therapeutic scalp massages that you get at the hairdressers if you agree to add ten pounds to your wash, cut and blow dry. Personally I thought the money was well worth it. The girl who did the shampoo at Lyle's, the most popular hairdressers in town, was always able to knead the right bits of the scalp in order to make me feel all floaty.

The first time I'd managed to persuade my mum to allow me to have my hair cut professionally was two years ago when I turned fourteen. In a way, Mum's reluctant agreement to put away her scissors had been my first victory in trying to gain some independence. Susan had been getting her hair cut at Lyle's since we were twelve. She'd had two whole years of a fashionable layered style while my head had resembled a bushy nest. On my first visit Lyle, the hairdresser, had put his fingers through my hair and grimaced. I still remember the tall, geeky looking man with no hair of his own dressed in a yellow shirt and brown checked trousers.

'My mum always cuts my hair,' I confessed, before he asked. Might as well blame the culprit, I thought. I didn't want Lyle to think I'd *chosen* to wear my hair like this.

He grinned and winked at me through the mirror. 'Darling, I will transform you now.'

And Lyle, my fairy godmother, did just that. He cut off about ten inches and layered the front to frame my face. I suddenly looked like another person . . . almost fashionable.

'You like it?' Lyle asked, holding a mirror so I could see the rear view.

'I love it,' I answered. 'I'm always coming here.'

The next time I had gone in for a trim, Lyle easily convinced me I needed a scalp massage and a bottle of his special shampoo and conditioner. I hadn't been convinced about his hair products, but the scalp massage performed by the girl who washed my hair had been amazing, and very, very different from the near torture that Ambreen-bhaji was now performing on my head. She was using her fingers to scoop the white base out of the pungent jar, rubbing it in her hands to turn it into a liquid and then depositing it on my head to soak my roots. Ambreen-bhaji then employed a vigorous rubbing technique – and it hurt. At one stage she tipped my head back and began the same technique at the base of my hairline. It hurt so much that tears sprang to my eyes.

'Ambreen-bhaji,' I implored.

'Shush, your hair needs oil,' she responded in a clear no-nonsense tone.

'Be gentle,' Nannyma advised, taking pity on me.

Ambreen-bhaji grunted, but thankfully did ease the pressure slightly.

'You foreign girls are so delicate,' she said. 'My friend Jannat . . . you know the one who works at the *haveli* . . . she says that Sehar-memsahib is just as bad. She squeaks like a little animal every time they try to oil her. She needs to oil her body or she will end up with stretch marks. When the baby grows inside it pulls the skin . . . like a balloon expanding with air. You have to look after yourself when bringing new life into world. But the foreign girl won't listen. Tut, tut.'

I exchanged a look with Nannyma, but neither of us said anything.

'And you know Jannat said –' Ambreen-bhaji was cut off as the subject of her disapproval climbed the steps of the veranda, followed by Farhat.

'*As salaam alaikum*,' Sehar greeted us.

We responded and I tried to grab my opportunity to get away from Ambreen-bhaji's fingers, but she was having none of it, yanking me back into place.

Sehar looked down at me in amusement. 'You look bad, girl.'

Through the pain I'd given no thought to what I looked like. Probably as if a pan of chip fat had been poured on to my head.

'No, no,' Farhat chimed in. 'You look good. I can see the tension is going from your face. You are so lucky to have Ambreen-bhaji give you this massage.'

'Farhat dear, would you like to have your hair oiled?' Nannyma asked.

Farhat immediately became flustered. 'Oh no, I couldn't . . . I really couldn't.'

'Nonsense,' Nannyma said. 'Ambreen-bhaji, I think Zeba is done. Why don't you use the rest of your remarkable energy on Farhat.'

I felt Ambreen-bhaji's hands make one final swoop over my head before releasing me.

'Come, Farhat,' I said, scrambling up as fast as I could.

'No, no,' Farhat protested.

'Oh, stop making a fuss and sit down!' Sehar commanded.

Farhat hesitated, the internal battle in her mind apparent on her face. Should she allow herself this luxury or not? Was it her position to accept?

'Fatty!' Sehar snapped.

Farhat almost tripped over to Ambreen-bhaji in her haste to obey.

Ambreen-bhaji began the ritual of scooping the solid white oil out of the jar as Farhat untied the long, shiny green ribbon from her hair. The girl proved to be a model client; not a sound came from her as she closed her eyes and allowed her roots to be rubbed by the other maid's strong hands. By the end of twenty minutes, when Ambreen-bhaji had retied the green ribbon into her long hair, Farhat looked blissful.

'*As salaam alaikum.*'

I spun around at the sound of my dad's voice. He stood next to Mum, stiff-looking and unsure whether to climb the two steps of the veranda.

Farhat and Ambreen-bhaji sprang to their feet.

'Please come up,' Nannyma invited.

My parents climbed the steps and stood awkwardly in front of us. The tension could have been cut with a knife.

Sehar stood up and made her excuses. 'We need to get back to the *haveli*.'

Nannyma nodded. 'Be sure to visit again, my dear.'

Sehar smiled at my parents as she passed them with Farhat in tow, looking at the floor out of respect.

'Please sit,' Nannyma said. 'Ambreen-bhaji, bring water for my daughter and son-in-law.'

Ambreen-bhaji hurried into the house as my parents sat down on the bench opposite the swing.

'So you are leaving for a month?' Nannyma asked. 'Can business really not survive without you?'

Dad stared at the floor. Finally he said, 'No, there are issues which require my attention.'

We waited to hear what the issues were, but he never told us. Instead he cleared his throat and said: 'We shall return for the wedding.'

I inhaled sharply at that statement. Until that point, the thorny issue of my marriage had almost become a distant event to me. My dad met my eyes directly for the first time since he'd arrived and cleared his throat again. It was as if he was preparing to deliver a speech to me, but I beat him to it.

'You might as well not bother coming back in a month because I'M NOT MARRYING ANYBODY!'

My dad shot to his feet. 'You will marry Asif!' he shouted. 'I have given my brother my word. I will not go back on it.'

I sprang up to meet Dad's glare head-on. 'I don't care what you have promised Taya-ji,' I spat out through gritted teeth. 'It wasn't your place to offer me in the first place!'

Dad looked like he was going to explode. His chest rose a couple of inches and his face turned crimson. He looked like he was having difficulty even finding his voice. Mum, who had been sitting looking quite horrified at the spectacle of her husband and daughter, suddenly stood up and placed a hand on Dad's arm.

'Ji, calm down,' she cried desperately.

Dad was taking deep breaths now, his hand resting on his heart. 'Tell her,' he rasped. 'Tell her that this is my *izzat*, my honour. Who is she to ridicule me in front of my family, my peers? I will die before I break my promise to my brother.'

It was like that evening on the rooftop again; I was the rabbit caught in the unrelenting glare of a speeding car's headlights. I stood frozen.

'Zeba, go inside.'

The order came from the calm voice of Nannyma. I turned to her, shell-shocked, still unable to move my feet.

'Your father needs to calm down,' Nannyma said patiently. 'He can't do it with you here.'

'Get inside!' Mum screamed suddenly. 'You will give him a heart attack!'

I heard the words in slow motion, as though a Bollywood record was being dragged on the turntable.

'Get away!' Mum screamed again.

I couldn't bear it any more. I turned and fled from the veranda and away from Nannyma's house. I did not stop running till I reached the riverside and slumped down on the grass, burying my face in my hands. I could not believe what had just happened. My parents were not my own any more. They seemed possessed, as if the traditions of the village had entered their heads like some demon, brushing away any love or compassion they might once have had for me. I had ceased to be the precious baby girl they had brought home from hospital, the toddler who had learned to walk by clinging to their fingers, the nervous child who had leaped into their arms after the first day at school. All those shared memories that should have invoked a protective arm around me seemed to have disappeared. I was no longer my father's *rani*, I was my father's honour instead.

As I tried to empty my mind of thoughts of my parents, various memories flitted through my head. My mind cast back to another betrayal that had happened at junior school. Jessica Harper had been the most popular girl in our class and, as everybody wanted to be her friend, she wielded complete power over who got to play in the lunchtime game of rounders. I'd always been on her team – until she had chosen to share her family's view that I, on account of being Muslim, was also responsible for the atrocities of 9/11. Susan had furiously accused Jessica of ignorance, but Jessica had insisted that she 'wasn't playing with terrorists'. I had put on a brave face, but only I knew the immense hurt I'd felt as Susan, ever the loyal friend, and I had watched our classmates play from the sidelines for the remainder of Year Six.

I thought about Jessica and what had happened to her. Her popularity had extended to the boys in Norland High and that – coupled with an ignorance of contraception as well as religion – had resulted in her getting pregnant at fourteen. The whole school had been shocked. Teenage pregnancies were not the norm in our school. The girls of St Mary's High were taught to be achievers, and their exam results were some of the highest in Yorkshire. Previous head girls and successful Oxbridge candidates were invited back to address assemblies with speeches themed: 'It Doesn't Matter Where You Come From – If I Can Do It, So Can You.'

Then my mind skipped momentarily to those aunties back home who discouraged too much education for Muslim girls. 'What are our girls going to do with all this education?' they would say. 'Their jobs are to be wives and mothers. Give them too much independence and they want to change things. It is not good for our community. Our sons won't know how to handle free-thinking women with degrees.'

I wondered what my exam results would be. I supposed it no longer mattered what letters of the alphabet were assigned to my subject list. My teachers had predicted A-stars for me, but what use were they now? My life was over. My destiny was not to be an empowered, educated woman, but merely to be a wife to a husband I did not want.

I thought of Susan and wished that I could contact her. She too had been predicted high grades, and I could just imagine her throwing her result sheet in the air and jumping for joy. A stab of envy pierced my heart as I wondered who she would be celebrating her results with instead of me.

At that precise moment, I hated Pakistan with all my being.

Chapter 12

I refused to accompany my parents to the airport. Everybody gave me their two-penn'orth about seeing them off but I was adamant in my decision. Deep down I knew that I would not be able to calmly watch my parents board a plane for home – while I was forced to remain against my will.

They came to say goodbye on the morning of their departure. We had not spoken since I had fled Nannyma's house two days ago, and it became clear that our wounds were still raw when we faced each other on the veranda.

'Are you sure you will not come to the airport?' Dad asked in a cracked voice.

I gazed up at him. He looked terrible. Pouches that had never been there before hung under his eyes and his cheeks had sunk into his face, giving him a haunted look. Suddenly I wanted to run up to him and fling my arms around his neck, beg him to make this nightmare stop. I knew in my heart that Dad did not want this marriage for me, that he did not want to leave me behind. Why else would he look so tortured? What kind of a hold did Taya-ji have on him? How was any of this honourable?

'Your dad asked you a question,' Mum said with a detached expression.

I fixed my eyes on her and wondered if she regretted the hurtful words she had shouted at me. Somehow, I doubted it.

'No, I'm not coming,' I answered quietly.

'Very well,' Dad nodded. 'We will see you in a month.'

He took a step towards me, hesitant, unsure. I willed him to take the remaining three so that he could pull me to him in one of his bear hugs. He didn't. Instead, he chose to turn round and walk off the veranda towards the waiting Land Rover.

At any other time in my life I would have been shocked by this goodbye from my dad – but I wasn't today. I didn't think anything could shock me any more. I stood stiffly as Mum stepped forward to place her arms awkwardly around me. I think she expected me to return her cold embrace, but I didn't bother and kept my own arms by my sides. I was making a point and wanted her to object, to say something, but she refused to acknowledge my rudeness and merely stepped back, murmured a goodbye and left.

I watched the procession of Land Rovers spray the dust in the air as they powered out of sight.

'Zeba.'

I turned with a fixed smile to Nannyma, determined not to cry. I didn't see the point. It's not like it made an ounce of difference anyway.

'Why don't you go and visit Sehar at the *haveli*?' she suggested.

I flopped down on the swing to stare moodily ahead. I could still see the tyre tracks the vehicles had left behind.

'Maybe later,' I replied. 'I'm not really in the mood for company.'

'As you wish,' Nannyma said, taking her place on the swing.

Burning up with inner frustration, I got up and retreated into the house. Picking up one of Nannyma's Urdu magazines, I stared at the front cover. It was a horrific picture of the aftermath of some sort of explosion. A handful of charred bodies lay on a road with the burnt shell of a truck in the background. I turned to the inside pages and came across a small column in English. I read the piece, which was about the spiralling violence in the North-West Frontier Province. Five suicide bombs had been detonated last week killing hundreds of soldiers near an army barrack. I thought of Asif and the everyday danger he faced along with the rest of the country's armed forces. Then I thought of my dad's uncle, Imran-chacha, the retired army officer who had talked about facing a Muslim enemy on the other side of the country's border. It was his belief that common faith did not matter when facing an enemy. Did he still believe that now that his great-nephew was in combat with his own people?

I wondered what Asif was like. Was he an honourable soldier, full of bravery and compassion, or was he a thug in uniform? I decided not to examine those thoughts; I didn't want to think about Asif. Discarding the magazine, I stood up and flipped through Nusrat-kala's old records, searching for something to match my depressed mood. Among the sounds of the 80s were some classic Bollywood tunes, including Sehar's favourite, *Umrao Jaan*. I placed it on the turntable and music filled the room. Violins and the sitar combined to produce a melancholy tune, and then the unmistakable voice of Bollywood's most famous female artist, Asha Bhosle, sang the lyrics of a broken heart. Settling into an armchair, I let the sounds wash over me.

'Hey, you!' Half an hour later the words jostled me out of

my daze. I opened my eyes to find Sehar grinning down at me.

'Hi,' I responded half-heartedly. 'What are you doing here?'

'Why? Do I need an invite to see my favourite friend?' Sehar asked, depositing her pregnant body heavily on the sofa.

I shot Sehar a dirty look. I wasn't in the mood for her bolshiness today.

'We thinking we coming to cheering you up,' Farhat announced from the doorway.

'Why don't you sit down?' I invited.

She smiled and sat, cross-legged, on the floor.

'Why don't you sit on the chair instead of the floor?' I said irritably, knowing full well she wouldn't.

Farhat looked at me blankly, not moving.

'Why don't you –'

'Oh, for crying out loud, Zee, enough of your class warfare!' Sehar erupted. 'She's going to stay on the floor. Making her sit on a chair isn't going to end your situation.'

I clenched my jaw. Yes, granted, affording Farhat some dignity was not going to make things better for me, but that didn't mean we couldn't treat the girl with some respect. I opened my mouth to make that point but Sehar was having none of it.

'I ain't arguing, girl,' she stated. 'We came here to have a laugh. Now get out of your mood because we are going to have some fun.'

I glared at Sehar and she stared right back, one eyebrow arched. Her expression said it all: *You haven't got it half as bad as I have, so snap out of it.* I gave in then. What was the point of sulking? These girls were my friends, and they had come to make me feel better.

It turned out that Sehar's plans for 'fun' involved painting Farhat's face with heavy make-up.

'It wasn't hard to convince her. She needs a rehearsal before her wedding day,' Sehar informed me, opening a big bag filled with cosmetics. 'Come here, Fatty.'

Excited beyond words, Farhat ran up to her mistress and offered up the blank canvas of her face. From my armchair I watched Sehar paint as the record played itself to a finish and then I got up and turned it over so we could hear the songs on the other side.

'There we go,' Sehar announced, sitting back.

Farhat turned her face in my direction and I inhaled sharply in shock. The maid looked like a transvestite. Her skin was a grey mask because Sehar's foundation was much too light and her eyebrows, shaded with a dark pencil, looked gruesome. The only saving grace of Sehar's work was Farhat's lips, painted a deep, luscious red.

'Sehar, I really don't think you should go near Farhat's face on her wedding day,' I advised, struggling to contain a gurgle of laughter.

'Hmm,' Sehar replied, frowning slightly. 'You might be right.'

'How is I looking?' Farhat asked eagerly.

'Uhh . . .' I was lost for words.

'You look like a geisha,' Sehar offered confidently.

'Geisha?'

'Yes, you know the book I have in my room? The cover with that Japanese girl?'

'Oh,' was Farhat's response. She didn't look so excited any more. Perhaps our expressions were a giveaway.

'Can I looking in mirror now?'

'You might die of shock,' Sehar muttered.

'What?' Farhat asked, looking around for a mirror. She spotted one on the far wall.

'Actually I don't want you to see my work yet,' Sehar announced.

Farhat gazed up at her mistress and frowned. 'As you wish.'

Sehar sat back on the sofa. 'Yes, go and wash your face and remember no peeking. I forbid it.'

Farhat nodded and stood up. I watched her walk around the sofa, but instead of heading for the door, she jumped over a small table and ran for the mirror. Sehar's head shot up and she yelled, 'I said no!'

It was too late. Seeing her reflection, the maid let out a gasp of horror. 'I looking awful,' she squeaked in a shocked voice.

Sehar, who was still stuck on the sofa with her baby weight, wagged her finger at Farhat. 'That was just practice. I will do better next time.'

Farhat turned indignantly towards Sehar. 'No thank you.'

The sight of the overly made-up girl trying to stand her ground was too funny and Sehar and I burst into laughter. Farhat gazed at us with hurt in her eyes and I tried to compose myself, but with little success.

'You is very mean,' Farhat said quietly. 'If I go looking like this to my Abdullah, he not marrying me. He will call me names. That fat man in circus who making everybody laughing. What is it?'

'Clown?' I offered.

'Yes.'

'You are right,' Sehar hiccupped. 'I did a bad job. Look, here, you liked this lipstick, didn't you?'

Farhat eyed the product in Sehar's hand.

'You can have it,' Sehar offered. 'You will be wearing red, right? Well, it will match your outfit. Perhaps on the day you can just wear lipstick, a bit of kohl and mascara. That should be enough to make you a glowing bride. Here, take it.'

Farhat remained on the spot but her eyes looked hungrily at the Western manufactured tube.

'For crying out loud!' Sehar erupted. 'Just take it.'

Farhat moved forward to claim her gift. 'Thanking you,' she said shyly.

Sehar held out her hands and the maid pulled her up with surprising strength.

'Let's put some groovy tunes on,' Sehar enthused, waddling over to the stack of records. 'I want to dance.'

Farhat clapped her hands. 'Yaah.'

Sehar selected a record and the music of the 80s filled the room. 'Dance, Fatty,' she commanded.

Farhat began to move her arms in an action similar to a hen beating its wings, and then overcome with sudden shyness, buried her face in her hands.

'Fatty, don't stop!' Sehar cried. 'Come on, I'll join you.'

I watched through peals of laughter as Sehar threw her hands in the air and swayed her hips, her baby bump moving with her.

'Come on, Zee,' Sehar urged.

I skipped forward and began to dance, and it was at that moment that Nannyma entered the room with a frail-looking elderly man. He wore a purple *ajrak* turban on his head and carried a very expensive-looking cane to support his weight. His black eyes were like twinkling buttons set in a heavily lined, smiling face.

'Always nice to have merry young women in the house,' the man remarked.

Sehar and I straightened our *kameez*es and pulled our shawls in place.

'Girls, this is Sahib Mohammad Ali Khan,' Nannyma informed us. 'He is the landlord of the neighbouring district. Sahib, this is my granddaughter, Zeba, and that is Sher Shah's daughter-in-law, Sehar.'

I noticed Nannyma did not introduce Farhat, who was now standing by the doorway trying to hide her face behind her shawl.

'Girls, would you leave us?' Nannyma said. 'Sahib and I have some land matters to discuss.'

'He seemed nice,' I said a few minutes later as we walked down to the riverside.

'Apparently he is the opposite of my father-in-law: kind, just and fair,' Sehar replied. 'That's why everyone calls him Sahib. It means 'sir' in English. They are giving him extra kudos because he is so widely respected.'

'Really?' I asked doubtfully. Could landlords be respected when the very structure of the feudal system meant there was always a master and a servant?

'Yeah,' Sehar nodded. 'They're not all bad, you know. Some actually care about their tenants. Sahib Mohammad's villagers are quite fortunate. He has a small medical centre for the poor and there is a school for peasant kids, which his wife opened before she died. The girls have to attend until they are at least thirteen and the boys till they are fifteen.'

'Why not sixteen like us?' I wondered.

''Cause this isn't England!' Sehar said flatly. 'Why do you keep comparing everything with home? This is another country, not even developed, and you keep applying the standards of a First World country.'

I suppose Sehar was right. At least the children benefited from some education, unlike the ones in this district.

'I think I know why Sahib is here,' Sehar said suddenly.

'Why?'

'There is a big meeting going on at the *haveli* later today about the elections. You know that Sher Shah is standing for election as the political representative of this part of Sindh, don't you?'

'No,' I replied. 'Why would I know that?'

'I thought your nannyma would have told you,' Sehar said with a shrug.

'Will he win?' I asked.

'Yes, of course. Why wouldn't he? Ninety per cent of his voters are illiterate and will do as he says. They will vote for him using their fingerprints as their identity. The idea of a democracy is a sham. The people don't have a choice with their vote. They will think of their stomachs and they will vote for the landlord. It's standard practice.'

'What about people in other districts?'

'Well, that's what the meeting is about. Sher Shah will get a commitment from the other landlords by promising something or other, and they will order their tenants to vote for him.'

'How do you know all this?'

'There are a lot of people in the *haveli* and they all talk.'

Farhat who had been silent throughout this conversation nodded her head vigorously, having managed to understand that last sentence.

'Yes Zeba-ji, lots of people in *haveli*.'

Something occurred to me. 'What about his opponents?' I asked, thinking of the elections we had in school every year for Head Girl. There were at least five or six girls from Year Eleven who would each try to persuade the rest of the school that she would make a fabulous Head Girl. 'Surely the meaning of an election means there is more than one candidate.'

Sehar laughed. 'They don't stand a chance. Money is what wins elections in these parts. If Sher Shah stood his donkey as the candidate and told everyone to vote for it, the animal would win. Most of the people around here can't read or write so they don't know better. People just do as they are told by their landlords.'

Chapter 13

I missed fish and chips.

I missed the big fat chunky slices of potato and large cod that our local chippie sold. I had mine with lashings of vinegar and I ate them sitting on a wooden bench on the high street. The bench was dedicated to a man named Jamie Simpson and the plaque read 'Husband, father, councillor'. I'd no idea who he'd been and I doubted the other users of the bench knew either.

My local chippie was run by old Mrs Smith, a woman past a certain age and very much set in her views. Mrs Smith had been a presence in my life for as long as I could remember. She was tiny and bent with age, and as I'd grown from a child to a teenager, Mrs Smith had seemed to shrink further and further into herself. My mum would say she could remember Mrs Smith when she'd had a straight back but I couldn't.

Dad said that Mrs Smith had played an important role in our lives. One fine day, back in the late 1980s, he had been on his way to Leeds from Manchester when his train had pulled into a quaint-looking railway station. He'd decided to get off for a while just to take in the scenery of the surrounding hills.

However he hadn't realized that the train would only stop for two minutes and it had left without him. Having been told he'd have to wait another hour for the next train, he'd decided to go for a wander and the first shop that had caught his eye on the little high street had been Mrs Smith's chippie. He had enjoyed a hearty meal using a stubby wooden fork to scoop his potatoes and fish out of old newspaper. But the best part of it had been Mrs Smith's friendly chatter.

Dad said it was on that full stomach and hospitality that he'd decided this was the town for him. Besides, the open countryside reminded him of home. Old Mrs Smith was a firm fixture on my dad's Christmas list, which was made up of his non-Muslim friends. In return, Mrs Smith never forgot to present us with a chocolate box every year on our festival of Eid.

Susan and I were always fascinated by the old woman's knowledge of our area's history. Her family had lived in our town for centuries and there were more stones belonging to her family in the graveyard than any other. Mrs Smith said she could trace her family back to the time of the Wars of the Roses, although the history teacher at St Mary's High, Mr Duffield, wasn't so convinced about the credibility of that claim. We'd touched on the Wars of the Roses in school once, but nobody could talk about old battles as passionately as Mrs Smith.

When we were younger, Susan and I had sat in Mrs Smith's shop window bay on quiet afternoons and begged her to tell us the story again. She claimed it used to be called the Cousins' War because the battles for the English crown had been fought over by the descendants of one king. On one side had been the

House of Lancaster and on the other the House of York, and Mrs Smith's however-many-greats-ancestor had fought for the House of York. The craziness had continued for decades until it had all ended when the Lancaster heir, Henry VII, married the daughter of a previous York King, Edward IV. Finally both sides were united . . . or so I had thought.

'So everybody lived happily ever after?' I'd once asked. 'Did your family marry into the other side as well?'

'Not on your life!' Mrs Smith had erupted. 'They killed our people. Slaughtered them! The kings might forgive and marry each other but we don't. It was our blood that was spilt.' And so Mrs Smith, a proud Yorkshire woman, carried around a centuries-old hatred for Lancashire.

Looking at Ambreen-bhaji as she prepared home-made chips for me, I wondered whether people here carried hatred from the ancient past that had been handed down from generation to generation. The only thing I knew was that the two most competitive provinces, Sindh and Punjab, were rivals in wanting their own countrymen to become prime minister of the country. One of Sindh's most famous prime ministers had been Benazir Bhutto, the first woman prime minister of Pakistan.

I found it strange that this country – where women still drew water out of a well – had been progressive enough to elect a woman prime minister. Pondering these thoughts, I said as much to Nannyma when I walked out on to the veranda.

'Well it's more dynastic power than elected power,' she said. 'Her father had also been prime minister and had been executed by his rival who had toppled his government, so people just voted for her as his heir, and for her reforming ideas. But don't underestimate it. The sight of a woman at the top still opens doors for other women. There are lots of women activists in her party that otherwise might not have been there.'

I pondered on Nannyma's words, but not for too long as an unexpected guest arrived.

'*As salaam alaikum.*' It was Sehar's sister-in-law Shabana.

'*Wa alaikum salaam*,' Nannyma greeted her warmly. 'Please come in.'

Shabana climbed the veranda steps and sat on the deckchair. 'I just wanted to come and say goodbye,' she said to Nannyma. 'I am leaving for England tomorrow morning and I am not sure how long I will be away. My father is ill you see.'

'Yes of course,' Nannyma nodded sympathetically. 'I did hear about your father's stroke. You must be very worried.'

'Thank you,' she said. 'He is in hospital, so he is being looked after by the doctors.'

I gave Shabana a sympathetic look but I wasn't sure what to say. A silence developed and I took a step backwards. My nostrils were filled with the smell of fried potatoes. It wasn't quite the same as Mrs Smith's chips but the handmade slices would have to fill my craving for now. As I turned to walk into the house, Shabana called out to me, 'Zeba, do you have a minute?'

I stopped and turned to look at her quizzically.

'I wondered if I might be able to speak with you.'

'Oh, right,' I mumbled.

Nannyma stood up. 'I will see how Ambreen is getting along with your favourite English food.'

'Oh no, you don't have to leave,' Shabana objected.

'I know, I know,' Nannyma smiled, 'but I want to make sure Ambreen doesn't add chilli powder to Zeba's chips. She has been craving them all morning.'

I watched Nannyma walk into the house before I took her place on the swing.

'So how are you settling in? 'Shabana asked.

I looked down at my fingernails and decided to be honest. 'Not very well, actually.'

'No? Well, that is sad news, but not surprising. You know sometimes it takes time to adjust to another country with its different weather and lifestyle, but you become accustomed after a while.'

I shrugged.

'You know I am so used to living here now that when I visit England it takes me a while to adjust over there. No servants, no chauffeurs. Life is very hard in England.'

I stared at Shabana. Was this woman for real? She seemed to sense my disbelief because she gave a small laugh and said, 'Anyway, enough about my preferences, I came to talk to you about Sehar. You know she likes you a lot.'

I smiled. 'I like her too.'

'So perhaps you could have a word with her?'

I hesitated and then asked, 'About what?'

'Well . . . to stop resisting her fate for one.'

I didn't say anything.

'Sehar has still not accepted that she is a married woman now, soon to be a mother. She needs to stop fighting this family.'

I felt uncomfortable. 'I really don't think it's my place to say –'

'You don't understand,' came the interruption. 'The deed has been done. She is married to this family now. She needs to accept it rather than argue and fight with everyone.'

There was silence for a few seconds and then I said, 'I don't think she is happy.'

Shabana made an unladylike snorting sound and rolled her eyes heavenward. 'Nonsense,' she dismissed. 'She is being stubborn and refusing to accept her situation. Her life will be so much easier if she just accepts the fact that she is married.'

I decided not to say anything and Shabana continued.

'Look at me. I'm the same as you both. I was born in England but my *kismet*, my fate, was written with my husband and he lives here in Pakistan, and so my children and I must too. I grew up just like you, went to school, to *madrassa*, spent Saturdays at the shopping centre. All I wanted was to get married and have children and when my dad suggested I marry my cousin, I was happy. Sehar should learn to be happy too. Look at this lifestyle: no housework, no cooking. It's the life.'

'I think Sehar wants more,' I mumbled.

'What more?' Shabana demanded, her voice suddenly sharp. 'She wants to go out and work, does she? Believe me it all seems glamorous, wearing a business suit and going out to work but it is not. Work is work, whether you sit in an air-conditioned office or clean the floor like Farhat and her relatives do every day.'

I didn't know what to say and the silence stretched. Finally I said, 'I think you and Sehar are two different types of people.'

'No, we are one and the same. We hail from the same traditions and family. She is no different. She just *thinks* she is different. Look, I found it hard to adjust when I came here in the beginning, but I did. Sehar even has a choice. She can go back to live in England with her husband when her baby is born. I never had that choice. My husband hates England. He thinks it's cold and wet, so I had to adjust to the heat and dust here. That is what we women do in our lives. We adjust. We fit ourselves around our husbands. That is the way to lead a contented life.'

'Did you want to marry your husband?' I suddenly asked.

Shabana looked taken aback. 'Of course I did.'

'Sehar didn't,' I said simply.

Shabana stared at me, her eyes slightly narrowed. 'That is neither here nor there. It is done now. She is married and she needs to accept it. Her sulking and moods put pressure on everybody in the *haveli*. She is such a drama queen. If you were a true friend you would help her accept it. God knows I have tried, but she treats me with contempt for being happy with my lot. And you know she has no respect for my father-in-law, Sher Shah. He is a highly respected landlord and soon-to-be politician and she talks back rudely to him when he enquires about the baby's health. I am surprised he has been so calm with her this far.'

What did she mean, *calm with her*? 'What would you suggest your father-in-law does?' I spat, unable to hold back. 'Beat Sehar like his son does?'

Shabana sucked in her breath and then stood up stiffly. 'It didn't have to be that way. Sehar brought it upon herself, always fighting her husband. That is why I am telling you to advise her to accept her situation . . . she will not win. She cannot. This is a man's world.' She got up. 'Anyway, it was nice talking with you . . . I will just go inside and bid your nannyma farewell.'

Within minutes Shabana had left and Nannyma and I resumed our places on the swing. Something was bothering me: Shabana had said that her husband had hated England and so she had settled here. What if Asif hated England? Would I, like Shabana, be expected to adjust to the heat and dust of this village?

For the second time I voiced my thoughts out loud, but on this occasion Nannyma had no words to say to me. She just looked at me sadly and let the silence linger between us until Ambreen-bhaji came out with a plate of chips.

I had no appetite left as my stomach fluttered with unease, but I took the plate and managed to eat a few just to keep the smile on Ambreen-bhaji's face.

Chapter 14

The days passed slowly and I put my worries about Asif to the back of my mind. Each day seemed to merge into the last until sometimes I didn't even know whether it was a Monday or a Wednesday – but I always knew when it was a Friday. The holy day's afternoon prayer was preceded by a sermon on the loud-speaker for all the villagers to hear. It was in Sindhi and I was confused that the imam's preaching was never political and made no mention of the upheaval that was happening in other parts of the country. But wasn't that why Asif was in so much danger in the army? How could the imam talk about the need to be a good person without mentioning the bloodshed we all knew about?

Most days Sehar would visit to get away from her in-laws, but sometimes I would walk over to the *haveli* on my own, passing the huddle of huts where the children would run up to me, chattering and laughing. I had been here a month yet they still seemed to be fascinated by me. If I asked them how they were they would collectively giggle, leaving only one or two of the most confident among them to respond with 'he's fine' or 'she's fine'.

One day, I decided to take some almonds. At first many of the children were too shy to hold out their hands, but they scavenged what they could from the few who did take from me. Eventually I handed the remainder to the ringleader, Abdul, a boy of about eight who wore the same grey, washed-out *salwar kameez* every day. It turned out he was the youngest brother of Farhat's fiancé, Abdullah.

Late one morning as I prepared to leave for the *haveli* to have lunch with Sehar, I couldn't find my usual source of almonds in the kitchen. 'But there was a whole packet,' I said to Ambreen-bhaji.

'Yes, my dear,' she replied drily. 'There *was* a whole packet until you emptied and fed it to the children.'

'Well, don't we have any stored away?'

'No!' Ambreen-bhaji snapped. 'We don't! And I was going to make special *kheer*, rice pudding, tonight. It's only special when it contains almonds. What will I do now?'

I smiled at Ambreen-bhaji. She always amused me when she got irritable. I strode over to where she was standing and placed my arm around her shoulders.

'You know what, you could always ask Kareem-baba to go and get more from the market . . . Actually, tell him to get two extra packets for the children.'

Ambreen-bhaji shrugged off my arm. 'Yes, yes, that is all my husband is good for, to go to the market to fetch almonds for the village children. You are spoiling them.'

My mind drifted to my dad's shop. 'Ambreen-bhaji,' I said gently, 'they are children. When I was their age I used to go through half the sweets in our shop.' I knew Susan would have raised an eyebrow if she could hear me now. I was lying when

I said that I had only ever raided the counter when I'd been younger. The truth was that I ate at least two chocolate bars and as many sweets as I could manage whenever I had to cover the till counter.

'Yes, well,' Ambreen-bhaji said, bringing me back from happy thoughts of cola cubes and sherbert lemons. 'There is nothing left to feed them now . . . But I will ask him to get an extra pack for you and your merry band of followers.'

I followed Ambreen-bhaji out of the kitchen. 'What can I give them instead, now?' I asked. 'I have to go and collect Sehar and Farhat for the *mela* this afternoon.'

The *mela* was a big event in the village calendar. According to Farhat it was the best gathering of the year, filled with fairground rides, entertainment and food. People from all parts of the region travelled with family and friends to join in. For the last week Farhat had done nothing but talk of the *mela*. She had regaled Sehar and me with tales of her previous visits, trying to persuade us to attend. I didn't mind, but Sehar was insistent that she would not go with her mother-in-law as our chaperone. Apparently we needed to be accompanied by an older female relative as it would not be appropriate for us to attend by ourselves. In the end, Nannyma took pity on Farhat and volunteered to come with us.

'You care too much about what the children think,' Ambreen-bhaji retorted, but then she softened when she saw my expression. 'OK, let me think . . . Rather than disappoint them, why don't you use the southern path to the *haveli*? The route is longer, but it will save you the embarrassment of empty hands.'

I nodded and Ambreen-bhaji gave me instructions to the

back of the *haveli*. I smacked a kiss on her cheek and she pushed me away, flapping her hands like a mother hen, but I knew from the rosy glow in her cheeks that she was secretly pleased at my show of affection.

The secluded pathway was quiet and I could hear crows cawing in the distance as I walked alongside the fields. My eyes searched for a scarecrow, but I couldn't spot one. I wondered how the farmers kept the crows from picking at the crops, but as I contemplated the question big, fat raindrops began to fall on my head. I looked up and saw dark grey clouds gathering. When did that happen?

I quickened my pace; I didn't want to get caught in a downpour. I remembered Memsahib's disapproving look when she had caught me in her hallway covered in mud. I couldn't turn up like that again, so I broke into a run. However I hadn't got very far when the heavens opened and within seconds I was completely drenched. Struggling not to slip on the dirt road, I slowed down until I saw a building with a dome and four minarets ahead of me.

The mosque.

I knew from Ambreen-bhaji's directions that I wasn't far from the *haveli*, but I didn't fancy walking through the wet field and mud in the pouring rain. Perhaps there was a women's section in the mosque where I could take shelter. I ran up to the wooden door and knocked. I waited but nobody answered and so I banged again, harder, and this time the wooden door creaked open under my hand.

Removing my sandals I tentatively stepped inside. I found myself in a large room the size of our main assembly hall at school – which had enough space for five hundred pupils. The floor was covered in black tiles and the walls were a cream colour. At the other end of the room stood the imam's box, from where he led prayers, and a wall cabinet in which I imagined copies of the Qur'an were stored.

I knew there was still time before the muezzin would call the faithful to afternoon prayers. The men all seemed to pray at an allotted time governed by the mosque, but women were free to pray in a wider space of time at home. Nannyma would always take an afternoon nap first and then pray at about two o'clock. As the mosque was empty, I decided to wait for the rain to stop.

I moved further into the room and slid down to the ground. The floor beneath me felt hard and I thought of how uncomfortable it must be for the men who knelt here bowing their heads to the ground in prayer five times a day. The floor of our local mosque back home was covered in a plush carpet. From the age of five till eleven I'd spent every weekday between the hours of five and seven in Imam Zahid's *madrassa*. In a class of about thirty children, we'd sat in a row on the floor and rested our Qur'ans on the low wooden bench in front of us while we learned to recite the words in Arabic. The last half hour was spent perfecting over and over again the prayer for everyday activities like eating, going to sleep and leaving the house.

I thought back to a girl from school, Mary, who was a devout Jehovah's Witness. At lunchtimes – in full view of the whole canteen – she would place her food tray on the table, fold her hands together, close her eyes and begin to mouth her prayer of 'grace'. When she'd first arrived at our school in the middle of Year Seven, the dinner ladies had looked at her and giggled while the rest of us just stared and sniggered. Admirably, Mary hadn't cared, whereas I would not be caught dead uttering a prayer in either Arabic or English in front of my classmates. All I'd ever wanted to do was blend in, and I'd succeeded in not standing out at school just as I merged right in with the other kids at the mosque.

At the *madrassa* I became good friends with a girl called Tasneem. Her dad owned an Indian restaurant in a nearby town, which was very popular with the local people. As there were very few Muslims and no mosque in her town, her mum drove ten miles every day to ours. Tas and I bonded over our frustration at missing *Home and Away* and *Neighbours* when we were confined to our *madrassa*. We both suspected that our popularity at school was affected by the fact that we couldn't join in the pre-assembly chats every morning about the latest storylines.

But this deprivation of daily soap-watching ended when Tas and I turned eleven. Imam Zahid announced that we were too old for his class and that if we wished to further our knowledge of Islam then our parents should seek out a female teacher. To my delight my parents couldn't be bothered to organize tuition, but Tas's mum drove her the extra miles to Leeds three times a week. Despite promising to keep in touch, our phone calls just dried up as we turned into teenagers. It was fascinating how people whom you saw almost every day could disappear from your life so quickly. *Like my parents*, I thought wryly. I wondered how Sehar and I would stay in touch when I went home, my mind still refusing to accept any alternative.

My thoughts wandered back to my surroundings as the

patter of the rain slowly died down and I decided to leave the mosque before a second downpour began. The path was wet and muddy outside but the sun was already peeping through the clouds as I hoisted up my *salwar* and began to walk as fast as I could.

Chapter 15

Within minutes the pink monstrosity that was the *haveli* emerged against a blue sky. I entered through the back entrance and was told by a maid that Sehar was asleep, but that Farhat was in the downstairs TV room. I wiped my feet clean so as not to mark the marble floor and set out to find her. I discovered her on her hands and knees wiping the floor with a wet cloth, while her attention was fully focused on an American programme on TV. I pulled up my *salwar* and crouched down on the floor to surprise her.

'What you doing?' she cried, springing up. 'You not get on floor. What people say?'

'Well . . .' I was lost for words as I stood up.

'Never minding,' Farhat said hurriedly. 'Come, let us wake Sehar-ji to go to the *mela*.'

I nodded, still reeling from the reminder that Farhat would never base our relationship on anything other than her status in the village. I don't think she would accept that I thought of her as a friend.

I followed her into Sehar's bedroom. Roused from a deep sleep, Sehar was annoyed about having to get ready to go out.

'There had better be some seats, Farhat,' she complained, rubbing her stomach. 'I can't walk around for long with this huge bump, you know.'

Farhat nodded but continued to fuss about, ensuring Sehar had everything she needed. Then we ate a lunch of rice and vegetables before Farhat's fiancé, Abdullah, came to collect us in one of Sher Shah's minivans. When it was time to leave in the mid afternoon, the sun was still high in the sky. We drove back to Nannyma's house to collect her, Ambreen-bhaji and Husna-bhaji. Farhat was unimpressed at having to travel in the same car as the outcast widow, but one look from Nannyma meant she kept her mouth shut.

'I don't think I should be going,' Husna-bhaji said nervously. 'You know who will be there . . .'

'My dear, you cannot hide,' said Nannyma, cutting her off. 'It is a public place and you have every right to be there.'

Husna-bhaji had looked pleadingly at Ambreen-bhaji, but found no support there. We all knew that once Nannyma had her mind set on something nothing would change it.

It was a long drive on the dusty inland roads and the bumpiness of the ride made me feel sleepy. I leaned my head against the seat rest and my mind drifted again to home. Our town's big holiday festival was based around Christmas. I'd always loved that time of year, mainly because it meant two weeks off school and a binge of entertainment shows on TV. Sometimes when it snowed Susan and I would take cardboard boxes from my dad's shop and race to the top of the nearby hill. There we'd use the flattened boxes to slide down on the snow alongside dozens of other locals. It was the best.

In the centre of town Christmas lights would appear, in the

shapes of Santa Claus, reindeers, little elves and stars. These decorations had been a feature of our town for as long as I could remember, but last year there had been a big dispute over them. I'd heard my mum and dad talking about it over dinner. Apparently our area had two new local government councillors who were insisting that the lights could not be used any more because Christmas lights were offensive to the town's small Muslim community.

'I'm not offended,' my mum had said.

'Exactly,' Dad had agreed, absolutely livid. 'They can't use our religion as an excuse for someone else's agenda.'

In fact, he had been so incensed that he'd organized a petition, which he urged all his customers to sign declaring their support for the Christmas lights. The petition stressed that although as Muslims we did not celebrate Christmas as a religious festival, we respected the right of the local people to celebrate their own festivals in whatever manner they saw fit. My dad presented the petition to the local council and in the end the two councillors were defeated and our town's Christmas lights came on in December as scheduled.

'A victory for common sense,' my father declared happily.

There were now only a few months left till the town's lights would be lit again and I wondered if I'd be home to see them turned on by some suited middle-aged councillor whom nobody knew, but everybody cheered. Our town was so small and unremarkable we didn't even merit a D-list celebrity from some long-forgotten reality-TV show.

The cold days of Britain's December seemed a million miles away as the minivan finally pulled up at a field filled with colour and bustle. The wealthy women were dressed in their finest clothes, the fabrics a heady mixture of red, yellow, blue and purple embroidered with gold and silver thread and topped with twinkling beads. Gold jewellery and colourful gems glistened against their necks, fingers and wrists. The poorer women wore fabrics just as bright, but significantly sparser in gold and silver embroidery and beads. Simple necklaces adorned their necks and on their wrists shone bangles made of glass instead of precious metal.

Compared to the locals, Sehar and I were quite underdressed, but neither of us cared and in such heat we were actually grateful to be dressed in simple white *salwar kameeze*s with light shawls draped across our shoulders. Farhat, on the other hand, was wearing a bright lavender-coloured *salwar kameez* with a matching ribbon in her hair and glass bangles on her wrists. She had even applied the same coloured eye shadow. She looked like a walking, talking lavender flowerpot and she made me smile with her excited chatter. Two steps behind, Husna-bhaji followed with a nervous step, fully garbed in her black *burka*. I imagined she was really hot underneath the folds of dark fabric as it absorbed the sun's rays. She held her scarf over her mouth and I knew she was trying to hide her face, lest anyone recognize her.

The *mela*, it turned out, was a cross between a funfair and a circus. As we walked around we stopped to watch the performance of a trained monkey. The little animal looked like something out of a Disney cartoon. A red Ali-Baba hat was perched on his head and he was wearing a matching waistcoat. The monkey was dancing to the tune played on his owner's flute with his paws waving in the air. Every time the music stopped the monkey would whip off his fez and hold it out to his captivated audience for money. As the locals obliged with plenty of coins, I couldn't help thinking that this display would probably be frowned upon back home.

'People are staring at Husna-bhaji,' Sehar whispered to me.

By now Husna-bhaji was covering most of her face with the end of her black shawl, leaving only her eyes peering out. I glanced around to see some peasant women staring and pointing at her. I looked closely at their faces – a combination of ridicule, anger and fear – and then it hit me. These women genuinely thought Husna-bhaji was a witch. She was such a spectacle to them that she could have been the star attraction of the *mela*. If the women could have their way, would they have tied Husna-bhaji to a wooden pole and thrown rotten fruit at her?

I thought of school history lessons about the treatment of medieval English witches. People back then had thought of water as a pure element, so accused women were tied up and dropped in the river. If the pure water accepted her – as in, if she sank, and probably drowned – then it was declared the woman had been wrongly accused and was innocent of witchcraft. But if she floated and survived? Well then she had been rejected by the water and was therefore a living, breathing witch. And so she would hang or burn at the stake.

I threw a sideways glance at Husna-bhaji, unable to stop my mind from playing out its own images of her in the role of an English medieval witch, her hands tied to her feet, ready to be dunked in the river. I must have been frowning because Nannyma placed a hand on my arm.

'Don't worry about the looks, my dear. Nobody can touch Husna-bhaji when she is with me.'

I had to bite my lower lip to stop the words from tumbling out. *But what will happen to her when she is alone?*

'Zeba,' Nannyma said, smiling at me. 'I want you to enjoy yourself. Please make an effort for me.'

I smiled back, nodding, and then Nannyma called Husna-bhaji to her side and asked if she could link arms to help her walk. I knew Nannyma didn't need to do this, but pulling Husna-bhaji close to her sent a message to everyone at the *mela* that the widow was under her protection.

We walked towards the rides on the other side of the field where a big wheel majestically rose up into the air. It was the only high-rise ride and there was a long queue of people leading up to it. Two men stood nearby, waiting to manually crank various pieces of machinery. There were no engines to power anything.

Farhat wanted to sit on the big wheel and begged Sehar to join her, but she merely pointed to her bump to make her refusal clear, which only left me to join the queue. After a long wait we climbed into the plastic seat, which was shaped like a teacup, and secured the lock on the metal security bar.

One of the men operating the ride swung his arm and we were abruptly pushed into the air. The teacup swayed back and forth, and although we were only four feet in the air, Farhat clutched my arm, her face suddenly looking nervous.

'Hey, it's OK,' I reassured.

She nodded but did not let go of my arm.

'Have you ever been on one of these before?' I asked.

Farhat mumbled a 'no'.

Oh no, I thought. The teacup would rise until everyone below would look like ants. I hoped Farhat wasn't going to panic. Was she afraid of heights? It didn't make sense; she had happily climbed the mango tree that day on Sehar's order. But then again the tree wasn't as high as this ride. Maybe she was just feeling dizzy from the rotation. I closed my hand around hers and squeezed tightly, then stole a look at her face. She was white with anxiety and I wondered if I would be seeing the contents of her stomach soon. I hoped not.

'It's going to be OK,' I repeated.

'Yaah . . . yaah,' Farhat nodded, trying to look brave as the wheel moved higher. For the rest of the ride Farhat kept her eyes firmly closed as she bruised my hand with her crushing grip. Thankfully it was over quickly and a grateful Farhat scrambled off. The wheel had only spun around once, but I suppose the men could only work their arms so much in a day. *They really should get engines*, I thought as I watched a group of overweight ladies, dressed in their finest, queue for a place in the rotating teacups.

Chapter 16

A few days later the fun of the *mela* was forgotten as I stared up one morning at the man known as Sher Shah.

This was the first time I had seen him in the flesh, and I realized that the huge portraits in the *haveli* did no justice to his fierceness. He was enormous: well over six feet tall and seemed almost as wide. His face was huge and he was bald, save for a few strands, which he tried to sweep across his shining head. His eyes were like his face – big and round and looked like they were ready to pop out of their sockets at any moment. His nose was long and hooked and a moustache – more fearsome than even Taya-ji's – dominated his upper lip, the curls at both ends defying gravity to rest halfway up his fat cheeks. This man was the stuff of children's nightmares.

He towered over me as we assessed each other. I imagined he was unaccustomed to women meeting his gaze head-on. I had noticed the village girls trying to merge into the walls when Taya-ji crossed their paths, and I imagined they behaved the same way with the landlord. When I'd first seen this behaviour, I hadn't been sure if it was out of fear or respect, but I knew now that it was one masked by the other.

'So you will be our Asif's wife?' Sher Shah said silkily, his mellifluous voice at odds with his vast bulk. I had expected it to be deep, masculine and gravelly.

I maintained the eye contact that many of the villagers would regard as scandalous. Etiquette dictated that I should show deference to his male strength and higher intellect by behaving coyly, almost pretending to be dumb so that he could feel superior. I had no intention of doing anything of the kind, or of raising my shawl to my head, which was a basic requirement to offer respect in Pakistani society. I left my hair uncovered, flowing free in all its glory as if it signalled my loyalty to Sehar. This man's wish had the final word here, and he could have put a stop to Sehar's marriage if he'd had an ounce of moral responsibility. But he was a leader simply because he had inherited his father's land, not because he had compassion. This was his power. This was feudalism.

'Are you going to continue scowling at me?' Sher Shah joked, but there was an underlying warning in his voice.

I racked my brain for some cutting reply, but lost the opportunity when Nannyma walked back on to the veranda. She had left us to find some papers Sher Shah had come to collect. I wasn't sure what they were and a few weeks ago I would have accused Nannyma of fraternizing with the enemy, but I knew now that in order to survive in the jungle the different beasts had to find ways to live together.

Nannyma ordered tea and Ambreen-bhaji brought out the best china. There was an extra cup on the tray. It turned out that my taya-ji was also coming to pay a visit. I'd not seen him or Mariam-chachi since the day I had left their house on an ox cart.

Arriving in a cloud of dust, Taya-ji jumped out of his Land

Rover and leaped up the two steps of the veranda. Noting the scene before him, he glowered at me and not a word of greeting passed his lips. I knew he had noticed my uncovered head and was probably fighting the urge to grab my shawl and cover me completely with it. I couldn't work out who was scarier: my uncle, with his thuggish demeanour, or Sher Shah with his malice disguised by a diplomatic veneer. But I realized I was insulting my nannyma by not respecting the village hierarchy in her presence, so I reluctantly pulled my shawl over my hair.

Nannyma greeted Taya-ji with *salaam* and pointed to a chair. He accepted the invitation before turning to me, his expression now no longer so furious. 'How are you?'

I was surprised by the question. I wasn't sure what I was expecting but a query about my wellbeing was not what I'd had in mind. 'Good,' I answered.

'So I hear that you have made friends with Sher Shah's daughter-in-law. Very good.'

I nodded. Of course he would know that. The entire village knew the actions of the foreign girls.

'She will help you adjust to this life,' Taya-ji said gruffly. 'Not long now until Asif returns from duty and you can both leave for the UK. It must be very boring for you here with your old grandmother. No TV.'

'Actually I prefer it here,' I said defensively.

Taya-ji's eyes widened at my tone of voice and he looked like he was going to bark at me, but then he thought better of it and simply said, 'Well, I am sure you will be able to visit often.'

'Visit from where?' I demanded.

'From my house of course. You and Asif will live with us after you get married and before you leave. We don't have this

Western business of young married couples living separately from their parents.'

Sher Shah made the appropriate guffing noise at the pointed remark.

'Taya-ji,' I said icily, 'I don't know what my dad has said to you, but I have no intention of marrying your son, or anyone else in this village for that matter. If you had been considerate enough to ask *me* about my plans, I would have told you.'

The silence that followed was so thick with tension that Ambreen-bhaji could have cut it with the knife she used to slash the throats of chickens. I didn't know where I had found the courage to confront Taya-ji, but the bravery in my veins was vanishing quickly under his murderous glare.

Sher Shah took charge. 'Young girls do not know what they want most of the time, and they definitely don't know what is good for them,' he said. 'We have come here on business; let's not allow a domestic dispute to waste our time. Zeba, leave us.'

I blinked. Was this man ordering me to leave my own home?

'Zeba,' Nannyma said. 'Go see your friends. I have some land business to take care of.'

As much as I wanted to protest, I knew that it was better to obey Nannyma's authority. At least it would irritate the men that I listened to her but not them. Stepping off the veranda I made my way to the river. I didn't want to go to the *haveli* and Sehar and Farhat would not wander over for another couple of hours.

I sat down at the usual spot and thought furiously about the arrogance of Sher Shah and Taya-ji. Who did they think they were? My blood was beginning to boil as I thought of several retorts I could've thrown at them.

'Are you all right?' a voice interrupted my thoughts. I looked up into the beautiful but concerned face of Husna-bhaji.

'Yes,' I mumbled.

'Do you mind if I wash my clothes here?' she asked, holding a small bundle under her arm.

I shrugged half-heartedly, not really wanting the company, but unable to be so directly rude. Sometimes when I'd passed the river in the morning, I'd seen the village women huddled in groups washing their clothes. They were always armed with bars of soap and wooden sticks that looked like cricket bats. They would soak each item in the river, create a lather with the soap and then beat the soapy clothes with the stick. According to Farhat, it was the traditional way of removing dirt.

Husna-bhaji crouched down and began to untie her bundle, revealing three *salwars* and two *kameezes*. She shuffled forward and dipped one item in the river.

'You are alone?' she asked. 'Does your nannyma know you are here?'

I nodded. Taking the hint that I wasn't in the mood to speak, Husna-bhaji busied herself with her washing. I leaned back on my hands and glanced sideways. Two men were walking on the crooked path that ran alongside the river. They looked like field hands and were heading in our direction. I expected the men to walk past but when they were just a few feet away they stopped in their tracks. They were staring at the side profile of Husna-bhaji. Having recognized the widow, they raised the fingers of each hand to clutch each earlobe and then crossed the fingers from side to side.

I recognized the Muslim gesture, which was normally accompanied by the word '*tauba*', meaning 'pardon'. As a child

I had been taught by my mum to make the sign whenever I wanted to voice my disapproval of something. I grew up uttering '*tauba*' whenever I saw a Muslim person stroke a dog, which was forbidden in Islam, or if I saw a classmate steal a sweet from Mr Sam's corner shop. For years I would religiously touch my ears in a self-righteous manner until I was told to stop by my *madrassa* teacher Imam Zahid, who deemed it 'ancient cultural nonsense'. Looking at the behaviour of these village men, it was clear that the practice was still popular here.

Feeling outraged, I must have been scowling at them as they hurried past us because Husna-bhaji placed a gentle hand on my arm and said, 'You don't have to look offended on my account.'

'I . . . uhh . . .' I stammered.

'Really, it's fine,' she reassured me. 'I am used to it. It is actually better this way.'

'How?' I asked incredulously.

'They think I am a witch. It is better this way because the men keep away from me. I would rather be alone and pure than have to fight off unwanted male attention.'

'Oh,' was all I could manage.

'And I am not alone. Your nannyma is my friend and I live with the main protector.'

I was confused. I thought Husna-bhaji lived on her own. Her smile widened at my puzzled expression, revealing perfect white teeth that any American actress would be proud of.

'I live with God,' she explained. 'He is always with those who are alone and vulnerable.'

'Why don't you remarry?' I asked.

Husna-bhaji's laugh was a light tinkle. 'Who would have me? I am an unscrupulous woman, remember.'

'But it's not true!' I objected. The look on Husna-bhaji's face explained more than she could say. It was too late to convince the villagers that she was anything other than what they had deemed her to be. 'So you can't win,' I said. It was not a question but a statement.

Husna-bhaji gazed into the distance and a shadow settled in her eyes, giving her the appearance of a very sad doll. And then she said the words that were so self-defeated in their nature and so much a consequence of her circumstances that I had no reply.

'I am a woman, Zeba-ji. I can never win.'

Chapter 17

A few days after my outburst with Taya-ji, my nannyma surprised me at breakfast.

'We will visit the imam today,' she said simply. 'Perhaps a man of God will be able to help and guide us through this darkness into the light.'

'Eh?' My mouth fell open and almost with it the contents of Ambreen-bhaji's lovingly prepared omelette.

'We must find a way to end your engagement with Asif,' she continued. 'I have been rereading the sayings of our Prophet – peace upon him – and he has said clearly that a girl's consent is required for a marriage to be valid.'

Relief flooded through me as I realized that my nannyma was going to take steps to end my nightmare situation. Now, as Nannyma's ox cart made its slow journey to the small brick house behind the mosque, I was barely able to contain my hope.

The imam was exactly as I'd expected. He was old with a flowing white beard and wore a white skullcap and long robes. He kept his eyes lowered until Nannyma spoke, and only then did he raise them. I took a deep breath as I gazed into his heavily lined face; it was wise and full of dignity. Since the news of my enforced marriage I'd carried a knot in my stomach, but now, today, looking into the eyes of this holy man, I felt the tight cords of my muscles ease slightly. Perhaps this imam was going to be my saviour.

'Imam Sahib,' my nannyma said in her quiet, serene voice. 'I fear that a great abuse will be done to my granddaughter. She is being married against her will. I do not wish it, but everybody else in our family does. Can you not speak to Mustaq Khan, her uncle, and guide him against committing this injustice? It is forbidden in Islam; it is against our religion.'

The imam's gaze fell on me and he seemed deep in thought. 'Is this true, child?' he asked.

I nodded.

'Imam Sahib,' my nannyma pleaded. 'Do not let my Zeba's fate be that of the landlord's daughter-in-law, whom you yourself married. I beg you.'

I could not believe it. This was the same imam who had performed Sehar's marriage? This was the man she hated! What had Nannyma been thinking? Why did she think that a man who had actually enforced this crime could help?

The answer was delivered in the imam's quiet and sad voice. 'Sister, it is my duty as the bearer of Qur'anic knowledge to speak against this coming atrocity. As for the matter of Sehar Shah, I did not know I was playing a part in that child's false marriage. She was behind the curtain when I asked her for consent, and all I heard was the word 'qabool'. How was I to know it was not the bride's voice confirming her agreement to the marriage?'

Oh my word. I could not believe it. I had to tell Sehar.

The imam continued: 'I will speak to Mustaq Khan. I will

tell them that God does not permit the subjugation of women. But will Mustaq Khan listen to me? I doubt it.'

'You are our last chance,' my nannyma pleaded. 'Our only hope. If he won't listen to you, then who else can stop them?'

'I will try, sister.'

And that was it. Within minutes we were back in the ox cart and heading home. It seemed too simple to think that this was going to solve my problems and bend the will of my family, but for now all I could do was believe that it might.

I hurried across the field to the riverside. Sehar and Farhat were already there. Sehar was holding a battery-operated fan to her face. I don't know why she bothered. It was only the hot air that charged back at her. I flopped down next to them on the blanket.

'You won't believe what I found out,' I declared.

'Oh yeah?' Sehar enquired, only slightly interested.

'The imam who married you now regrets it,' I stated, matter of factly.

Sehar switched off her fan and looked down at me, disbelief shining in her eyes. 'And who told you that tripe?'

'The imam himself,' I revealed, and replayed the morning's event to her.

'So he thought that *I* had said *qabool*?' Sehar said. 'That I had accepted?'

I nodded.

Sehar set her chin forward in a determined way. 'He should have checked,' she insisted stubbornly.

I had been expecting this reaction. 'Sehar,' I began. 'It's not his fault. He didn't know. He came to perform a marriage by invitation. He followed the procedure. How was he to know that it was not your voice giving consent? That it was not your permission? There was a curtain between you.'

Sehar didn't say anything for a long while. Instead she gazed down at the grass and began picking the blades, first gently and then harshly. I saw her eyelashes flutter and I knew then that she was desperately fighting back the tears.

'It's OK to cry you know,' I said quietly.

'I won't give in,' she croaked.

I placed my hand over hers. 'The people who have hurt you are not here to see you like this . . . there's only me and Farhat.'

Sehar bit her lip, trying to control her face, but it didn't last long. Her shoulders slumped and the tears began to spill. Farhat glared at me. Sehar and I had spoken quickly in English and although the maid had been straining to catch the flow of the conversation, I knew she was none the wiser. I could tell that she wanted to comfort Sehar, but did not know how, and so she remained seated behind her, not saying anything.

I reached forward and placed my arm around Sehar. I wanted to comfort her too. We were like sisters, not joined by blood but united through the circumstances that we were facing.

Sehar cried for a very long time and seemed unable to stop. The dam had finally burst, her eyes became puffy and the tears mingled with snot on her upper lip. The ever cool, composed Sehar looked vulnerable at last. We sat under the giant tree for hours, saying very little to each other, but letting the sense of sisterhood wash over us as we knew we were safe with each other. Farhat sat quietly, understanding the need for silence. I wondered what she was thinking. In contrast, all her prayers were being answered by her marriage to Abdullah. I suspected she still couldn't understand our strange Western ways, but she knew better than to say anything.

When the sun finally set, Sehar turned to me. 'You mustn't go through with it,' she said. 'It's not right. It's your life.'

I nodded absently, not sure how to respond. It was all very well to believe my enforced marriage was not right, but how would I fight it?

'There has to be a way out,' Sehar continued. 'If even the imam says its wrong . . . that it's not allowed in our religion, then there has to be a way out.'

'There is no way out,' I whispered. 'If he can't convince my taya-ji then I have no other choice.'

'You do,' Sehar said firmly. 'I'm going to give you the contact details of that woman at the charity that works with the Forced Marriage Unit. Tara . . . you remember I told you about her? She would have helped me if I'd left home. She will come and rescue you. All you need to do is get on the internet and send her a message.'

I stared at Sehar doubtfully. 'If it's so easy, why don't you contact her about your own rescue?'

'Because I can't access the internet,' Sehar admitted, shrugging her shoulders. 'Sher Shah won't let me out of this village and the internet at the *haveli* has secure passwords. Nobody will give them to me. But you live with your nannyma. She is on your side. Tell her to help you. She can take you to Karachi and you can contact Tara.'

I chewed on my lower lip. It seemed so easy. All I had to do was get to an internet shop in Karachi.

'Or you could just send Tara to rescue me when you get back home with the baby?' I suggested.

Sehar gave me a mocking look and I couldn't blame her. I was a coward. If I had been on the *Titanic* I would have refused to get on a lifeboat, just in case I survived. Despite all my protests against the forced marriage, when it came to the crunch I was too frightened to really do anything about it.

'It's always better to be prepared,' Sehar insisted. 'I thought you would find another way out but now I'm not so sure. I know Tara's email by heart. Fatty, give me the knife.'

Farhat handed over the knife she always carried in the small basket of fruit and snacks for the permanently hungry Sehar.

I was hit by a wave of sadness as I watched my friend carefully scrape the email address of a woman I didn't know on a tree trunk. It was tragic. Most girls our age carved out heart shapes and filled them with the initials of boys they fancied. Sehar, on the other hand, was carving out the name of a faceless stranger in London – a fairy godmother who felt about as real to me as a fairytale ending.

Two days later the outcome became clear. The imam had not been successful.

My taya-ji had become so enraged that he had the old man ousted from the mosque with the blessing of Sher Shah. Then, to prove their point, Sher Shah and Taya-ji dragged the imam outside Nannyma's house.

'Fatima-ji,' Sher Shah called, 'come and witness what you have caused with your silly ideas and meddling.'

Nannyma and I dashed out of the house on to the main road. A short distance away, Husna-bhaji stood frozen with her water-pot hanging by her side. It was like a scene from a Bollywood movie. Sher Shah, my taya-ji and a host of other men were surrounding the imam. In the harsh glare of the midday sun, it struck me how frail and old he was. His immaculate white robe had a dirty, brown stain running from his right shoulder to his knees. It seemed to be an imprint of the mud from where he had fallen . . . or been pushed.

There was a quiet dignity in his eyes as he looked squarely back at the landlord and Taya-ji.

'Be gone!' Taya-ji shouted at him. 'You are not welcome here. Corrupting our womenfolk with ideas, daring to speak against our traditions.'

From the corner of my eye, I saw Nannyma slowly cover her mouth with her hands.

'Forty years we kept you in employment in our mosque and this is how you repay us!' Sher Shah boomed.

'It is a crime not to speak up against injustice,' the imam said quietly. 'And you are committing an injustice against this young girl.'

Taya-ji and Sher Shah both looked like steam was going to blow out of their ears and their sharp intake of breath seemed to inflate their protruding fat bellies to bursting point. For a mad, fleeting second I thought that would actually happen and we would be covered in half-digested gobbets of food.

I wanted to giggle. It was a mad urge in response to the appalling scene in front of us.

'Be gone!' Sher Shah shouted before turning around to storm off with Taya-ji by his side.

The imam stood like a statue in his position. I knew it was irrational of me but I couldn't help wondering if he was think-ing of collecting his belongings. Suddenly, to my horror, one of the men stepped forward and pushed the imam, sending him sprawling face down in the mud. A couple of the men laughed. Ignoring them, the imam raised himself off the ground, but was unable to stand up immediately. He seemed to be fighting for breath.

I was just about to run over to him when a loud clattering sound diverted my attention. Husna-bhaji had dropped her water-pot, which smashed into pieces as she ran to the imam still lying on the ground. She put her arm around his back and slowly urged him up. The mud on his clothes now stained the black *burka* she wore. Tears were running down her face and she nearly buckled under the weight of the imam when he finally got to his feet. Surrounding them, the group of men stared; at first open mouthed at this defiance of the landlord's wishes, and then with a gleam of malice as they prepared to humiliate the woman as well as the old man.

'Don't you dare!'

Nannyma's voice was a whiplash – unusually high-pitched and shrill. It had the power to halt the village men in their tracks. 'Get out of here!' she ordered.

They turned and left.

Nannyma hurried over to the imam and Husna-bhaji. 'Come inside,' she offered quietly.

The imam shook his head slowly.

'You cannot leave like this,' Nannyma begged. 'You have served our community for forty years. What these men have done to you brings shame on our village. Please.'

The imam shook his head again. 'I am an imam and they have done this to me. You are a woman and what they will do to you does not bear thinking about. For your own welfare, I will leave.' And he disentangled his arm from Husna-bhaji's firm, protective grip to walk away, slowly and painfully, but with a dignity no corrupt landlord could match.

Helplessly, we watched him go and then Nannyma turned around and walked slowly into the house. I followed her but she closed the door to her room, locking me out. Feeling abandoned, I leaned against the door, trying to reach out to her. I stood there for what seemed like hours, listening with growing misery at the wretched sobbing coming from the other side.

Nannyma may have well been the arbiter of justice and a commanding voice in the village, but only for those who were considered to be beneath her. She was not equal to the powerful men who ran this village. They were in a class of their own, and there was nobody to balance and check their arrogant wishes. It seemed they feared no one, not even God.

Chapter 18

It did not end there. In our quest for justice we had unleashed a storm of malice and arrogance that damaged everything it touched. Sher Shah was in the eye of the hurricane, spinning his evil round and round and round until the destruction was complete.

Back home there were always stories in the newspapers about Asian women who suffered honour-based violence. I had only noticed them because my English teacher, Mrs Malson, had set an assignment about the language used by journalists to cover certain types of stories. Susan and I had picked 'honour violence' and Googled the stories. There were endless cases in the local and national newspapers of women being beaten and even killed by partners or family members. I remember feeling horrified by the articles, not really understanding why people would behave this way. Could someone actually kill a person they claimed to love just because they hadn't behaved in the way they wanted?

But looking at the way events were unfolding in the village I felt scared. For men like Sher Shah it was not enough that an old man should be beaten and kicked out of his home.

The landlord would not be satisfied until every dissident was crushed beneath his leather shoes. His dilemma, however, lay with the figure of Nannyma for she could not be humiliated physically. She was, after all, revered by the villagers. But in questioning Taya-ji's decision to marry me to Asif, Nannyma had challenged the patriarchal structure that was the foundation of the power and control wielded by Sher Shah and Taya-ji. That sort of defiance could not go unchecked.

Mr Duffield had once told my history class that revolutions in the past had often been sparked off not by years, decades or even centuries of oppression, but by a single act that enraged people. He gave the example of Rosa Parks from Alabama in America, who focused attention on racial segregation in 1955 by refusing to give up her seat on a bus to a white person. In this village, thousands of miles away from America, a direct, physical violation of Nannyma would be considered such an act. The villagers would not stand for it, and throughout history successful tyrants knew never to rock the boat if they wanted to maintain their iron grip.

But there was always another way. Mr Duffield had also taught us that prisoners sometimes confessed to crimes not as a result of the torture inflicted on them, but through the fear that a loved one was being tortured on their behalf. And that was what Sher Shah did to Nannyma. He hurt a person she protected in order to hurt her.

It was the day after the scene with the imam, and Nannyma and I were sitting on the swing in silence. Nannyma's face was set in a grim expression and the light in her eyes had dimmed somewhat. I didn't know what to say to her. I knew she regarded the humiliation inflicted on the imam as her own. She had tried to help me and she had failed, and in the process an old man had lost his home and his job. I wanted to put my arms around her and reassure her that everything would be OK, but I didn't know if it would be.

'Fatima-ji! Fatima-ji!' Kareem-baba came racing up to the house, clutching his side and keeling over as he reached the veranda.

'What's happened?' Nannyma cried, rushing to him.

Ambreen-bhaji, having heard the commotion from inside the house, came running out to her husband's side. She made him sit down on the steps and urged him to take a few calming breaths. Finally he said, 'Sher Shah is destroying Husna-bhaji's hut. Her belongings have been flung out and he has got his men swinging axes to break the walls. The roof has already caved in.'

Nannyma's face paled. 'You saw this with your own eyes?' she demanded.

Kareem-baba nodded.

'Then let us go and see for ourselves.'

The four of us marched along the dusty path to the outskirts of the village where Husna-bhaji's hut was located. On the way we came across Farhat, who was standing outside a small mud hut, which I presumed was her home. She stared open-mouthed before falling into step with us.

Reaching a scene of chaos, we found a sobbing Husna-bhaji squatting on the floor, a broken sewing machine cradled in her arms. It was not enough to demolish her home; they had to destroy her livelihood too.

I'd expected Nannyma to comfort Husna-bhaji, but she walked directly up to the five men who were still swinging their axes against the single remaining wall.

'Stop!' Nannyma ordered. 'Why are you doing this?'

The men hesitated, their weapons frozen in mid-air as they contemplated the question.

'They are doing so on my orders.'

We all whipped around in the direction of the voice to find Sher Shah sitting on a deckchair, relaxed and comfortable in the shade of a large tree. He had been callously viewing the destruction from a ringside seat.

'That is my property you have destroyed,' Nannyma spat out icily.

'Granted, but it has been built on my land,' came the counter attack.

'Shah, why are you doing this?' Nannyma asked, deliberately addressing the landlord only by his last name.

It did the trick. His chest rose an inch or two as he physically fought to suppress the gathering rage just under the surface.

'That woman,' Sher Shah growled through gritted teeth, pointing a stick at Husna-bhaji, who was still lost in her own world of wailing, 'is bringing disrepute to the village.'

Sometimes on the news I'd seen people – desperate people – throw stones and shoes at political leaders. I'd always wondered about the point of throwing a pebble or a slipper. It was not as though you could hurt your enemy. But I felt like doing that now. It was an action that communicated desperate rage. Previously I had felt helpless for myself, but today I felt fury on behalf of Nannyma, Husna-bhaji, Sehar and all the wronged women of the village as well as the imam. I wanted to crouch down, pick up a stone and hurl it in the face of this monster.

'Pick up Husna-bhaji's belongings,' Nannyma ordered Ambreen-bhaji and Kareem-baba. 'She will stay with me.'

Sher Shah sprang to his feet and stomped over to us. 'I said she cannot remain in the village,' he forced out through gritted teeth. 'Her presence dishonours us.'

'What about the way you dishonour the village?' Nannyma snapped back. 'What about your mistresses in Karachi?'

Sher Shah looked as if he had been slapped in the face. 'How dare you?' he spluttered, spittle spraying the air. 'Who do you think you are?'

Nannyma did not shrink from him. She met his glare directly with flashing eyes, her head raised in a defiant gesture.

'I will tell you who I am,' she said icily. 'I was a bride here before you were even conceived. Your father was a good man. He cared as a landlord should for the poor and vulnerable, for the widows and the orphans. He would be ashamed to see what his own son has become. You dishonour your entire *zaat* of landlords. Who do you think *you* are? Accusing and throwing out a poor, helpless widow without any evidence of wrongdoing? You use a vulnerable human being to get at me, who dared to question the way you play with innocent lives. And you call yourself a man!'

Sher Shah stared at Nannyma, outrage etched on his entire being. She had attacked him about his *zaat* – the very essence of who he was. It translated loosely to mean 'tribe'. Nannyma had once mentioned that according to some traditional belief systems, a Pakistani was born into a *zaat* just as a Hindu was born into a caste. Neither could be mistaken for class because a person was allowed to move up the social ladder, whereas *zaat* and caste remained with you from birth till death.

As I watched Sher Shah's face turn purple, I knew we were just moments away from a dam of rage bursting . . . and it did.

'How dare you!' he erupted. 'You are an old woman! That is all you are!'

'Enough!'

I spun round at the voice that dared to halt Sher Shah's tirade. It was Sahib Mohammad Ali Khan, the neighbouring landlord whom I had met at Nannyma's house. We all stared at him as he slowly approached from his Land Rover, aided by his cane.

'What are you doing here, Sahib Mohammad-ji?' Sher Shah asked silkily, his face now devoid of the earlier malice and fury.

'I was on my way to your *haveli*,' Sahib Mohammad replied. 'And I noticed this commotion. Why is that woman wailing?'

We all stared at Husna-bhaji who was still oblivious to us.

'Sahib Mohammad-ji –' Sher Shah began, but he didn't get very far.

'Let Fatima-ji explain,' Sahib Mohammad interrupted.

My nannyma gave a quick summary of the situation, but did not include the points about my wedding or the imam's fate.

Sahib Mohammad looked disapprovingly at Sher Shah. 'You will not enter paradise if you treat widows in this way,' he admonished gently. 'We landlords have a duty to care for and protect the vulnerable. You were taught this from the time you could speak.'

Sher Shah's face clouded over with anger, but he did not say anything, respecting the older man's status.

'This has to be resolved,' Sahib Mohammad continued. 'I will not have Fatima-ji upset like this. Make your peace, Shah.'

'The woman cannot stay on my land,' Sher Shah insisted.

'She can stay on Fatima-ji's land,' Sahib Mohammad countered firmly. 'I do not know what your dispute with the widow is, but you cannot treat her in this way, Shah. It goes against the basic teachings of the Qur'an.'

Silence followed as Sher Shah contemplated Sahib Mohammad's words. Finally he nodded his agreement and retreated to the tree's shade, plonking his vast bulk on the deckchair. He was like a child who had been scolded and sent to the naughty step.

I watched the scene with amazement. I could not believe there was a person alive who could keep Sher Shah in check. He was a tyrant, but it was obvious now that his political ambitions outside his own land depended on the generosity of his peers, the other landlords of Sindh.

'Go home, Fatima-ji,' Sahib-Mohammad advised. 'Your work here is done.'

'I am grateful,' Nannyma replied. 'You truly are one of the just landlords.'

With those words Nannyma turned around, crossed the few feet to the sobbing Husna-bhaji and tried to help her to her feet. But my frail Nannyma couldn't manage it, while Husna-bhaji seemed unable to stand of her own accord. I was about to run over but Farhat beat me to it. She grabbed Husna-bhaji around the middle and urged her to her feet, whispering soothing words in her ear.

The six of us traipsed back to Nannyma's house, laden down with Husna-bhaji's belongings. Kareem-baba was holding a long roll of material while Ambreen-bhaji, Farhat and I carried odd bits of household goods and clothes. Husna-bhaji walked in a daze next to Nannyma and when we arrived home, burst into tears again.

Nannyma let her cry for a long time. 'You are not alone, Husna,' she said eventually. 'Sher Shah cannot hurt you in my house.'

'He did this because I helped the imam to his feet?' Husna-bhaji managed.

'Maybe,' Nannyma answered. 'But, even if you had not helped the imam, Sher Shah would have done this. It is less about your help and more about my challenge to his authority in this village. He wanted to hurt me. He has scored his point and so as long as I do not retaliate he will leave us alone.'

And that was the point at which I knew I had no choice but to accept the marriage to Asif. Sher Shah wanted this marriage to go ahead because a cancellation now would be regarded as a direct challenge to the authority of Taya-ji, and in turn his own authority. It was pathetic, but in Sher Shah's eyes a simple act of disobedience could unravel the thread on the centuries-old village tapestry in which women and peasants were the property of rich, unjust men. If Nannyma continued to pick at the thread by helping me to escape their plans, then he would find a way to target her again.

Chapter 19

I resigned myself to the marriage after that, declaring as much to Taya-ji, whose initial scepticism soon gave way to pure glee.

Two weeks later my parents returned and it was announced that the engagement would take place within days as Asif had also returned from duty. The wedding was scheduled for the following month. Mum and Dad were like strangers to me now. I didn't feel I knew them at all, and they treated me with aloofness in return. I think it was easier for them to avoid the accusing look of betrayal in my eyes.

I was pretty sure Taya-ji never told my parents of Nannyma's attempt to stop the wedding. The whole thing was like a shameful secret. Nobody spoke about it. Since the episode with the imam, Nannyma had become a shadow of her former self. I think it was a shock for her to discover that she was nothing but a silly old woman in the eyes of Sher Shah and Taya-ji.

I knew there were many people who would argue that because I was no longer putting up a fight it meant that I had given my consent to be married. I had not. I just had no choice. My heart and my mind would never consent to the marriage and I hoped that eventually Asif would grow to hate me because I would never be able to accept or love him.

It was not the future I had planned for myself.

Sehar's bump was growing bigger and she was impatient to give birth. I think she was just fed up with the burden of carrying the weight. Sometimes she could hardly move; her ankles and feet were so swollen and her back ached. This made it harder for me to see her: she sometimes couldn't leave her room and I would not set foot in Sher Shah's property. One of the worst moments of my life had been explaining to her that I had decided not to resist my marriage to Asif. I felt as if I was betraying her, even thought we both knew I was doing it only to protect my nannyma.

On the days when Sehar felt well enough, Abdullah brought her over in a Land Rover. She made poor Farhat sit in the passenger seat while she languished on her own in the back. The poor maid was mortified every time, as it was against village custom for an engaged couple to be seen together so openly. I did try to have a word with Sehar, but quite typically she laughed it off.

'What? They're engaged! Anyway,' she would say, stroking her protruding stomach, 'baby and I chaperone from the back.'

Two days before my engagement ceremony, Sehar and I were sitting on the swing with Farhat in her usual position on the floor. There was something about Sehar that was mesmerizing. She was absolutely blooming. That was the only way I could describe her. Her skin and hair were shining with good health while her bump seemed to have taken over the middle of her body. She was in her own words 'ready to pop' but she still had two weeks left before her due date.

'I wish this baby would stop kicking,' Sehar grumbled.

'Shall I get you something?' Farhat immediately offered, springing to her feet.

'And you can stop fussing!' Sehar snapped. 'Honestly, between you and this baby, I'm feeling stifled.'

I grinned at Sehar. 'Yeah, right. The baby's your passport to freedom. It's coming soon like a package in the post.'

Sehar grimaced. 'Not sure you can compare giving birth with a letterbox.'

'Are you nervous?' I asked. 'A bit,' Sehar answered. 'Not really got too long to go now, but I'm sure it will all be OK. They'll get a doctor to deliver the baby for me in the *haveli*. As soon as it pops, I'm going home. Can't wait.'

I nodded, trying to smile but the gesture did not reach my eyes. I couldn't help feeling envious. Sehar would be going home.

'Water people coming,' Farhat announced, pointing to the group of brightly dressed women sauntering over to us with their water-pots.

'*As salaam alaikum*,' they greeted in unison, smiling warmly.

I answered and informed them that Nannyma was out on an errand with Kareem-baba.

'We have not come to see Fatima-ji,' said one woman in Sindhi. 'We come for Memsahib.'

Sehar and I stared at the women. Who were they looking for?

'They mean Sehar-memsahib,' Farhat said quickly, clearing up the confusion. Of course. Sehar belonged to the landlord's family.

'Not long to go now,' one of them said to Sehar, showing a gap in her front teeth. 'Are you ready?'

'Umm . . .' Sehar seemed lost for words.

'It will feel like your insides are being ripped apart,' said one from the back. 'The earth will move and the volcano will erupt.'

'Don't let your husband be near you when the pains start,' piped up another. 'You will want to kill him with your bare hands for putting you in this situation.'

'Maybe he *should* be around for the birth then,' Sehar muttered under her breath.

The women continued sharing their experiences and advice, completely oblivious to the alarm they were raising in Sehar. Another woman made a crude joke and they all burst into fresh peals of laughter, and then the joyous, happy sound was abruptly cut off by the sight of something behind me.

Curious, I turned around to find Husna-bhaji standing nervously by the door.

The women glared at the widow.

'Witch!' one woman spat.

'Hey,' I cried indignantly. 'Don't you dare call her that!'

'Yeah, don't you dare,' Sehar piped up, struggling to get off the swing and on to her feet.

'It's OK,' Husna-bhaji said hurriedly. 'I will go back inside.'

'No, you won't,' I said, grabbing Husna-bhaji's arm and pulling her further on to the veranda. 'You live here and are entitled to join in.'

'Zeba-ji,' a woman at the front said in a patronizing voice, 'you and Memsahib are foreign. You do not know what these village witches are like. They put spells on you to make them take you in. Your poor grandmother has been manipulated. You all have. You must follow our advice and throw her out before she eats your liver.'

Sehar burst out laughing.

'Do not laugh, Memsahib,' another woman said gravely. 'You do not know what we know. Beware of the –'

'Enough!' It was Farhat.

We all stared at the maid.

'Husna-bhaji is a poor widow and not a witch!' Farhat exclaimed hotly. 'We are supposed to be Muslims and you should treat her with kindness and mercy so that on the Day of Judgement God will treat you with mercy and kind-ness.'

A pin-drop silence followed Farhat's outburst. *Well*, I thought, *someone's been paying attention to Nannyma's pearls of wisdom; talk about regurgitating word for word.* But one woman from the back made a hissing noise and then another joined in, and another. They only stopped as a vehi-cle pulled up behind them. Asif jumped out and the women scampered away, pulling their *ajrak* shawls to cover their faces.

I watched anxiously as Asif approached the veranda. I hadn't seen him since I'd first arrived. What did he want?

'*As salaam alaikum*,' he greeted us.

'*Wa alaikum salaam*,' Sehar answered, a look of interest on her face. I couldn't even croak my response. My voice was trapped somewhere in my throat.

'May I speak with you, Zeba?' Asif asked. He was dressed in his army uniform. Was this guy ever off duty?

'Not sure that's allowed, Asif-sahib,' Sehar said. 'My maid and I will have to chaperone.'

Asif gave Sehar a quizzical look. 'You're not serious?' he drawled.

'Very much so,' Sehar said coolly.

'I do not follow your customs,' Asif declared.

'They're your customs, not ours,' Sehar countered. 'We're British but we are respecting your traditions.'

Asif rolled his eyes and turned to me. 'Zeba, please ask your friends to leave us. It is important that I talk to you alone and I am not one to follow such customs in important affairs like marriage.'

A wild thought struck me. Perhaps Asif had come to tell me he was in love with someone else and he wanted to call off the wedding. I gestured to Sehar to go inside the house. Reluctantly she did so with Farhat and Husna-bhaji in tow.

I met Asif's eyes as he lowered himself on to the deckchair. Was he about to give me my freedom?

'Zeba, I want you to know that I fully respect our parents' decision in arranging our match,' he began. 'Strengthening our family bond means a lot to them and I can see the benefits.'

'Oh,' was all I could manage as the gush of hope that had entered my body leaked away in drips.

'I was surprised when you agreed to this match,' Asif continued. 'You're so young and I thought . . . Anyway, I can see that you are just as respectful of family and tradition, and I like that about you.'

Agreed to this match? Could someone really be so blind?

'Do you have a preference for a honeymoon location?'

I wanted the ground to open up and swallow me.

'You know . . . is there anywhere you'd like to visit after the wedding?'

I continued to gape at him and I think he took my speechlessness as shyness. He smiled and got up.

'I'll be off,' he said. 'I just wanted to spend some time with you before the wedding. Perhaps it is not so appropriate here in the village.'

'No,' I whispered.

'We'll have to get to know each other after the wedding.'

With those words he descended from the veranda, climbed into his Land Rover and sped off. The dust from his vehicle was still in the air when Sehar and Farhat emerged again.

'I heard every word,' Sehar admitted. 'You mad girl, why didn't you tell him you don't want to marry him?'

'Would it have made a difference?' I asked through stiff lips. 'He seemed pretty happy about the wedding. He's planning the honeymoon.'

'Still . . .' Sehar's voice trailed off.

'He wouldn't have listened,' I insisted. 'Why should he?'

'You should have tried,' Sehar said stubbornly. 'Clearly he isn't aware that you are being forced into this. How would he know? You were sent to live here so as not to cause a commotion in his house and he has hardly been here to notice anything that has gone on. Bet he doesn't even know what happened with the imam.'

'But what difference would it have made?' I asked.

'A lot,' Sehar said quietly. 'He looks like a proud bloke to me. It will probably hurt his ego to think his bride ain't willing. You know I bet you he's got this fantasy in his head that you're besotted with the fact that he's a man in uniform. Every other girl in this village is.'

'Too bad I'm not.'

'And when will he find out? On your wedding night when you start screaming at him not to touch you?'

I burst into tears and ran back in the house. Sehar followed.

'Oh, Zee,' she said, stroking my hair as I sobbed into a cushion. 'I just don't want you to go through what I did. You can still find a way out. I'm sure your nannyma will be fine – she has the whole village on her side.'

'But how?' I asked.

'Contact Tara,' she said.

'It's too late,' I sobbed.

'It's never too late,' Sehar said firmly. 'We all deserve happy endings but sometimes we have to work at them.'

Chapter 20

I wasn't ready to ask for outside help. Even if Tara came and collected me I would be completely disowned by my family. Was I really ready to leave behind everything I had? Never see my family and friends again? I couldn't make that decision. Deep down I still loved my parents and I had to find another way to get myself out of this situation.

Lying awake at night, I decided to confront Asif. He was in the dark about what was expected of him as much as I was when I had been lied to about the reasons for this trip. I decided to tell Asif the truth.

Early the next morning, I walked over to Farhat's house and asked her if she could get a message to Asif through her fiancé, Abdullah. I wanted to meet Asif in the sugar-cane fields behind Nannyma's house at four in the afternoon.

'You sure meeting Asif in sugar-cane fields good idea?' Farhat asked doubtfully.

I stared at Farhat. What was the problem?

'Sugar-cane fields is where people meeting to have affairs,' Farhat explained patiently. 'Very bad reputations. Like Joey in *Friends* . . . sleeping with girls who not his wife. Very bad.'

I'd had no idea that sugar-cane fields acted as illicit locations for people having affairs, but it was the best place for me to meet Asif. We would have little chance of being spotted by anyone.

'Farhat, please tell Abdullah to pass the message to Asif,' I said firmly.

I arrived at the sugar-cane field just before four o'clock. I'd thought about what to say all day, from an angry tirade to words pleading for mercy. In the end I decided to judge his mood. If I could detect kindness in him, then I would adopt a soft manner. If he was abrupt and impatient, then I would give as good as.

'Zeba, *as salaam alaikum*.' He approached me without a sound and I jumped. Was the ability to creep up like a killer panther part of his army training?

I replied in kind, my voice barely above a whisper. My hands had started to sweat and my heart hammered in its ribcage. This was it. I had to tell him. It was my only way out.

'You wanted to see me?'

I nodded. 'There is something I think you should know.'

He waited for me to go further. I swallowed. Perhaps I should build up to my revelation I thought . . . break the ice a little.

'So are you having a good time in the army?'

'What?' The question took him by surprise.

'The army. You love it, right?'

He gazed down at me from his great height, a slight frown creasing his forehead. 'It is my life,' he said simply.

Here was my chance to tell him that the people who loved him the most wanted to end that life. I opened my mouth but he was already talking.

'I'm glad you asked about the army. It *is* my life. My fellow soldiers are my brothers. We are united in a cause. A cause to save this country from everything that threatens it. It is important that as my wife you know about the type of life I will lead and how you will fit in as an army wife.'

Army wife!

'I wanted –' I began but he cut me off, and to my shock his eyes filled with tears. I couldn't believe it.

'I was going to request that we delay the wedding.'

My heart leaped with hope.

'My best friend died in a special operation a month ago. That was why I had to disappear when you had only just arrived here.'

For the second time my hope seeped away like water in a drought.

'I knew it was rude of me to leave as soon as you came, but I had to.'

'Your friend died?'

'Yes. His name was Sarfraz Khan and he was from Lahore – an only son with five sisters. His parents were devastated and I thought it right to stay with them awhile before I returned here. He was killed doing his duty for his country,' he added, clearing his throat. 'It was his destiny.'

I didn't know what to say. Asif seemed lost in his own thoughts and the silence between us stretched. I tried to suppress my own thoughts but with little success. I couldn't escape from the fact that I had an obligation to save Asif from the same fate as his dead friend. I shut my eyes. Somewhere in the background I heard the cawing of the black crows. They were ever-present in the fields, but only now did I hear them. Now their sound was like a siren warning that it was all over.

'What else did you want to say to me?'

My eyes flew open. There was one last chance. Could I tell him? The image of a shrouded body floated before my eyes.

'Nothing.' I shrugged, an awkwardness developing between us.

'I have to leave with my father for some business shortly,' he said.

I nodded. 'Thanks for coming.'

I watched him walk away and then made my way slowly to the river, hot tears streaming down my face.

Sehar and Farhat were already there. Sehar was standing in the water with her *salwar* hoisted up to her shins. I knew she found the cool water soothing when she was hot. Farhat was holding Sehar's hand firmly to make sure she didn't topple. They hadn't seen me approach and so I stood under the shade of the giant tree, wiping away the last of my tears.

'You coming in?' Sehar yelled, spotting me suddenly.

'Not today,' I called back, not in the mood to splash around.

I watched Sehar carefully make her way back to the bank and then lower herself slowly on to the grass with Farhat's aid.

'You been crying?' was the first thing Sehar said to me.

I crawled on to the blanket that Farhat had spread in the tree's shade. Stretching out on my back, I fixed my gaze on the branches.

'No,' I denied.

'Why are you lying?'

'Yaah, Zeba-ji,' Farhat chimed in. 'Your eyes puffy and red. Making you look very ugly actually. Yaah – too much ugly.'

My lower lip trembled and Sehar shot Farhat a dirty look.

'Yes, thank you, Fatty,' she snapped. 'We don't need your opinion.'

Farhat shrugged. 'Only saying Zeba-ji looking more pretty when not crying. Actually everyone look ugly when crying. Sehar-ji, you look most ugly when crying.'

'Shut up!' Sehar shouted.

Farhat opened her mouth one more time, but then thought better of it and sat quietly.

Sehar turned to me. 'Did you speak to Asif?'

'I'm going to go through with it,' I said.

Sehar didn't say anything.

'I know you don't agree, but I don't think I have a choice,' I said miserably. 'If I don't marry him, then he will die in the army and then I will have to live with that guilt forever.'

She still didn't say anything.

'Please say something,' I begged.

Sehar looked at me and I could see sadness in her eyes.

'You have to do what is right for you,' she said quietly.

'So the engagement is tomorrow,' I persisted. 'Will you come?'

She smiled and nodded. 'Nothing will keep me away.'

My parents came to see me that evening. They wanted to take me back to Taya-ji's house, but I refused, insisting that I would go in the morning. Mum looked like she wanted to argue but Dad held up a hand to silence her.

We were sitting at the dinner table finishing our meal, although most of it lay untouched. Nannyma, my parents and I did not seem to have much of an appetite.

'Zeba,' my father said, 'come out with me on to the veranda. I would like to talk to you.'

I dipped my hands in the water of the finger bowl to clean them and followed Dad on to the veranda. He was sitting in Farhat's usual position on the steps. I joined him and he did not waste any time getting to the point.

'Your Taya-ji told me you met Asif in the sugar-cane fields today.'

I gasped slightly, remembering Farhat's words about the reputation of the sugar-cane fields and feeling embarrassed in front of my dad.

'It wasn't like that,' I mumbled.

He made a strange sound – like a cross between a laugh and a contemptuous snort.

'I know you would never shame me like that,' he said, turning to look directly in my eyes, 'but I need to know what you said to him.'

'How does Taya-ji know I met Asif?' I blurted suddenly.

'It doesn't matter.'

'It does! Did Asif say something?'

'He didn't. But Taya-ji has men everywhere keeping an eye on you. Surely you know that?'

I sprang to my feet. This was too much. It was like being a prisoner.

'Sit down, Zeba.'

It was a command. I sat.

'Did you say anything to Asif that could jeopardize tomorrow?'

My blood was fuming. I bit my lip.

'Did you?'

'Maybe.'

'What did you say?'

The fury coursing through my veins urged recklessness. 'I told him the truth about the marriage . . . that we were getting married so he would leave the army.'

My dad was as still as a statue and we both sat there waiting for the other to speak. Finally he said, 'You didn't say anything like that did you, *beti*?'

A part of me wanted to carry on lying to provoke a stronger reaction, but then I thought: what was the point? My dad had always been able to tell when I was lying.

'No, I didn't.'

'Then why did you meet him?'

I took a deep breath. 'It *was* to tell him the truth, but I couldn't in the end. He told me about his best friend who died.'

My dad closed his eyes. '*Beti*,' he whispered, 'you did the right thing.'

'Whatever.'

'We all have our duties,' he continued. 'We owe Taya-ji.'

'Yeah,' I said standing up. 'You owe your brother as a brother, but clearly you don't owe me anything as my father.'

With those words I turned and walked back into Nannyma's house, knowing the sanctuary it had offered me so far was about to end.

Chapter 21

I was back at Taya-ji's house for my engagement ceremony.

My mum placed a pink shawl on my head and then began fussing with the fabric. I looked at her through the dressing-room mirror and was reminded of how she looked when she arranged a bouquet of flowers in a vase. The arrangement had to be perfect. It had to be her way; rose petals got plucked and stems got cut off until it was to her liking. I always picked up the discarded velvet-like petals before she could bin them, keeping them in between the pages of old scrapbooks.

Mum tipped my head slightly to secure the shawl to my hair with pins. The fabric was heavy and I wondered how many fingers it had taken to create this monstrosity. Every single pearl and bead was hand sewn.

I pulled a face at my reflection as Mum continued to jab at my scalp. I looked like a Christmas tree from top to bottom. All I needed now was a star or an angel on top of my head to complete the outfit. The floor-length skirt and short top were beaded as heavily as the shawl. I looked so hideous that I could've auditioned for one of Cinderella's ugly sisters in a pantomime.

'Do I have to wear this?' I asked meekly. 'It's hot and I'm going to boil.'

'It's your engagement outfit, and as the lucky girl you have to wear it,' my mother insisted.

Lucky? I pulled a face.

'Come on,' she said. 'It is time.'

I shuffled along slowly behind my mum. She was leading the way and on either side of me were two girls brought in by Mariam-chachi to act as my friends, companions, bridesmaids . . . sidekicks. I had no idea who they were, only that they were from Karachi. Both were giggling for no reason at all, and I had to quash the urge to send them flying with karate kicks.

After what seemed like an eternity, we arrived at the top of the stairs and it was time to navigate the steps. Knowing I was likely to trip, I hoisted the skirt up around my ankles and raised challenging eyes to the girl on my right. She looked absolutely horrified at my inelegant behaviour and rolled her eyes at her friend. For a second I thought they might grab my hands to force me to release the material, but they didn't. Instead, with disgusted expressions they looked ahead and preceded me. I followed clumsily.

At the bottom of the stairs I released my skirt and took a ragged breath. With my heart suddenly pounding inside my ribcage, it hit me that I had to enter a room and allow someone to slip an engagement ring on my finger. My mum turned to me and gave a small smile. I didn't return it, instead taking another shaky breath. I knew I had to do this – there was no way out any more – but all I wanted to do was turn round and run.

We walked through the main door and into a hushed room.

I kept my eyes lowered and allowed myself to be guided by the two girls. Their grip on my arms was firm.

I thought of Sehar and wondered where she was in the crowd of people. I had expected her to come to my room as soon as she had arrived. Was she even here? Maybe she had decided not to come and see the *bakri* being led to the altar.

I shuffled along slowly, following my mum's *salwar*. Finally she stopped, turned around and guided me to sit next to Asif by placing both her hands on either side of my shoulders.

Asif was already seated on the plush two-seater sofa and even with my lowered gaze I could see he was wearing his army uniform. I wondered if he owned any civilian clothes at all. Gritting my teeth, I tried to think of a happy place. I thought of walking to school with Susan, smiling and content. I thought of playing in the park when we were kids: warm sunny days on the swings, down the slide and around the merry-go-round.

I was suddenly jolted out of my memories by someone trying to cram a sweetmeat into my mouth. I recoiled and pushed the hand away. There was nervous laughter.

'Zeba,' I heard my mum say. 'It is tradition. It's your day to be fed with sweets by your well-wishers.'

I swallowed first and then parted my lips to allow what was really just a chunk of fried sugar into my mouth – and that's how it continued. For another ten minutes I was fed *jalebis*, *laddus*, *mithai* and *halwa*. By the end of it I felt quite sick and was ready to retch. I gulped the air and someone must have noticed my discomfort because a fan suddenly materialized. I closed my eyes, wishing I was miles away, but then I was rudely jostled to my feet. This time it was Asif's mum, Mariam-chachi, who was manhandling me.

'Time to exchange gifts,' she said loudly. 'Asif and Zeba will give each other rings to mark their commitment to each other.'

I didn't know if this was the custom or not, but my hand was held up by someone and Asif slipped a diamond ring on my finger. I stared down at it. The white sparkling monstrosity might as well have been handcuffs. My mum came to stand beside me and placed a ring in the palm of my hand.

'Now you put this on his finger,' she instructed.

Asif held out his hand and waited. I gazed down at the band of silver but I couldn't will myself to do it. Again there was nervous laughter.

'She's shy,' I heard my mum explain to the amassed audience before nudging me with her shoulder.

I knew I had to get this over with. The longer I stood like a zombie, the more I would have to endure. I fumbled with the ring and managed to slip it on to Asif's finger. It would not go on easily, so I just left it halfway and let my hands drop to my sides.

A silence followed, broken eventually by Asif's soft laughter. He pushed the ring into place before clutching my chin with his right hand. Forcing my face up to meet his, he murmured, 'So shy.'

I knew that in the view of the guests, Asif looked like a man who was cheekily trying to share a glance with his fiancée. For the next two hours I sat there staring down at my lap as Asif chatted away to his guests. People no longer seemed concerned with me. With the rituals performed, they all seemed more interested in having a good time with each other. I raised my eyes and they fell on my dad. Since his return we had barely exchanged more than a few words. He was standing with a group of men, seemingly part of a group discussion, but I knew my dad, and I recognized the glazed look in his eyes. He was physically here but his mind was somewhere else. He looked glum. Today was his only child's engagement ceremony and he looked like he had the world's worries on his shoulders. There was not a hint of happiness on his face, only misery. I knew in my heart that he didn't want this for me, and I just couldn't understand the obligation he felt to his older brother.

I looked for Taya-ji in the crowd and I spotted him not far off, deep in conversation with another man. I found Mariam-chachi too. She was talking in a circle of women, hands gesturing, hair swishing and diamonds sparkling at her throat. She looked happy, but then why shouldn't she be? Her son was getting engaged, just as she'd planned, and it was going to save his life.

I did not know anyone else in the room aside from my parents, Nannyma, Taya-ji and Mariam-chachi. I did not spot Sehar or Farhat, and even Nannyma's household of Kareem-baba and Ambreen-bhaji were not here. Husna-bhaji had not been allowed to attend the party. Nannyma and Sher Shah's encounter had made waves across the village and Mariam-chachi had personally rung Nannyma to ban the widow. I had tried to object, but Nannyma had insisted it was not worth it. She said Husna-bhaji would only be ridiculed by the other women, guests who had come all the way from Karachi, if she was to attend.

'But surely the so-called "educated" people will know that she is not a witch!'

'She may as well be,' Nannyma replied wisely. 'Husna-bhaji's beauty pulls the glances of the men, and although many wives will tolerate competition from women of their own *zaat*, they will not tolerate the attractiveness of a peasant woman. Trust me; Husna-bhaji is better off at home tonight.'

Finally the torture was over and I was allowed to retire to my room. The two girls who had escorted me rushed forward, but I informed them haughtily that I had no need of them. They shrugged and sidled back to the party, in particular a small group of young army officers. I knew my parents would be returning home in the weeks between the engagement and my wedding, so I managed to force a farewell that I hoped looked genuine to onlookers, before I escaped. There was something satisfying in the fact that my dad looked so consumed with guilt he could barely look me in the eye.

Alone in my room I took off the scarf, the heavy skirt and top, the jewellery and the engagement ring. The whole costume had felt like a prisoner's uniform. I felt hot, tired and angry. I was furious with Sehar for not coming tonight. I had needed her and she had let me down. Suddenly unable to suppress my rage any longer, I picked up a book and threw it against a mirror, causing it to smash. At the sound of the glass shattering, Feroz-baba, the house servant, ran in.

'Zeba-ji, are you all right?' he asked, eyeing the broken glass.

I turned angrily towards him. 'Sehar did not come!'

'Sehar-ji is having her baby today,' Feroz-baba explained calmly. 'Farhat told Abdullah to tell me. I think we will have good news before morning.'

I stared at Feroz-baba. I couldn't believe it. Sehar's baby was coming already? But it was a few days early and . . . Oh, what did it matter; her passport to freedom was about to arrive. Had it not been my engagement today I would have made my way to the *haveli*, but it was late and I knew my parents would not let me leave at this hour. Besides, Sehar had Farhat with her. She would be OK.

Still desperate for some air, I turned towards the open window, only to jump back in fear at a sudden clap of lightning. The storm had come from nowhere and it lasted all night, an outburst to echo my own.

Chapter 22

Sehar's son was born on that stormy night.

There was thunder and lightning and rain. It was just like the opening scene of the Bollywood movies she loved so much, except that there was no three-hour journey to a happy ending.

Apparently her baby boy had come out quite still, and so the midwife had been forced to turn him upside down and tap his tiny chest to get him to breathe. The rumours were that it had seemed unlikely he would, however, in the seconds that had followed, the baby boy had breathed air and embraced life . . . just as the life had seeped out of his mother.

Sehar died from internal bleeding caused by the complications of giving birth in a medieval village. They should have taken her to a hospital, but they hadn't. The understanding was that women had given birth like this for centuries, so why did Sehar need a modern hospital? All that feudal wealth, and a qualified doctor could not even be summoned. But I knew the truth. I guessed it. Sher Shah was scared of Sehar. He feared that the excruciating labour pains would loosen her tongue and she would rant and rave against his family in a public hospital.

My friend.

Sehar.

Dead.

Three days passed before they buried Sehar. They kept her in a fridge type coffin that Sher Shah had arranged. She was locked away in a room all by herself in the grand *haveli*, while they breached the deadline dictated by Islam that a dead body had to be buried as soon as possible. The reason was Sehar's family; they had not attended her marriage, but vast numbers of them were flying in to bury her.

Sehar's funeral was to be a grand affair. This was an occasion. A young woman had died in childbirth – a foreign woman, and in the house of the great landlord too. Nannyma said the *haveli* would host hundreds of people under its roof: from peasants to neighbouring landlords as well as industrialists and politicians from Karachi. She also commented that, ironically, there would be more of Sher Shah's enemies in attendance than his friends.

Schadenfreude, I immediately thought.

In Year Nine, my English teacher had gone to great lengths to explain the German word, which describes the joy felt by one person at the misfortune of another. She had even made us write our own stories to prove our understanding of it.

I knew there were probably many who hated Sher Shah, but their *Schadenfreude* was misplaced. The simple truth was this: Sher Shah had not lost anything through Sehar's tragic death. It was another man's daughter who had died – not his son. In fact, he may even have got exactly what he'd wanted; Sehar with her feisty personality had been an embarrassment to him.

I climbed the steps to the *haveli* slowly and painfully. My legs felt as though lead had been poured into them. Actually my whole body was shrieking at me to run from this place, to hide. Denial was still an option; if I didn't see Sehar in death, then I would not have to accept it. I paused at the top step and leaned against a pillar, trying to still my racing heart.

'Zeba-ji.'

It was Farhat's voice, small and scared, almost unrecognizable.

Three days had passed since Sehar had died, yet Farhat had not sought me out. She had disappeared. I was so angry with her. This was a time when we needed each other, but she had abandoned me. I was in no doubt that she was devastated. She had loved Sehar like a puppy loves its owner – completely and loyally – but that didn't mean she had to hide herself from me.

I raised heavy eyes and was not shocked by what I saw. The maid's devastation was reflected in her appearance. Her cheeks and eye sockets had sunk into her face giving her a drawn, haggard look. For the first time since I had met her, there was no coloured ribbon in the plait that sat on her left shoulder, and her clothes were crumpled and stained.

The anger that had accumulated in the last seventy-two hours dissolved and I reached out to her, my arms seeking her. She stepped into my embrace and the tears spilled over both our faces and on to each other's shoulders.

'Are you coming in?' I asked when we finally pulled apart.

'Naah,' she said simply.

'Have you seen her?' I asked, my voice trembling.

'Not for three days.'

'Why won't you come in?'

'I cannot.'

I nodded my head. Perhaps it was too much for her. I wished I too could refuse to enter the *haveli*, but I knew I had to face Sehar one last time. Not to see her now would be to betray her. I squeezed Farhat's arm and then turned to walk in.

Sher Shah's *haveli*, even in the simplicity adopted for the funeral, looked splendid. Every piece of furniture had been removed to make space for the mourners, leaving only the white pillars, tall and erect, and the grand chandelier hanging ominously over the massed throng. The room was a vision of white; not a single bright dye could be seen on the bodies of the women who were sitting on the floor. Most were hushed, but there were a few who were wailing with their arms in the air and screams of anguish emerging from their throats. I looked closely at these women. Why were they so upset? They hadn't even known Sehar.

I pulled my white scarf firmly on my head, trying to stop it slipping and revealing my hair. I took a step forward, my bare feet touching the cold marble and my eyes searching for a gap in the white maze. Somewhere hidden among this crowd was the person who had been one of my few friends in the most desperate time of my life. I had been told by one of the maids that they had taken her body from its refrigerated coffin and laid it on the floor so people could see her for the final time. I had to find her.

'Zeba.'

Someone said my name. I didn't know who it was, but slowly a pathway opened before me as women shifted to the sides to let me through. I walked slowly down the path. Now the marble floor felt warm from the heat of the women's bodies. I didn't want to continue. Looking at Sehar's body, taking it all in, would make it real, and suddenly I didn't want to believe it. I turned abruptly, ready to run, but I didn't get far.

I felt a warm hand on my arm and looked up into my nanny-ma's clear eyes.

'You need to see your friend,' she said.

'No,' I whispered through stiff lips.

'Zeba, *beti*.' My nannyma's voice was gentle. 'You will regret it if you don't. You need to say goodbye.'

I stifled a sob and remained frozen on the spot, but Nannyma took my hand and led me into the crowd. I could feel every pair of eyes on me. It was as if for some reason I was the one expected to provide the entertainment.

'Where are Sehar's parents?' I asked. 'Aren't they coming?'

'They have arrived,' Nannyma replied.

'Where is she?' I asked, blindly looking around.

'Right here,' Nannyma said softly.

And there she was. My friend, Sehar, wrapped in a white shroud with only her face visible. She wasn't in a coffin, just on a white sheet on the floor. A crazy part of me wanted to object. Sehar would find the marble hard, it would be digging into her back . . . and then I remembered she couldn't feel it.

My nannyma urged me to sit and I did, falling to my knees to gaze down at Sehar. I had never seen a dead body before, and Sehar seemed . . . well, she looked like she was just asleep. I reached out a hand to touch her face, but it was grabbed by another and flung away harshly. I looked up and saw an older version of Sehar. The same face shape, eyes, nose and mouth, all the way down to the same smooth skin. I stared at the woman. Her face was a contortion of grief as she gazed down at her dead daughter's face. Suddenly I wanted to slap her. How dare she pretend to be upset when she hadn't cared about her daughter when she'd been alive?

The forced marriage.

The beatings.

The humiliation.

I opened my mouth, ready to fling a torrent of abuse at Sehar's mother, but my nannyma's index finger came to rest on my lips, stopping me.

'This is not the time, Zeba,' she said quietly.

I flicked my head slightly and Nannyma's finger fell away.

'Zeba, *beti*,' Nannyma's voice was hushed. 'Let Sehar have some dignity in death. These people gave her none while she was alive. Act as her friend and let her have some now.'

'But . . .'

'There is nothing you can say to that woman that she isn't feeling already.'

I looked at Sehar's mother. Perhaps Nannyma was right; perhaps I should just let it go. I glanced around and my eyes fell on Memsahib, sitting two paces away, her face set in a grim expression. Again, I had to resist the urge to reach out and slap her. How dare she sit in Sehar's *mehfil*, this gathering to praise Sehar, to give the impression that she cared. The memsahib of this grand *haveli* had never cared about Sehar. Instead she had encouraged her son to beat her daughter-in-law to break her spirit, to try to reduce her to a cowering shadow of her former self. I could not work out who was worse. The woman who had given birth to Sehar and then sold her like a chicken in the market, or the woman who allowed her son to beat his wife.

I must have been scowling at Memsahib because Nannyma leaned forward again, a warning in her eyes. Taking heed, I sat back on my heels and picked up a *misbaha*, a Muslim rosary that was lying spare. These people were praying for Sehar and I would pray for her too.

'God is one,' I repeated again and again as I flicked the rosary beads between my fingers. It was strange but the ritual calmed me down and made the whole thing more believable.

Sehar was dead.

'God is one.'

Sehar was dead.

'God is one.'

There were ninety-nine beads in the *misbaha* and I had only got halfway through when a wave of wailing began at the edges of the room and cascaded through to its centre. I wanted to press my hands over my ears against the shrieking and I looked around trying to figure out what had unleashed this agony . . . and then I knew.

The men had come to collect Sehar. It was time to bury her. I turned back towards Sehar to find that her mother had thrown herself against the body. She was crying hysterically.

The handful of men walked slowly along the pathway that had magically appeared from the doorway to where Sehar lay. I didn't recognize them. In the Muslim tradition, only the male relatives of a dead woman were allowed touch her corpse. I imagined these men to be Sehar's family: perhaps her father, her brothers, her uncles, her husband. Men who had never asked her what she wanted.

I watched as the grim-faced men lifted Sehar into a simple wooden coffin and then raised it on to their shoulders. This was it. She was being carried out to a lonely graveyard where she would be buried six feet under the earth.

Sehar, my friend, who had so wanted to live.

Sehar, my friend, who never got her own happy ending.

Chapter 23

I held Sehar's son in my arms. The three days of mourning since the burial were now over and the white sheets had been cleared off the floor. Farhat had let me into the nursery. She was caring for the baby, an over-protective surrogate mother. The baby was tiny and my eyes filled with tears. I wanted to scream. This baby was never going to know his mother. Ever. He was never going to know her laughter, or her sarcasm.

Sehar had been desperate to live her life. She had wanted to climb a mountain, swim in the sea, ride a horse, run a marathon, pick wild flowers, become a Bollywood star. So many things . . . and she was never going to be able to do any of them. And her son, this tiny baby boy, was going to grow up and know nothing of what his mother had wanted for him. Life was so cruel. This baby's paternal family were animals, and as far as I was concerned they were responsible for his mother's death.

The baby began to whimper and I rocked him gently, trying to ease his discomfort. It seemed to do the trick and he lay content in my arms.

'He is liking you,' Farhat whispered with a smile.

I nodded, gazing down at the little bundle. This little boy

was supposed to have been his mother's passport to freedom.

'Farhat,' I said, 'were you with Sehar when she died?'

Farhat's eyes welled up and she nodded her head. 'Yes, Sehar-ji and I were very exciting to coming to your engagement . . . not in good way,' she said hurriedly when I frowned, 'but like to supporting you. Sehar-ji kept saying, "Hurry up, Fatty. Zee needs us."'

A pang of guilt shot through me as I remembered how I'd mentally sworn at Sehar for abandoning me that evening.

'Sehar-ji was getting ready; she was putting on her blue suit. Making her looking very pretty and she put on matching eyeshadow too. Then her waters broke and baby started coming. I said to Memsahib to take her to hospital, but they said no time.'

'The baby was quick?' I asked.

'No!' Farhat cried, and then she stepped close to me and began to whisper. 'There was time for hospital in big speeding car but Memsahib said no. Sehar-ji crying for medicine to make pain stop, she kept saying she needing drugs. She holding my hand so tight, begging me to help her. I could not do anything. Her screams were very much loud all through night. I am surprising that whole village did not hear her. Then just before the muezzin called the *adhan* for morning prayer, Sehar-ji starting to bleed and it not stop. Blood all on bed and then on floor. Midwife mopping blood and getting very scared, saying take girl to hospital because she need doctor. But Memsahib said no.'

I closed my eyes, trying to imagine the pain Sehar must have felt, and beside me Farhat relived our friend's death in sobbing whispers.

'Sehar-ji screaming, I crying, Mensahib shouting, "Push, push, you useless English *guri*."'

I bit down hard on my lower lip. Was there no end to that woman's wickedness?

'It was horrible,' Farhat continued. 'Then baby came with one last push, but it was very silent. So midwife turned him other way round – you know, feet facing roof – and tapping his chest and then baby crying. I was so happy now. I put my head next to Sehar-ji and said to her, "Look, your son is born," but her eyes was closed. I thinking she sleeping and so let go of her hand. It was limp . . . you know like loose . . . but I thinking Sehar-ji having no energy, is tiring, so I leave her to look at baby who is crying and being cleaning by midwife.

'Then Memsahib is screaming. She said Sehar-ji is dead. I ran back to Sehar-ji and no heart beating and no tickety-tick-tock in top of her hand or in neck . . . you know . . . what word . . . pulsing?'

'No pulse,' I supplied through stiff lips.

'Yaah.' Farhat nodded. 'Then I was sending out of room to find Sher Shah Sahib. He not in house. Abdullah tell me he is at his mistress house. But who is mistress? No one knows. I tell Memsahib that Sher Shah Sahib at mistress house and she slap me and tell me to leave house.'

My eyes were still closed when Farhat finished relaying the death scene.

'Zeba-ji?' Farhat's voice was nervous and I opened my eyes.

'I'm so sorry,' I managed. 'It must have been horrendous.'

'Yes.'

'You told Sher Shah's wife that her husband was with his mistress? Is that why you were banned from the funeral?'

Farhat nodded miserably.

'And now she is buried you are allowed back in the *haveli*?'

'Nobody else better to look after baby. It was Sehar-ji's husband's order. Salman Sahib said only I can. Memsahib not happy, but she not want to look after baby and anyways she has to listen to wishes of her son. He is man.'

I pondered on Farhat's words about Sehar's husband. I had never met him. Sehar had only ever referred to him as 'the git' and he had existed in our world as the mysterious bogeyman. Why would he order Farhat back into the *haveli*? Perhaps he knew how much the girl had adored his wife and so would treat his son better than anyone else. Maybe he was going to be a better father than he was ever a husband.

'Oh, he is here,' Farhat said in a low voice and pulled her shawl over her head.

'So you are Zeba?'

The voice was almost feminine, squeaky and soft. I looked up into the angelic features of Salman Sahib, the younger of Sher Shah's two sons. His skin was smooth with no trace of stubble, his shiny sun-kissed hair flopped over his feline eyes and he had a skinny body that was just an inch or two taller than mine. Sehar had never mentioned that she towered over him.

In those first few seconds, I understood why Sehar had been so repulsed by this man. She had always gushed about the heroes of her Bollywood movies, who were masculine and courageous. Salman Sahib was nowhere close to being the hero of her dreams, and the angelic features could not hide his petulance.

'You look so natural with my son,' he said, eyeing me strangely.

With one hand supporting the baby, I used the other to pull my shawl fully over my head.

'You know it's a shame that you have the ring of another man on your finger.'

I gaped at him. What was he talking about?

'You could have made an excellent mother for my son.'

Instinctively I took a step back, appalled. This man was disgusting. The earth had not even settled on his wife's grave and he was already thinking of marrying another woman.

'You know I would be willing to move to the UK with you, unlike Asif,' Salman continued, oblivious to my revulsion.

'What?' I gasped.

He gazed at me with an odd expression. 'Asif is very much the hero, the adventurer, but Pakistan is not a fairy tale. Death is but a step away in this country. Heroes do not live happily ever after. They die, so why tie yourself to him?'

'You don't know what you're talking about,' I blurted out. 'Asif will be moving with me to England. He won't remain a soldier.'

Salman's face was malicious in its glee. 'Who told you that? Mustaq Khan? The old man is fooling himself if he thinks Asif will leave the army. Obviously you don't know your fiancé very well. He will remain here in this country, fighting the extremists, and you will reside in this village with his parents, your life withering away.'

Something snapped in my mind. My life was no longer my own. And Sehar had no life left. Was I doomed to remain in this village like my friend – to die here?

Would I ever see England again?

Sehar had wanted to escape, and the reason she hadn't was because she had been biding her time, foolishly thinking she would be allowed to return home if she just stuck it out a little longer. Except she never got to go home. Events . . . destiny . . . whatever it could be called, robbed her of her one hope.

I knew then that I had to escape. Sehar would have wanted that.

'I have to go,' I muttered, handing the baby back to Farhat before fleeing with my heart in my mouth.

I ran to my nannyma's house in the midday sun. Halfway there my slipper broke and the useless plastic and rubber hung off my foot as I navigated around the mud, ditches and cow pats. I kept my face half covered with my shawl, but I knew from the stares I attracted that I had not succeeded in hiding my identity. The villagers knew I was the foreign girl . . . the one who was still alive.

The midday sun bore down on me like a laser beam and I stopped against a tree to catch my breath, but only for a second. I wanted . . . I *needed* to be free and nothing and nobody was going to stop me now.

I owed Sehar.

I adjusted the slipper and clenched my toes against the plastic in an attempt to hold it on. I went five paces before the slipper broke completely and fell off. Abandoning both shoes, I began to run in my bare feet. The hot earth scorched my soles, but I did not care. I was running towards freedom. All I could think about was Sehar's face.

Sehar laughing as she paddled in the river.

Sehar clutching the branch of a tree with one hand as she plucked its fruit with another.

Sehar trying not to look awed as the baby kicked her in the womb.

Sehar lying dead, wrapped in a white shroud on the *haveli*'s hard marble floor.

189

The images of Sehar flicked through my mind like a digital photo frame, and I ran faster and faster. My breathing was now rapid and I had a stitch in my side. I knew I should stop to ease the burning sensation but I couldn't . . . I wouldn't. And so I carried on, running like a mad person who had escaped from the asylum, desperate to get away from the people who were preparing to put me in a straitjacket for the rest of my life. Minutes later I was running up to Nannyma's veranda, and she jumped up from the swing and rushed forward, arms held out to catch me.

'Zeba, what has happened?'

'I have to leave,' I gasped. 'I cannot marry Asif. If I do, I will die like Sehar.'

Nannyma stared at me. 'Hush, child,' she whispered.

'I mean it! I don't want to die!'

'You won't die,' she assured me.

'I will if I marry Asif,' I insisted, and burst into tears.

Nannyma led me inside the house, where Ambreen-bhaji bathed my feet in cold water. One of my toes was bleeding. Eventually I calmed down. The panic was replaced by a new-found determination. Only an hour ago I had thought that I would end up the same as all the other women in this village: confined, restricted and woven into a culture that was organized to suit the power and status of men. Well, I wasn't having any of it. I was not a citizen of this country. It did not matter who my ancestors were. What mattered was who I was, here in the present.

I waited till Ambreen-bhaji had placed a towel on the floor for me to dry my feet, and then turned to Nannyma. I told her about the email address etched on the tree trunk. I was going to contact my country for help.

She looked at me doubtfully. 'How can they help you? You are thousands of miles from what you call British justice. This is another country.'

'I have to try, Nannyma,' I said determinedly. 'All I need is an internet connection. I just need to be able to send this woman an email about where I am, and they will come to rescue me . . . Please.'

'The only place in this village with an internet connection is Sher Shah's *haveli*, but you will not be able to use it. It will arouse suspicion.'

'There must be somewhere else,' I pleaded.

Nannyma thought for a moment then announced: 'Your auntie Nusrat is due to arrive from America this weekend. You can go to Karachi with her and use the internet there,' she said. 'You will have to be very careful, Zeba, but that plan may just work.' Nannyma leaned forward and held my face in her hands. 'Please don't get your hopes up, though. What you are suggesting sounds like a fairy tale. I will ask Nusrat to help you, but in return you must also prepare yourself for the idea that you will marry Asif. Do not let this dream cloud what may be the reality.'

Chapter 24

My auntie Nusrat-kala was an angel sent to set me free.

She was exactly as I remembered: pretty face beaming with a smile. Nannyma had confided everything to her younger daughter in a letter and Nusrat-kala had not hesitated in getting on a flight with her husband. I knew it meant a lot to Nannyma that her daughter still remembered what life in the village was like, and therefore knew how shaken her mother would be by recent events. She put my own mother to shame.

It seemed everyone was delighted to see Nusrat-kala. Ambreen-bhaji's eyes followed her around affectionately while Husna-bhaji hung off her every word. Even the water-collecting women came up to the veranda every day to exchange pleasantries with Nusrat-kala. She was like a celebrity come home. Uncle Tahir was content to remain in the background while the village women oohed and aahed over his wife. At first I couldn't see why everyone loved her quite so much, and then I realized it was because she made every person feel special. She enquired after their elderly parents, their children, the monsoon season and how it had nearly ruined last season's crops, and a vast array of other things that affected their lives. And at no stage did she boast of her Western life, and if she did talk about it, it was only because she was asked. Watching her, I wondered if it was an American thing to be so cheerful.

Two days after Nusrat-kala and Uncle Tahir arrived, we prepared to go to Karachi along with Nannyma. The three adults had discussed what they could do to help me, but as my passport was in my dad's possession there was really nothing they could do. I really was a prisoner in this country and the only people who could help me escape were British government officials. We didn't tell anybody about the trip. Precisely at seven in the morning, Kareem-baba parked an old jeep outside the porch.

'Who does this belong to?' I asked.

'It used to be my dad's,' said Nusrat-kala in her unique accent, which was part South Asian and part American. 'Mom keeps it secure in the old barn around the back and she uses it occasionally.' Then switching to Sindhi she called, 'Kareem-baba, have you checked it for oil and water?'

He nodded, beaming at her.

'Well, let's go then,' she said cheerfully.

I climbed into the back with Nannyma and my aunt while Uncle Tahir took the front seat with Kareem-baba.

'What if someone asks where we're going?' I suddenly said aloud.

'Don't worry, Zeba,' said Uncle Tahir, twisting around. 'We're free people. We're visiting Karachi for clothes . . . you know, for your wedding.'

'Won't they think it's strange that we didn't ask Mariam-chachi to come with us?'

Nusrat-kala laughed. 'You know, kid, you think too much. You need to chill.'

'That's easy for you to say,' I said. 'You have your freedom.'

An uneasy silence descended on the car. 'Zeba *beti*,' said Nannyma. 'Your auntie is only trying to help.'

I turned to look out of the window and touched the piece of paper in my pocket. The day after my encounter with Salman Shah, I had run to the riverside and crouched under the giant tree, searching the bark for Sehar's engraving. After copying the address I'd sat under the tree for a long time, remembering my friend.

I knew she would have been proud of me.

The journey to Karachi took five hours, and as we approached the city my heart grew heavy with dread as the time neared for me to take steps towards regaining my freedom. I peered out of the window at the bustling crowd. The streets were packed with people wearing both modern and traditional dress. Beards and *burkas* mingled with clean-shaven faces, tight jeans and sleeveless tops. The roads were packed with scooters swerving to avoid stray goats, and trucks heavily loaded with goods decorated like Bollywood stage sets. After the serenity of the village, the city was buzzing with noise and commotion.

'It's kinda crazy,' I muttered.

'There is some order in the chaos,' Nannyma said. 'You have to look for it, but everything and everyone is heading somewhere.'

Back home I'd ventured as far as Leeds city centre with Susan and I'd thought that was mega-busy. I had never been to London and I wondered if it was like this – but somehow I doubted that our capital would have roads where a line of four vehicles raced against each other to get ahead in a three-lane road, and animals would certainly not be part of that same traffic.

'I love the crowds,' Nusrat-kala announced, turning to me with a grin. 'It reminds me of Chicago.' She grabbed my hand and squeezed it. 'I'll show you one day.'

Our first stop was an internet shop, which was inside a modern shopping mall. Uncle Tahir quickly paid the money and then led me to the computer in the middle of a large room. I looked around at the other customers, who were all immersed in their own screens, oblivious to me, but I still felt nervous. What if someone recognized me? There had been hundreds of people at Sehar's funeral and many had noticed me as the other foreign girl who was engaged to the army officer. What if one of Asif's friends or Sher Shah's associates saw me? The landlord seemed to have a spider web of contacts from the top of society all the way to the lower ranks. Sher Shah would immediately inform Taya-ji and then we'd all be asked some serious questions.

'Zeba *beti*, perhaps you should get started,' Uncle Tahir advised.

Nodding, I pulled out a chair and sat down under the whirring ceiling fan. I logged on to my email account and found about twenty messages from Susan. I nearly burst into tears at that point as a feeling of homesickness washed over me. Fighting to swallow the lump that had formed in my throat, I opened her most recent email and read the sentence demanding to know where I was.

I minimized Susan's message and opened a new message window and typed as fast as I could. I'd memorized what I wanted to say so I didn't waste time when I got the chance. It was simple and straight to the point.

Dear Tara?

My name is Zeba Khan and I am a British citizen. I am being held against my will by my father's family in Pakistan. They are forcing me to marry my cousin. I do not wish to and need help to escape. My friend Sehar Shah gave me your details. She is now dead. I am at the following location . . .

I set out the details of the village in terms of the distance from Karachi and I also added my UK home address as well as my school's name and address. I wished I'd memorized my passport number, but I hadn't and there was nothing I could do about that now. I wish I'd also known my National Insurance number, but the card was tucked away in my desk at home. Pushing aside thoughts of identity numbers, I quickly researched the email addresses for my local MP, the Foreign Office and the prime minister's office at 10 Downing Street and copied the message to them. I prayed that Tara would pick up the message, but if not her then somebody, somewhere.

Next I quickly wrote to Susan, explaining the situation and asking her to contact our school headmistress to see if she could help.

In half an hour I was done. This was it. I had contacted the people who could help me.

My stomach still full of butterflies, I made my way back to where Nannyma, Nusrat-kala and Uncle Tahir were waiting for me.

'All done?' Nusrat-kala asked.

I nodded. It felt so simple and fast. Could this really work?

Back in the jeep, Nannyma squeezed my arm. 'Our God is full of justice, Zeba,' she said quietly. 'He will help you escape.

You have taken the necessary action and now all you can do is wait and pray to him.'

I nodded and stared out of the window at the people scuttling past. Suddenly the vehicle braked and our bodies lurched forward. A cold dread filled my heart. *Taya-ji has found out what we have done. He has sent Sher Shah's thugs to stop us and . . .*

'Sorry,' Kareem-baba said from the driver's seat. 'The fool pulled out in front of me.'

Biting my lip, I peered forward and saw a small car was blocking our way. The driver was a young man who looked apologetic as he attempted to restart his vehicle.

'Be careful, Kareem-baba,' Nannyma advised calmly.

My heart returned to its normal pace as we sat waiting for the car to move. Then we were off again. Our next stop was going to be the clothes market. Nusrat-kala needed to buy some new outfits . . . it was going to be our cover story for the visit if anybody in the village asked.

The next few days passed in a blur. Every hour of the morning and afternoon I stood at the edge of the veranda and stared out at the distant road, hoping, yearning and wishing for this faceless 'Tara' to come and rescue me. Nusrat-kala sometimes stood silently beside me while Nannyma sat on her swing, her fingers flicking through a *misbaha*, praying for my freedom.

I knew it would be highly unlikely that I was rescued within days of having sent the emails. The real world did not work like that, especially given that it would be a miracle if I was rescued at all. Tara, or someone at any of the other offices I had written to, would have to notice my email first and only then could a rescue process start. I knew all that, but I also knew that time was passing. We were now only two weeks away from my wedding and I had never known the clock to tick so fast.

I stayed away from Taya-ji's house where I knew Mariam-chachi was having daily meetings with wedding planners. Because my parents would not be back until just before the wedding, it was going to be the wedding that Asif's mother wanted for her son. Even if I wasn't being forced to marry Asif, the idea of getting excited about celebrations so close to Sehar's death turned my stomach. I didn't care what I was going to wear – in fact, the less I liked it the better. I'd never been the type of girl who spent her childhood imagining herself on her wedding day and thinking about all the preparations. But I knew that, if I had been, this wouldn't have been the vision that I'd have conjured up.

Chapter 25

Farhat's wedding day arrived. She was finally going to marry her Abdullah.

Unlike Asif's family, Farhat had tried to cancel her *nikaah*, her wedding, but her parents had insisted it go ahead as the arrangements had been made. The view was that there was no point in delaying a good occasion, and I agreed that Sehar would have wanted Farhat to be happy.

The week before, Sehar's family had left for England and taken her baby son with them. I'd been to say goodbye with Nusrat-kala, and Sehar's mum had confided to my aunt that she was going to raise him, give him a British education until he was ready to return as an adult to his father's home. Sher Shah had agreed to it and his will was the only one that mattered. Sehar's mum kept calling the baby Ishfaq – I was not sure who named him – certainly Sehar had never mentioned any names. I'd held her baby in my arms before they left. Farhat had been sitting at my feet on the floor, crying. She'd made no attempt to stop her tears. She was heartbroken that they were going to take the baby away. Farhat had convinced herself that Ishfaq would remain in the village and she would be his nanny, caring for him like she had her beloved Sehar. She couldn't understand how the baby had a British passport when he had been born in Pakistan. I'd tried to explain that the baby was British by descent and it did not matter where he had been born. That was just geography. His mother had been British and that meant he was too.

When the moment of departure arrived, Farhat had wailed like an old woman who was losing her entire world. Sehar's mother had looked at her sympathetically and then climbed into the Land Rover with Ishfaq in her arms, closing the door in Farhat's face. I'd watched helplessly as the maid had stepped forward and pressed her nose against the tinted window, her tears marking the smooth glass as she desperately tried to catch a final glimpse of the baby.

'Eh, move the girl.' It had been Sher Shah who'd spoken as he peered down at Farhat.

I'd been about to place a hand on Farhat's shoulder to urge her to come away, but she stepped back herself as she tried to stifle her sobs in her shawl. Despite her grief Farhat knew that she had to stifle her emotions in front of her employer. At that moment, I had felt like kicking Sher Shah's shins for his lack of compassion.

The Land Rover had roared into life and I'd reached out to grab Farhat's hand as we watched the vehicle drive away. Every day since we had sat by the riverside, crying and laughing as we remembered Sehar. We couldn't help it. It had become a routine. My heart physically hurt; it was tight and heavy and I knew Farhat's was too, and that her pain was much worse because it was intermingled with guilt.

'Zeba-ji, I should have letting Sehar-ji escaping.'

I knew the admission had not come easily. It spoke against everything Farhat had been raised to believe. I'd tried to make her feel better.

'It would have made no difference you know. So you keeping quiet would have given Sehar a head start of what . . . ten minutes? They would have found her. This village is in the middle of nowhere. Nobody would have supported her, or helped her and she would have been lost in the wilderness.'

Farhat had nodded, still sobbing. 'Yaah, but Sehar-ji blaming me. She only wanted me on her side, naah? I never getting to say sorry.'

I hadn't known what to say. I'd reached out and hugged the girl as she cried the guilt out on my shoulder.

Today, however, was Farhat's wedding day and I was determined that we would remember it as a happy occasion. After all, Farhat was actually excited to marry her Abdullah. When I entered her small hut, I was struck by the genuine happiness it contained. The dry, mud walls were decorated with red glittery shawls and colourful balloons hung from the ceiling. Farhat's mum, Rachida-bhaji, greeted me with a shy, surprised smile. She knew Farhat and I spent time together, but she did not expect me to attend her daughter's wedding. It was not the norm in the village for the rich to attend the peasants' celebrations. In another world, perhaps if I had been born and raised here, I would not have set foot in this hut and I definitely would not have hugged the bride's mother.

Rachida-bhaji seemed shocked when I reached forward to press myself against her stiff body. Her arms remained by her side and, when I stepped back, she lifted her shiny scarf to her blushing face and tried to hide behind it.

'In England we always hug the bride's mother,' I explained, trying to put her at ease. 'Thank you for including me in this happy occasion. Now where is the lucky bride?'

Rachida-bhaji relaxed a little and pointed to the sheer green scarf, glistening with gold plastic stars that was acting as a veil to shield the bride from the guests before the ceremony. I hesitated. Should I walk around?

'Zeba-ji.' It was Farhat calling me from the other side of the veil. 'Come, come, you is my bestest friend now. You sit with me, isn't it?'

I hurried around to find a beautiful bride on the other side. Farhat was wearing a deep red wedding outfit made up of a full ball-gown skirt and top. On her head rested a red shawl, heavy with beadwork, and her plait lay on her left shoulder, coiled with a shiny matching red and gold ribbon.

'You look gorgeous,' I gasped.

'They rubbing turmeric on my skin last night,' Farhat explained, blushing furiously at my compliment. 'You know mixed with yoghurt to make my skin nice and lovely. I always wishing to have shining skin like you and Sehar-ji . . .'

She paused, but I was determined to make her feel beautiful.

'And you have shining skin today,' I whispered in her ear. 'Abdullah won't be able to keep his eyes off you.'

Farhat blushed furiously again and then she held out a hand. 'Zeba-ji,' she said, 'this is the lipstick Sehar-ji gave me. Would you putting it on for me?'

I took the tube and applied the red shade to Farhat's lips. Neither of us said anything. It had been wishful thinking on my part to think we could have got through today without feeling sadness for Sehar. But it was lovely to know that she was a part of it.

I settled down next to Farhat on the wooden bed, which was covered in a shiny red fabric, and waited for the ceremony to begin. Glancing around at the simplicity of the event, I couldn't help thinking of my own wedding on which it seemed no expense was being spared. Two days earlier I'd been subjected to a dress fitting by Mariam-chachi at Nannyma's house. She had arrived in the morning accompanied by two seamstresses and my mum, who had returned before my dad to help with the final preparations. We had embraced awkwardly.

Nannyma had remained on her swing, but Nusrat-kala had joined us in my room. I'd been ordered to try on the red skirt and heavily embroidered and beaded top so that it could be amended to my measurements. I tried not to pay too much attention to the dress, or even comment on it, just to annoy Mariam-chachi and my mum. As the seamstresses pricked me with pins, Husna-bhaji had come in to offer her help but the widow had been shooed out by Mariam-chachi, who had seemed offended by her presence.

'You know Husna-bhaji is one of the best seamstresses I've ever come across,' Nusrat-kala had announced.

'Well then you obviously haven't come across many,' Mariam-chachi had shot back.

'Whatever,' Nusrat-kala had muttered, scowling.

My outfit wasn't the only thing that was extravagant. Mariam-chachi had then begun gushing that Sher Shah had offered his *haveli* as the wedding venue. I had swayed on my legs as this fact registered with me. It was too obscene to even think about. Were they seriously expecting me to enter the very place where Sehar's funeral had been held dressed in a red costume sparkling with enough dazzle to make a Las Vegas showgirl proud?

'Why can't we have the wedding here?' I'd asked.

Mariam-chachi and my mum had stared at me as if I'd asked the most ridiculous question.

'This house isn't big enough to accommodate all the guests,' Mariam-chachi had sniffed. 'So many people are coming. Important people: politicians from Islamabad, artists and writers from Lahore and businessmen from Karachi. It is going to be quite an occasion in the social diary. After all, it is my son's wedding.'

'Well, you know Zee should get a say,' Nusrat-kala had said suddenly.

'Nusrat, will you stop interfering,' my mum had snapped.

'Someone has to!' Nusrat-kala had exploded. 'You obviously don't give two hoots about your own daughter's happiness.'

'How dare you!' my mum had raged. 'Who do you think you are?'

'Someone who cares about –'

'Nusrat!' It had been Nannyma standing by the door. 'Come away,' she'd said to her younger daughter. 'Let Nighat and Mariam get on with what they came to do.'

Nusrat-kala had looked like she was going to object, but then changed her mind and walked out. I watched her leave helplessly as another pin poked my waist.

'Ow!' I yelled.

The seamstress had started to apologize but Mariam-chachi interrupted. 'It's OK, just get on with it.' Then turning to Mum she said, 'Nighat, the *haveli* will look lovely. We will hang fairy lights all around the building to light it up in the night. We will have fresh flowers hanging from every nook and cranny. The best sweetmeats from Karachi have been ordered. The food will be an elaborate buffet of chicken and meat kebabs, biryani, vegetable dishes, fish, the most exotic of fruits, a chocolate fountain and . . .'

I closed my eyes as Mariam-chachi gushed on about her plans . . .

That had been two days ago and I'd only managed to get through the dress fitting with the hope in my heart that Tara would come and rescue me. I was still hoping and I was still waiting, but today I wanted to celebrate Farhat's wedding, a more joyous occasion than mine could ever be, despite all the money being spent on it.

The new village imam arrived, a young man in his twenties. Presumably someone malleable whom Sher Shah could control from the outset. He remained on the other side of the curtain with Abdullah and his family while he gave a short sermon and recited some verses from the Qur'an. Then he came round to speak to Farhat. Standing over her he asked in a deep, clear voice, 'Do you Farhat Usman Sulaiman Mehmood agree to this marriage. Is it *qabool*?'

'*Qabool*,' Farhat whispered.

'I did not hear you. *Qabool*?'

'*Qabool*,' she said clearly.

The imam then returned to Abdullah and officially asked him if he agreed to the marriage. We heard the groom's accept-ance, his '*qabool*', from the other side and after another quick recital from the Qur'an, which concluded the ceremony, the cries of *mubarak*, congratulations, went up on the other side as the men embraced each other. Rachida-bhaji, who had been standing behind us, rushed forward to hug her daughter, crying with joy. Gazing at the two of them, I felt a stab of jealousy in my heart, a piercing pain because I did not have a mother who cried with exhilaration for my happiness.

Chapter 26

I waited and waited but nobody came for me. Days passed and yet Tara's cavalry did not ride to my rescue. I had foolishly thought that I could become master of my destiny. I had been wrong. I had been arrogant to think that I was different from the peasant women who came for their water every day. I was the same as them: restricted, confined and powerless. It did not matter that I carried a red passport engraved with the emblem of a unicorn and a lion. Crying into my nannyma's lap, I gave up the last fragments of hope.

I walked around like a zombie. It was just a matter of days now until my wedding. I felt as though the hours and minutes that ticked away led to my execution. My bridal outfit was ready. In our culture red was a celebratory colour, but I knew that it was also a martyr's colour. I couldn't help thinking of myself in this way. I felt cold all the time and I couldn't eat.

My nannyma prayed for me. Even my Nusrat-kala was showing signs of strain. She was no longer on speaking terms with my mum. Both sisters had decided they'd had enough of each other. They really were chalk and cheese. My mum was preparing to lay me down as a sacrificial lamb for her husband's honour, while my aunt paced the veranda in worry.

I was no longer speaking to my dad. He had returned from England three days ago for the wedding and Nannyma had invited him and Mum to dinner. It had been a tense affair. Mum and Nusrat-kala had ignored each other, Dad had hardly said a word and even Nannyma had looked glum. It had been left to poor Uncle Tahir to keep a form of conversation alive, but even he had given up halfway through the main course. When we had finished eating, Nannyma had spoken up.

'Kamran,' she had addressed Dad. 'There is still time. Back out of this. Don't condemn your daughter to this life in the village.'

My dad had stared down at the half eaten remains on his plate. 'I cannot,' he'd replied tersely. 'You know I cannot.'

Nannyma's hand had slammed down on the table and made us all jump.

'The boy will never agree to leave for England,' she had cried. 'He will remain here. Think about it. She is your only child. You will have her part from you like this?'

My dad's chair had scraped back violently and then his own fist had come down hard on the table.

'Perhaps you are right,' he had said through gritted teeth. 'But what can I do? It is too late. I have given my word. My honour depends on this marriage going ahead.'

The mention of the word honour had stirred something inside me. I had walked over to my dad and knelt in front of him. 'Is your honour more important than my happiness?' I had asked with tears streaming down my face. 'I don't want my life ruined. I don't want to die like Sehar!'

My dad had turned pained eyes towards me before rising violently to his feet and walking out. As usual my mum had followed closely behind. I hadn't heard a word from either of them since. It seemed they couldn't face me and I wasn't really surprised. I couldn't face them either.

There were now only three days left until the first of my ceremonies. My henna night was scheduled first, followed by the *nikaah* and reception the next day. After the wedding I was expected to move in with Asif at Taya-ji's house. This was the custom: a daughter-in-law moved in with her husband's family.

The thought of living with Mariam-chachi filled me with dread. How was I going to face seeing her every day, especially if there was going to be no return to England? I knew there wasn't. Everyone knew there wasn't. Asif had already announced that he was going to return to the army for a special mission in the North-West Frontier Province five days after the wedding. To my knowledge nobody had questioned his plans. Not my dad, not Taya-ji, his mother . . . no one. It seemed that they just wanted the marriage to go ahead first and then they would deal with informing Asif about the move to the UK. To me it just seemed like wishful thinking on their part.

I was sitting now with Nusrat-kala on the veranda. Nannyma had retired to her room for a siesta, as had Uncle Tahir.

'If Taya-ji wants Asif to move to the UK, why doesn't he order him?' I asked. 'What's all this stuff about him going off on another mission?'

Nusrat-kala grimaced. 'Does Asif strike you as a man who will listen to anyone but himself?'

I didn't say anything and Nusrat-kala looked at me sympathetically.

'Look, Zeba,' she said. 'I don't know why Taya-ji is holding back. You'd think he could stand up to his own son, but it appears that in terms of stubbornness the apple did not fall far from the tree.'

I had no idea what she meant and I just stared at her.

'Asif is as stubborn as his father,' Nusrat-kala explained. 'Look, all I know is that Taya-ji will urge Asif to leave for the UK once the wedding has happened. According to your mum, Asif will be made to feel guilty about your unhappiness at remaining here and it is hoped that then he will agree to make the move.'

'It is *hoped*?' I repeated bitterly. 'It is hoped . . . well, that's all right then. Let's live on that rare hope that Asif might take pity on me one day and chuck in everything he loves in order to put a smile on my face. And then, once he's in England, he can start resenting me because he misses his home, his job, his friends.'

Nusrat-kala gazed at me helplessly. 'I'm so sorry,' she gasped, close to tears. 'Are you sure Sehar had all the facts about this Tara?'

I shrugged. There was no point in going over it again with my aunt. Nusrat-kala had asked me the same question countless times and I had relayed to her everything Sehar had said. What was the point of going over old ground again? Either I was going to be rescued and taken home by some miracle, or I was going to wither away in this village.

Chapter 27

My henna ceremony was to begin in four hours. The evening of food and traditional song and dance was being held at Taya-ji's house.

My hands were already painted with henna. Last night a village girl, Sabina, had arrived with Mariam-chachi and my mum and spent four hours weaving her intricate design on my palms. My feet remained to be painted and she was going to decorate them tonight at the ceremony. Apparently the henna task was a long, laborious one that had to be divided over two days. I stared down at my hands. Somewhere, buried deep in the pattern, the name of my future husband was hidden. Sabina had told me it was traditional for a groom to search for his name on the wedding night. I knew that I wouldn't be able to help Asif; his name was written in Urdu.

It was four in the afternoon and I was with Farhat on Nanny-ma's rooftop garden. She was here to help me dress for the party and then Abdullah was going to take us to Mariam-chachi's house.

I stood gazing out at the endless green fields ahead of me while Farhat immersed herself in arranging the dozen or so bangles I had to wear on my arms. In the middle of the fields was a dusty, bumpy road, which had been carved out by the vehicles en route to the main road. In the distance I could see a white jeep approaching; guests for my wedding ceremony the next day, no doubt. People I didn't even know were coming from far and wide to celebrate the beginning of my doomed life.

The vehicle got closer and closer and I expected it to speed past, splashing dirty water and mud at the villagers with its giant tyres. But instead the jeep slowed down and pulled up outside Nannyma's house. A woman wearing a white cotton *salwar kameez* and a blue shawl emerged, a black leather bag on her right shoulder.

There was something vaguely familiar about her. It was like I could relate to her despite the distance between us. It was something in her walk, in the way she held herself and the quiet confidence that oozed from her every pore. And then it hit me. This woman was foreign. She was not Pakistani. It was obvious in the way she slapped away flies. The woman looked around and, seeing no one, called to someone inside the car.

'I think this is it.'

The English she spoke was delivered in a Midlands accent. She sounded just like Sehar. A flicker of hope ignited in my chest, but I ignored it. Perhaps she was a Birmingham relative come to visit Sher Shah's family.

A white man with blond hair emerged from the car.

I saw Uncle Tahir approach the couple and exchange words. Then Uncle Tahir called out to his wife urgently and Nusrat-kala ran outside. She listened intently to her husband, shook hands with the couple and then turned to run back into the house. I frowned and leaned forward over the roof wall to try and catch their words, but the only sound I could hear was the frenzied clicking of Nusrat-kala's kitten heels as she hurried up the stone steps leading to the roof. I turned to face her just as she emerged into the sunshine.

'Zeba,' she panted. 'They are here.'

I stared blankly at my aunt.

'It's the British High Commission. They've come to take you home.'

'But . . .' I couldn't believe it.

'You must hurry,' Nusrat-kala urged. 'Tahir has given five hundred dollars to the man outside. It should pay for your ticket home. We need to get you out of Pakistan urgently.'

'I . . .'

'Zeba, my darling, we have no time. Just grab a shawl and go. Tahir and I really can't be seen to be helping you. We must pretend we know nothing for the sake of Nannyma, or your taya-ji will unleash his fury on her. We will say that you crept out without any of us realizing. We won't sound the alarm until we think you have passed a safe distance. Now go!'

For someone who had been yearning for this moment of escape, I hadn't prepared for it at all well. My hands began to tremble as my mind registered the seriousness of what I was about to do. All I had to do to escape was run down the stairs, out of my nannyma's house and into that jeep. Nearly a year ago, all Sehar had had to do was walk out of her house, get to the railway station and she would still be alive.

'I'm ready!' I cried.

'Come on then!'

Nusrat-kala turned to run back down the stairs and I was

about to follow when a voice called out to me. I had forgotten all about Farhat sitting quietly on the wooden bed.

'Where is you going?' she asked in a small voice. 'Is your henna party tonight.'

'I am going to leave with those people down there.'

'But is your henna night,' Farhat insisted in a small, stubborn voice.

I took a step forward towards the door and Farhat moved to block me. 'Is my duty to let Abdullah stop you. Zeba-ji, you is not shaming Taya-ji's family like this.'

'You don't work for Taya-ji,' I spat out.

Farhat looked perplexed. 'But this is reputation of the village. The *izzat* of village. The promise has been making by your father. You have to marry.'

'I won't!' I gritted my teeth, trying to control my anger. 'I won't let them kill me like they did Sehar.'

At the mention of our friend, Farhat's eyes widened and she took on a wounded look as if I'd hit her.

'They killed Sehar!' I cried. 'You can't let them kill me!'

Farhat gulped and then nodded her head slightly. 'Go,' she whispered. 'I say nothing.'

I threw a look down below to make sure the couple was still waiting. They were looking around anxiously. It was enough to make me bolt, but I skidded to a halt when I reached the door. I turned to look at Farhat. She remained standing, looking strangely serene. I knew that if I escaped today then I would owe my life to this peasant girl. I reached Farhat in a few strides and flung my arms around her.

'I love you, Fatty,' I whispered, using Sehar's nickname for her. The words caught in my throat.

Farhat blushed furiously at the open display of affection. 'You need leave. Go.'

I turned and ran as fast as I could, down the stairs, through the courtyard and on to the veranda. The couple were staring at something, which stopped me in my tracks. I turned in the direction of their gaze and saw my nannyma. She was on her swing, her feet lightly pushing the floor to maintain the swaying motion.

'Go, my daughter, go,' she said simply.

I burst into tears. Would I ever see my nannyma again? And Nusrat-kala and Uncle Tahir? For the first time I realized that by escaping I was potentially sacrificing contact with my entire family.

As if sensing my thoughts, Nannyma stood up to hug me and I clung to her.

'My prayers have been answered, Zeba, my *beti*,' Nannyma said, untangling herself from my grip. 'I want the world for you. Now go!'

Chapter 28

We sped through the wilderness of Sindh, over rocky paths and then smooth motorways until the glistening lights of Karachi appeared as a speck in the distance. From the moment the vehicle had left the village, I'd been tempted to look over my shoulder to check we weren't being followed, but I hadn't had the courage. Somehow I didn't think I would be able to bear it if Sher Shah or Taya-ji crept up on us, and so I sat grim-faced with my rescuers, none of us uttering a word during the five-hour journey. Introductions didn't seem important as I spent the time tense and in shock.

Day had become night by the time the car pulled up outside a two-storey house. I climbed out of the vehicle and gazed up at the red brick building. It looked like the outside of a railway station, a bit like St Pancras station in the Harry Potter movies.

'Is this the British High Commission?' I asked.

The woman looked at me kindly. 'No,' she said. 'It's a safe house, but it is the property of the British government.'

'Safe house? So I will be safe from my relatives?'

'Yes, you will,' the woman assured. 'Nobody will be able to locate you here.'

I wasn't convinced about the 'safety' that the safe house would provide for me. How could it? Sher Shah, who outranked Taya-ji in wealth, status and power, would be helping the search for me. I was sure he would know people in Karachi who could find me.

'My name's Saima by the way,' the woman introduced herself. 'And that there is Damian.'

I nodded.

Saima put her hand on my arm. 'We're sorry about what happened to your friend.'

I couldn't respond. I didn't know how to. What should I say? *Hey, thanks for rescuing me instead.*

We entered the empty house in silence and Saima led me to a room on the upper floor.

'I'll bring you something to eat,' she offered.

'No, thank you,' I said. 'I don't want anything. I'm not hungry. I just need to sleep.'

Saima nodded and left the room.

That night I hardly slept. I lay in the stark white room on a single bed expecting the door to be broken down any minute. Perhaps I had watched too many movies where the villains caught up with the heroine. I wondered what commotion was happening in the village. I knew Taya-ji and Dad would blame Nannyma and I felt awful, but I knew she would be able to hold her own. Plus, she had Nusrat-kala and Uncle Tahir with her for support. I looked at my watch. It was just after ten. Had I been at the village, my henna ceremony would've been under way with girls dancing to the *tabla*, the traditional drum, and the women singing folk songs. Like Farhat, a yellow turmeric paste would've been rubbed into my skin to create a radiant glow and my hair oiled to make it silky soft.

I buried my head under the pillow trying to block out the thoughts that invaded my mind. I didn't want to think about what should have been happening right now. I'd wanted to escape and I had succeeded. There was no point looking back now. The minutes slowly turned into hours and I must have fallen asleep because suddenly Saima was jolting me awake.

'We have to leave,' she was saying. 'You have a flight to catch.'

I bolted out of bed. The magic word was flight. I was going home to England.

'There's a shower room at the end of the hallway and perhaps you could fit into these clothes,' Saima said, handing me a pair of white linen trousers and a long shirt.

I took them gratefully and ten minutes later I was ready. Saima offered me some tea and biscuits, but I knew I wouldn't be able to swallow anything. My heart was in my mouth I was so nervous. Damian came into the room with a rucksack flung over his shoulder. Finally we were ready to leave. I walked down the steps of the house and climbed into the jeep. My breathing was rapid as the vehicle pulled out of the gates and I prayed with all my heart and soul that we would reach the airport safely.

We arrived fifty minutes later and thankfully my worst fears of a car-jacking were not realized. But I couldn't help constantly looking over my shoulder as the three of us walked briskly through the airport . . . and then something awful occurred to me.

'I haven't got my passport!' I exclaimed.

Damian grinned at me. 'Do you think you're with a couple of loonies?' he joked.

I stared at him. I wasn't sure how to answer that.

'It's all arranged,' Saima said. 'We have a copy of it.'

'You do?' I was dumbfounded. 'Will they accept that?'

'Relax,' Saima assured. 'We'll get you home.'

I took a deep breath and felt like I could finally just trust Saima and Damian.

Then suddenly, like a predator emerging from nowhere, Asif stepped out from behind a pillar and stood barring my way. I froze in my tracks as my heart began to thud in my chest. This was like one of Sehar's Bollywood movies. In the space of a split-second I knew my instincts had been right; men like Sher Shah and Asif wielded too much power in this country. You couldn't just escape them. It wasn't possible.

'Going somewhere?' Asif said coolly as he towered in front of me.

I just gaped at him. Saima and Damian moved swiftly to my side.

'Who is he?' Saima asked in a small whisper.

'My fiancé.'

I heard her sharp intake of breath.

'Well, he's keen on you, ain't he, love,' Damian muttered.

'He's going to drag me back to the village,' I said, my voice shaking.

'No he won't,' Saima said firmly. 'You're British and he can't kidnap you from this airport. Perhaps we should try and get security, Damian.'

I wanted to believe her but the sight of the three men forming a triangle behind Asif persuaded me otherwise. There was no way I was going to be able to escape.

'Can I help you, mate?' Damian said casually, as though

being ambushed like this was the most ordinary of events.

'I am not your "mate",' Asif replied tersely in English, the fingers of one hand rolled into a fist, his knuckles white. 'And furthermore you have my bride-to-be. I want to know why you've kidnapped her.'

'I think you'll find,' Damian countered, 'that she's here of her own free will.'

'Let her tell me that,' Asif demanded. His hand was now resting on his hip, forcing back his army jacket to reveal the top half of a handgun tucked into his jeans.

I stared at the lethal weapon. This was crazy, I thought. I was a simple girl from a small town in Yorkshire. How could this be happening to me? What was Asif going to do? Shoot Damian and Saima and then drag me back to the village? Sehar had been wrong about him. There was no honourable pride in Asif, just a need to impose his own will like his father.

It seemed Damian had noticed it too. 'Take it easy,' he said.

'No!' Asif snapped. 'You take it easy!'

'There's no need for all this,' Damian said quietly.

'Keep quiet!' Asif ordered.

'Look,' Damian began, 'what is it you want? You can't seriously think you can shoot us here? We're officers of the British High Commission. It doesn't matter who your father is or your family connections, you won't get away with it.'

Asif was staring at Damian with disbelief. 'You think I'm going to shoot you?'

'Of course we think that!' I burst out, finding my voice from a combination of fear and outrage. 'What else would we think?'

Asif's eyes widened in further disbelief. Then, as if he were noticing the exposed gun for the first time, he pulled his jacket over it. Finally he said, 'I just wanted to talk to you before you left. Why did you do this? Why run away?'

'I want to go home,' I whispered. 'I don't want to marry you. These people are helping me.'

'And you've decided now?' Asif demanded incredulously. 'A day before the wedding? Why didn't you say anything when I came to see you?'

'Because I didn't think you would listen.'

'And this is your way of getting me to listen?'

'I never agreed to this marriage,' I mumbled, close to tears.

'Our marriage has been arranged by our parents,' Asif said tightly. 'I am respecting their wishes. Why aren't you?'

'Because I don't want to marry you,' I cried, then added feebly: 'I want an education first.'

Asif looked baffled. 'So what's the problem? You can attend a ladies' college in Karachi. I won't stop you.'

'In Karachi?' I repeated. Salman Shah had been right. Asif had no intention of leaving Pakistan – no matter what Taya-ji said. Before I knew it, the truth was tumbling out of my mouth. 'Your parents want you to come to England with me. They don't want us to live here.'

Now Asif seemed affronted. 'I am an officer in my country's army. I will not be leaving Pakistan.'

'But Taya-ji and Mariam-chachi only want us to marry so that you will leave Pakistan for the UK,' I argued. 'They don't want you here in the face of danger. That's why my dad agreed to the marriage even though he knew I didn't want it!'

Asif stared at me. 'How do you know this?'

I explained what Nannyma had told me, but left out the conversation with Salman Shah. Asif listened silently, his scowl deepening with my every word. Finally when I finished, he simply said, 'Go home, Zeba.'

'What?' I gasped.

'Go home,' Asif repeated.

I stared up at him. Was he letting me go? Or was this a ploy to . . . what? I didn't know.

'Don't look so shocked,' Asif said. 'You are free to go. I suggest you return to England as soon as possible, otherwise I don't know what my father will do to you.' With those words he walked away from me.

'You OK?' Saima asked.

'He said I could go,' I mumbled.

'Yeah well, what are we waiting for?' Damian said. 'Let's get out of here before the guy changes his mind.'

The three of us hurried to the check-in counter. I was trembling. I could not believe Asif had just let me go like that. It was a miracle.

'You know, I gotta say this,' Damian said, as he handed me my boarding pass. They had been allowed to accompany me to the gate to make sure I boarded the flight safely. 'You are one of the lucky ones.'

'Oi!' Saima warned him. 'Don't scare her.'

'It's OK,' I whispered. 'I know, you're right. My friend wasn't one of the lucky ones, and it's thanks to her that I made it this far. I owe you all. Thank you for everything.'

'You're welcome,' Saima smiled. 'And say hi to Tara for me. Tell her I'll meet her for coffee back home when my time is up here. Remember, someone will be there to meet you off the plane at Heathrow.'

I nodded, unable to say anything as a lump formed in my throat. I wanted to throw my arms around these two strangers to express my gratitude for what they had done for me. But I didn't. A big part of me was desperate to board the plane and have it take off into the air before Asif changed his mind, but, resisting the urge to run, I attempted to articulate my thanks again. Saima stopped me by placing an arm around me.

'You don't need to say anything. You are going to be just fine,' she assured me. 'Isn't she, Damian?'

Damian winked at me and when he took a step back I knew it was time to go.

Smiling my goodbye, I turned and walked through the door, which led to the steps down to the tarmac. The bus ride to the plane took about two minutes and then I was climbing aboard the 747 direct to London.

I couldn't believe it. I was going home. The words were like a song in my heart.

Chapter 29

The plane was circling Heathrow, waiting for authorization to descend. It was evening, but there was still plenty of light and I could clearly see the tops of houses through the little oval window. It was my first sight of London, my capital city, which I had never visited, and although the view was dull, the joy in my heart threatened to explode. However, the surreal feeling of coming home only lasted until the plane's wheels hit the tarmac. As the Boeing 747 slowly made its way to its stand, there was only one thought nagging in my mind: what would happen to me now?

As soon as I left the plane, I was met by an airport official whose job it was to deliver me to the Foreign Office representative.

'You look nervous,' he said, looking down at me sympathetically. 'Don't be.'

I managed a weak smile as I tried to erase the fear and fatigue from my face. Heathrow airport was huge and the journey down the endless corridors was taking its toll on me. My mind was screaming its one relentless question: how was I going to survive on my own?

My answer came in the shape of a tall, statuesque Asian woman dressed in sneakers, jeans and a T-shirt. I knew it was Tara as soon as I saw her. Her big brown eyes lit up when she saw me, and immediately I felt better. Was she used to working with girls who looked like me – scared rabbits fleeing the foxes? Whatever the reason, she bounded up to me on her long legs and reached down to grab me in a hug.

'Welcome home, Zeba,' she said in a warm, husky voice.

I managed a slight nod as some of the fear trickled away.

Once we were in the car heading into the city, Tara told me she had organized a place for me in a refuge in Whitechapel, which was in East London. I repeated the name of the place in my head several times; it sounded familiar. Hey, wasn't that where Jack the Ripper had killed all those women? I hadn't realized I had voiced the question aloud until Tara burst out with a rich, heavy laugh.

'Yeah, that's right,' she said. 'But I don't think you have to worry about him any more. He's long dead . . . More importantly you will merge into the crowds and become anonymous. That's what we want for now.'

The women-only hostel was a big three-storey Edwardian house. A total of twelve people lived there, including the on-site supervisor, Alice. There were another two Asian girls and the rest were all white.

Tara spent some time helping me to settle in. Before leaving, she hugged me tightly. 'Be strong,' she said, smiling down at me. 'I will be back tomorrow. I'm leaving you in very safe and capable hands.'

I tried to look cheerful and confident, but inside my stomach was churning with nerves. Then I remembered Sehar, and why I was here, and immediately everything felt a little better.

I didn't talk to anyone once she had gone. I felt like I was in a daze. Too much had happened. Locking the door of my new room, I crawled under the duvet fully clothed and stared at the ceiling. Was this going to be my life now? Was I going to have the courage to make it on my own?

I wanted to phone Susan, but thought better of it. Tara had warned me not to contact anyone from home – not for now anyway. She'd said it was too dangerous. I'd asked her if she thought men with guns would turn up to kidnap me. I'd meant it as a joke, but she'd taken me seriously.

'Well, that has been known to happen in the past, but that's not what I'm concerned about.'

Really? *Is there anything worse than men with guns coming to kidnap me?* I thought.

Apparently Tara had thought so. She told me the first forty-eight hours were crucial. Most girls who escaped were so overwhelmed by being alone in a strange place that they succumbed to that very fear and allowed themselves to be talked into returning home.

Feeling as I was feeling now, I could see Tara had been right to be concerned.

One of the Asian girls struck up a conversation with me over breakfast. Her name was Surjit and she was from the West Midlands. I glanced at her wrist and noticed a silver bracelet, a *kara*, which identified her as a Sikh. Surjit was a fifteen-year-old chatterbox with short hair and a gothic dress sense.

Her story was similar to mine. She was the youngest of four sisters who had all married men from the Punjab state of India.

Surjit claimed none of her sisters were happy and that two were the constant victims of domestic violence. She didn't want the same future as her siblings so she ran away from home as soon as a trip to India was announced. Although no wedding was ever mentioned by her parents, Surjit said she knew one had been arranged for her. 'Girls who don't learn from the mistakes of their older sisters are very foolish,' she said confidently.

When Surjit asked me about my story, I told her the truth. Well, all of it except the part about Sehar. I found it too painful to talk about my dead friend. When I'd been in Pakistan, it had been Farhat who had been plagued with guilt. However, here, now, breathing in the air of the country both Sehar and I had pined for, a creeping guilt had started to overtake me. An escape to London was meant to have been the first steps to Sehar's happy ending. It was supposed to have been her beginning, but it wasn't, it was mine . . . and my friend's body lay six feet under the ground of the country she had hated.

On the second day Surjit and I attended a counselling session in a small room next to the kitchen. Nasreen, the other Asian girl, joined us although she never spoke a word. She was a tall, big-boned girl with long dark hair pulled back in a ponytail. Her face seemed permanently set in a sad expression and her nervous eyes darted continuously around her as if she was expecting to be attacked from any direction at anytime. I had tried speaking to her at breakfast – small talk about the weather – but she'd just looked at me vacantly and carried on eating her cereal. I couldn't help wondering what trauma lay behind the silence.

The counselling session was something like the Alcoholics Anonymous meetings that featured in TV dramas, except that we were Forced Marriage Anonymous. There weren't many of us, just us three girls and an Asian guy called Habib who looked about nineteen. He had a long, skinny body, a toothy grin and short, spiky hair. Although only women lived in the hostel, Alice had explained that occasionally young men attended some of the group sessions during the day.

'So you're the latest one to join us,' he said, when I sat down next to him on a chair.

I nodded.

'It's a shame, innit,' Habib said, shaking his head. 'Our parents just don't get us.'

I nodded again, surprised at his willingness to talk.

'You're shocked, innit?' he said, grinning. 'I can tell you're thinking "what's this bloke doing here with these girls", ain't you?'

'No,' I denied, although that was exactly what I was thinking.

'I ain't bothered if people think it's weird for me to be here,' he laughed. Only I know what I've been through is just the same as you girls. I know what's it like when they try to force you to marry someone you don't want.'

Now I really was surprised. This guy had been forced too? I thought it was only ever the girls. My face must have revealed what I was thinking because Habib was shaking his head.

'Yeah, girl, it happens to us blokes as well. My mum was ill and she wanted me to marry her sister's daughter in Kashmir. She nagged me and nagged me and nagged me, but I wasn't having any of it. Her brother, my uncle, even threatened to have me beaten up. Can you believe it? That was it, man, when my mum sided with her brother, that's when I left.'

I didn't know what to say so I just stared at him.

'It's all right,' Habib said, the grin back in its place. 'I'm all right, you know. Getting by now and . . .' He stopped talking as a middle-aged Asian woman walked in.

'Hello, everyone,' she greeted us before turning to look at me directly. 'And you must be Zeba. I'm Aisha, the centre's counsellor. Tara's told me all about you.'

And so our session began. I didn't really talk much about myself except to say that I was from the north. Habib needed no encouragement to launch into his life story when requested.

'Well, I already told you about what was happening at home with my mum and her brother bullying me and the chick from Kashmir. Well, I weren't having any of it so I ran away but I ended up on the streets. Man that was rough. The streets ain't a fun place to be when you got no proper friends. I can't even remember the last two years. It's all a blur. But then I got saved by this charity. They said they could help me and I knew I couldn't handle living on streets forever so I went with them. And now look at me. Been trying to get my life back together for over a year, but I ain't been home to see my mum yet. I'm gonna find me a nice girl, marry her and then I'll take her home as my bride.'

'Habib, that was really good of you to share your story again for the benefit of Zeba,' Aisha said, smiling broadly.

Habib gave another toothy grin and shrugged. 'Happy to help, man.'

'Well yes, it is important that you girls realize that young men go through the same kind of problem,' Aisha continued. 'We're here to help you all. Now, Nasreen, how about we hear from you today.'

Nasreen stared at her hands.

'Nas,' Aisha coaxed, 'talking helps us to deal with the issues we have locked inside. Why don't you try and say a few words?'

The silence stretched.

'Well, we want to hear Zeba's story, but we can't hear hers until we hear yours,' Aisha said. 'I am sure Zeba is very keen to tell us what happened to her, so we'll think about both of those things for next time, shall we?'

I could see that Aisha was trying to coax Nasreen to talk, but that she didn't want to push her. I was pleased that no one was being forced to do anything. I wasn't sure if I would be able to tell my whole story, including the bit about Sehar, when my time came.

For the rest of the session Aisha talked to us about confidence, and how to think positively about our futures. Although I wasn't at that stage yet, it was nice to imagine that I could have those thoughts one day.

Afterwards Surjit asked if I wanted to go for a walk. I wasn't sure if it was allowed but Alice nodded her agreement. I wished she hadn't. I really didn't want to leave the security of the hostel. Despite its impersonal feel with its clinical white walls and odd plants placed here and there, I felt safe here. I knew my fear was irrational; nobody knew me here. How could they? I was a Yorkshire girl who had never visited London before. I had no relatives here or friends, but still I felt wary about stepping outside.

Surjit sensed my hesitation. 'The fresh air will be good,' she said.

I decided she was right. I had nothing to fear.

We wandered through the narrow back streets near the hostel

until we emerged on to the high street. Looking around I was slightly unsettled by the immediate thought that I may as well be in Pakistan – or rather in Bangladesh. We were smack bang in the middle of the Bangladeshi community. Sari shops, kebab takeaways and travel agents lined the street and a small market crowded the same pavement. Stalls were piled high with *hijab* head coverings, Bollywood DVDs and fruit and vegetables. I watched a group of women crowd around the fishmonger's stall impatient for their turn. Salmon, trout and cod lay with eyes and mouths wide open as women draped in saris and cardigans poked the scales to check for freshness.

'Gross smell, ain't it?' Surjit said, leading us away from the fish stall.

I thought of Imran-chacha, my great uncle, the retired soldier. The Bangladeshis were another people he had been at war with. My dad had told me that when the British Empire had ended in 1947 and India was partitioned, Mohammad Ali Jinnah had carved out two pieces of land, which were named West Pakistan and East Pakistan, to form a new Muslim state. But the two areas were separated by 1,600 kilometres of Indian land in the middle. The Governor-General and former Viceroy of India, Lord Mountbatten, who had been given the task of handing the land back to its people, had warned Jinnah that a country divided could not succeed, but his advice was ignored. Whenever my dad told me the story of his country's birth he would grudgingly concede that Mountbatten had been right when he'd predicted there would be disputes over resources and wealth that would tear the new Muslim nation apart.

In the 1970s, the East Pakistanis had demanded an independent state and fought for it. Imran-chacha had been one of the

West Pakistan troops who had tried to quash the uprising, but failed. The East Pakistanis had won with the aid of India's first female prime minister, Indira Gandhi, and renamed their land Bangladesh. My dad always referred to her as the woman who knew how to play political games.

'That was one woman who knew that her enemy's enemy was her friend,' he would say.

I marvelled at how people were able to move on from war and destruction. Two decades ago my family and the relatives of these people had been killing each other, and yet here I was now living within this community, hidden in their numbers, accepted as a Muslim sister.

I looked across the road. An imposing, old-looking building stretched from one end of the street to the other.

'That's the Royal London Hospital,' Surjit said, following my gaze. 'Sam, the cleaner at the hostel . . . you ain't met her yet, well, she says that's where a lot of the dead and injured were taken after the July 7 bombings. Aldgate East station is just up the road near where a bomb went off. Do you want to go see?'

I mumbled no. I felt weary again. Surjit's mention of bombs and death just reminded me of Asif and I didn't want to think about him. I decided to change the subject.

'So what's up with that girl Nasreen?' I asked.

'How do you mean?'

'Well, she's like a . . . a . . . zombie,' I said, unsure how else to describe it.

Surjit shrugged. 'I don't know really. I've been here about two months and she was here before me. She keeps herself to herself. I've never heard her speak. Everyone's intrigued by her, but I've only heard some rumours from the other girls about what happened to her.'

I waited for Surjit to tell me but she became mesmerized by a shoe shop's window display where fake diamonds glistened on a pair of pastel-coloured sandals. I glanced at Surjit. Surely the pretty footwear didn't really appeal to her with her preference for black T-shirts, leggings and clunky boots?

'Me mum used to love these shoes,' she said in a small voice. 'She kept buying me pairs when the sales were on after the summer wedding season. Said I should dress like a girl. You know every time I walk past this shop it reminds me of me mum.'

'Do you miss her?' I asked, firmly blocking out any thought of my own mum.

'Yeah, course,' Surjit said, nodding. 'But not me dad though. He couldn't bear looking at me most times 'cause I weren't born a boy.'

I wasn't sure what to say to that, but I didn't want a gloomy silence to develop. 'So you were telling me about Nasreen.'

'Oh yeah, well, there are so many rumours. Some say she was abused by her father then married off and then beaten by her husband.'

'What?' I gasped.

'I don't know if it's true,' Surjit said quickly. 'There are other rumours too. She ran away from home to be with her white boyfriend. He tried to kill her so she had to escape him.'

I raised an eyebrow. 'Do you know the truth at all?'

Surjit seemed to think about it. 'I guess not. Anyway, whatever the truth is, she's safe and secure and that's what matters. That's what Aisha and Alice keep telling us.'

I nodded.

'What do you want to do tonight?' Surjit asked. 'Shall we get a DVD?'

'Up to you,' I said, looking around at the cars and buses thundering down the road. I didn't tell her that what I really wanted to do, standing in the middle of this chaotic inner-city area, was return to my hometown. I missed the familiarity and tranquillity of my Yorkshire streets where people acknowledged each other with smiles. Everything I knew was there, and Susan and . . . perhaps my parents too by now. I wondered. Would I ever be able to call it home again?

Chapter 30

The first week passed slowly and my nights were filled with a combination of relief about the past and fear for the future.

Tara had arranged for me to receive some state benefit. It wasn't much, but I managed to live on it. I bought a few clothes from the market and returned the items that had been loaned to me by Alice. I frugally saved the little money left over under my mattress.

Surjit's company helped. She always had something to talk about and although sometimes her constant babble did not register in my head the sound of her voice was reassuring. It didn't take long for the other women to welcome me into the fold. It was as if we were sisters in a special club. Surjit and I were the youngest there. Although none of us knew Nasreen's exact age, we thought she was in her twenties. She looked older to me – maybe her traumatic experience had aged her.

The first time I actually felt comfortable with the others was on a Saturday night watching *The X Factor*. Together we laughed, cringed and hollered at the TV screen as contestant after contestant appeared. For the last two years I'd watched this show with Susan. I missed my best friend more than ever. In Pakistan I'd been so consumed with my escape I could think of little else, but now back in England I wanted to see her more than anything. I wanted to ask her what she'd thought when I didn't return from my holiday, and if she'd got my email. I was desperate to know what my parents had told her. I doubted she would believe for one moment that I had decided to stay in Pakistan and marry a stranger.

I thought about getting in touch, but I was petrified that if I did my parents would be able to trace me. Everyone had told me in no uncertain terms not to contact anyone, and Alice had sat with me while I deleted all my emails without opening them, so no one could see I'd even had access. There were literally a hundred from Susan alone, which made me feel better even if I couldn't read them. Surjit had told me she was sure a private detective had been hired to find her. She said all the women in the centre lived in fear of the past catching up with them. As I'd reluctantly pressed 'delete', I'd decided that for the moment my safety would have to come first.

A week later I decided to log on to my email again and delete any new messages. Just seeing that people had tried to get in touch was enough to make me feel better, even if I didn't open them. I had been watching pop videos on YouTube, catching up with all the music I had missed in the last few months, and I felt happy and relaxed enough to do it. But as soon as I signed in to my account, one email caught my eye. It was from Nusrat-kala. Usually I would have deleted it, worried that someone was trying to pretend to be her, but in the subject line it simply said 'I want the world for you'.

These were the words Nannyma used when she'd said fare-well to Nusrat-kala when she moved to America. They were the words Nannyma had uttered to me when she had handed me over to the protection of strangers on the day of my henna ceremony. The words were like a secret code between me, Nannyma and Nusrat-kala, and my gut instinct told me that this email had to be genuine.

I opened the message with a pounding heart.

As *salaam alaikum*, my lovely Zeba,

Here's hoping you are well, my girl. Mom and I have been worried sick about you but we knew you were in good hands. I'm still in Pakistan. I'm staying at cousin Bilal's in Karachi at the moment and I just thought to email you about what's been going on.

After you left all hell kinda broke loose here. Your Taya-ji stormed over to Mom's house and threatened her with all sorts unless she gave details of where you were. Your parents were with him. Mom said she didn't know, which was the truth. They left after that, vowing never to set foot in her house again. That promise didn't last very long – they returned the next day, or at least your parents did. I'm sure you can guess why.

Asif had returned home after letting you go to demand what Taya-ji's plans were for him. Your dad explained that shortly after the marriage it was expected that you would both move to England. Your poor dad tried to convince Asif that he could run the grocery store for him. You can imagine Asif's horror at seeing such a future for himself. Of course he was having none of it and shouted at the top of his voice that he would never leave Pakistan. In turn your dad made it quite clear that you could not be expected to remain in Sindh. It was crazy. Your dad was still assuming that you would marry Asif. He seemed to believe that the issue was not about convincing you to marry, but rather to persuade Asif to move to England. To cut a long story short, Asif said he refused to marry you now that he knew the arrangement had been all about getting him to emigrate. There was no shifting him and he left for Islamabad the very same day.

Anyway, your Taya-ji then turned on your parents. He demanded that after the shame you had brought on the family, you needed to be publicly disowned. You'll be pleased to hear that your dad finally developed some backbone against his older brother. He said you were his daughter, his child, and he was not going to do anything of the kind. He publicly acknowledged that he had only agreed to the marriage arrangement because of Taya-ji's fears for Asif. He had wanted to help, but now that Asif had made it clear that he would not move to England the agreement was void. Hey presto, your parents were kicked out of Taya-ji's house! They stayed here at Mom's until their flight home was rearranged.

Since they got back your mum has been calling me desperate to find out where you are. They cannot locate you. Nighat says she's been crying to some friend of yours called Susan to get her to reveal where you are, but the kid insists she doesn't know anything. You might not want to hear this, Zeba, but Mom and I think you should get in touch with your parents. They just want to meet up and reassure themselves that you are all right. When the time is right perhaps you can also go home. I think you can trust them now.

I couldn't believe it. My parents wanted me to come home? After everything they had put me through, they thought they could just turn the clock back? Before I could think too much I pressed reply to the message and started typing:

Wa alaikum salaam, Nusrat-kala,

I am well and safe. Please don't worry about me. I am not ready to meet them, let alone go home to Mum and Dad.

Please respect that.

With much love

Zeba

Later that day Tara came to see me.

'Hey, I've got something you might be interested in.'

I looked up half-heartedly; she held out an A4 brown envelope.

'What is it?' I asked, fumbling with the opening. Of course I could have ripped it apart but for some reason I was afraid of what I would find. Finally I reached inside and pulled out two sheets of paper.

My breath caught in my throat. It was my GCSE results.

My eyes scanned the grades. I couldn't believe it: eight A-stars. Overwhelmed, I burst into tears.

'Hey, they can't be that bad,' Tara said hurriedly. 'And so what if they are – you can always resit and . . .' Her voice trailed off as her eyes stared down at the paper. Suddenly she exclaimed, 'What are you crying for, you silly girl! You've topped it.'

I cried even harder.

'Oh, you silly girl,' Tara beamed, reaching out to hug me. 'You should be proud. You are one very, very clever girl.'

I hiccupped against her shoulder. I didn't know why I was crying. I should have been happy. These results were what I had worked so hard for. Susan and I had slaved over revision charts and guides. My bedroom wall had been covered in notes to help me memorize maths formulae, French phrases and diagrams of the human heart. It had all been worth it, and yet somehow, looking at my surroundings and feeling the emptiness inside me, I couldn't help thinking that somehow it had not. I should have opened my results in front of my parents, not a charity worker, and they should have been proud of me.

Tara seemed to guess my thoughts. 'Hey, look, I'm not your family, but let me take you out to celebrate tonight,' she offered. 'It will be my treat. We'll take Surjit too.'

A feeling of shame immediately took over me. I had to be the most ungrateful human ever. Tara had gone to the trouble of getting my results, and now she was offering to take me out to celebrate. She had also just hugged me with genuine warmth and concern for my feelings – something I couldn't recall my mum ever doing. I nodded my head in agreement. 'That would be nice, thank you, Tara.'

'You know,' Tara said gently, 'it's OK to miss your parents and your home.'

'I don't,' I lied, not convincing either of us.

That evening Tara, Surjit, Nasreen and I tucked into a lavish Chinese meal.

Nasreen had been sitting by herself in the TV room when Tara had spotted her. Although Tara didn't work with her she had kindly invited her anyway. Nasreen never spoke a word, but seemed content to be with us, heartily eating every fish and vegetable dish that Tara offered. I thought Tara would treat the dinner like a counselling session, but she didn't.

Instead she spent the entire evening talking about her favourite Bollywood movies. Surjit, another film buff, joined in with her own list.

'What about your number one movie, Zeba?' Tara asked me.

I thought of the doomed dancer Umrao Jaan, and Sehar's pain over the heroine's unhappy ending. '*Pakeezah*,' I replied, ignoring the image of the beautiful Umrao in my mind and opting instead for the dancer whose dreams did come true. 'I loved how she got her happy ending.'

'Good choice,' Tara said. 'Into classics, are you?'

'Yes,' I mumbled. 'But it was a friend's favourite. She kept making me watch it again and again until I fell in love with it too.'

'Well, your friend's got good taste,' Tara laughed.

'Yes, Sehar had the best taste,' I said, biting my lip. I knew I had just turned a corner. This was the first time I had spoken Sehar's name out loud without bursting into tears.

Tara smiled at me and I could see something in her eyes. She had never known Sehar except for that rushed telephone conversation when she had urged her to escape. I wondered what Tara felt about my dead friend.

Unaware that a sensitive moment had just passed, Surjit moved the conversation on to her fascination with a certain actor's biceps. Once that topic was exhausted, Tara asked if I'd thought about her suggestion to go to college to do my A levels. I knew I should, but I just couldn't will myself to enrol at the local college. Tara, however, didn't let up. She bugged me about it and by the end of the meal I'd given in.

The next day Tara didn't let me forget, and she took me down to the college first thing to enrol. History, law, politics,

English . . . But within days I was glad that I had done it. Surjit, meanwhile, had enrolled in Year Eleven at a local school. She instantly made friends whereas I had none at my college. But that was how I wanted it. The textbooks were my escape from the boredom at the hostel, and the only friends I wanted were my old ones.

The emails from Nusrat-kala were constant and repetitive. She begged me to meet with my parents who were still searching for me. I couldn't understand why she was pushing this on me when she'd been instrumental in my escape. Surely she could understand that I couldn't just forgive them. After another email to tell her that I wasn't interested, I began to ignore her emails and delete them along with the rest.

I wasn't a fool.

Chapter 31

I was going to my first pop concert. Some of the other women at the hostel thought it was amazing that I was a sixteen-year-old who had never been to a music concert. I'd just shrugged, not bothering to explain the reason. My parents had never allowed it because they were convinced concerts were an epicentre for drugs, alcohol, boys and, above all, the ultimate in Muslim parental reasoning: what would people think of a young Asian girl allowed out past seven in the evening?

I was so excited. Susan had been going to concerts since we were fourteen and she always told me about how amazing the live performances were. I couldn't wait to experience it for myself. I was dressed up in black skinny jeans and a red sequinned top I had bought from the market after an agonizing deliberation. Surjit, on the other hand, went to the extreme with her gothic style: black lipstick and nail polish completed her black ensemble. Standing next to her, I was sure I looked like a disco queen.

The concert was incredible and I loved it, but going to sleep later that night I was struck by a bolt of guilt. My parents had been very clear about the rules I needed to follow. Until this bizarre marriage proposal with Asif had popped up, I'd led a carefree life within the boundaries set by my religion and culture. There were certain things that were not allowed: alcohol, drugs and boyfriends, but I was fine with that. I'd never wanted those things anyway. But what about the endless opportunities that were available to me now? I could come and go as I pleased. I could do whatever I wanted and nobody could stop me. But did I want to do all the things that I could?

I decided that just because I could didn't mean I had to. The only thing my parents would've disapproved of was the pop concert. Other than that, I was still behaving appropriately, and boys were the last thing on my mind after what I had just been through with Asif.

No, I thought, falling asleep, *those aunties will have nothing on me to gossip about at their weekly tea parties* . . . Well, apart from the fact that I had run away from my wedding. Actually, I didn't think the auntie-jis needed anything else. That bit of information was enough to last them a lifetime.

My nannyma was a woman of words. She also thought that the tragedy of the Muslim world was that there were neither enough writers nor enough readers. She asked me once when I was in Pakistan: what was more important, reading or writing? I answered that we needed to have writers in order to have material for readers.

'But if the writers thought there were more readers, Zeba, they would write more,' she'd pointed out.

Pushing my feet against the ground to sway the swing on

that lazy afternoon, I could not see what the fuss was about. 'Readers, writers, what does it matter?'

'It matters,' my nannyma had said, noting my dismissive expression, 'because written words articulate history, tradition and thoughts. Without the reflections of society captured by writers, we cannot learn about the past, we cannot make sense of the present and we cannot improve our future.'

So that was why my nannyma kept a diary, and that is why Nusrat-kala posted me a package: a hardback journal, written with dried black ink. She sent it from Pakistan to the Forced Marriage Unit in London, and through Tara they passed it on to me.

When it arrived, I held the precious item in my hands. I flicked through the pages lovingly, knowing it had belonged to my nannyma. I remembered sitting with her on the swing, watching her fountain pen scrape across the handmade paper as she drew the script of her language. I had never asked what she was writing. It had never occurred to me.

I raised the journal to my nose and breathed in the scent of my grandmother. It was her Lilies of the Valley talcum powder mixed with the aromatic smell of the cloves that always swam in her tea. Lowering the book, I turned the pages more slowly. The writing was in Urdu and I could not read it. But Nusrat-kala had included a letter for me in English, in which she had translated a part of Nannyma's diary, dated July.

Tuesday, 3pm

Zeba is sitting on the swing with me. I grow to love this girl more every day and it breaks my heart to think about what they will do to her. Of course what they have planned for her is nothing different from what has been planned for centuries for the girls born into these ancient parts of our land. But times have changed. She is not a product of her ancestors; she is not what her own mother is: a subordinate of the men surrounding her.

I see myself in Zeba when I was young. In the stubborn set of her chin, her flashing eyes when she is angry, passionate and even very rarely . . . happy. She has a mind of her own that cannot fathom the traditions of this village. And that is what the practices are: tradition, not religion.

The tradition of a father choosing his daughter's husband.

The tradition of marrying cousins to keep land and wealth within the family.

The tradition of a woman never voicing her own likes or dislikes – her own desires.

The tradition of this rural, feudal land has nothing in common with the modern world.

My heart aches for my Zeba and it literally cries when I see her friend Sehar. Sher Shah's family have been relentless in trying to break the spirit of this beautiful, bright young woman and I think they are not far off. How much more will she be able to take? Does her mother never wonder what is happening to her child? Does the same fate await my Zeba?

Sometimes I think women without daughters are the worst culprits against the daughters of others. They treat them so badly because karma cannot come back round to them. They will never shed tears knowing their own precious daughters are being abused. This invincibility strengthens the malice and spite in their hearts, eroding the compassion and love that should reign there.

My Zeba is my child now. She means more to me than she does to her own mother. Nighat is an empty shell, devoid of the protective instinct she should feel for her baby. So the task falls to me. I shall do what I can, but I do not have much hope. How to stop a man like Mustaq Khan is a matter that haunts my sleep. This charade is happening because he wants it. A British passport for his son now that the angel of death hovers a few paces behind the soldiers of our army. What has happened to our country? Suicide bombs in our cities placed there by our own citizens. The threat of an American invasion unless our army takes control of the growing insurgency. It is a daily worry for us all, but more so for the parents of a beloved son.

And Asif? The soldier, the hero, who is oblivious to his parents' concern about his welfare and even more ignorant about the reasons behind the choice of his bride. He is brave or foolish depending on perspective, but he will never leave Pakistan. He will never abandon his comrades to flee his homeland. And my Zeba. What will become of her? She will wither away in this village and before long she will become the young widow of a man she was forced to marry.

I spoke to her father before he left for the UK. I told him plainly what I thought and he listened quietly and then broke down in tears. He reminded me of the little boy he'd been all those years ago, constantly in the shadow of his older brother. Their father had been right to organize his younger son's passport and residency visa to the UK. He had wanted his youngest to build his own life, away from the intimidating older son. But this village hasn't changed over time. The people have grown older, but the power structures have not changed. My son-in-law is still as much in the shadow of Mustaq as he was when growing up. I know he does not want this marriage for Zeba. He is a man of words and dreams and he wanted more for his daughter, but he says his hands are tied. Obligations to the family must come first, he insists. I objected. No, I said. Your daughter is not a possession to give away. She has her own life, her own desires. She is not a lifeless doll. Would he be able to live with her unhappiness on his conscience? He replied that he would have to. After all, what choice did he really have? It was either to give Zeba up or to be banished from his family.

He has made his choice. It is slowly killing him to do this to his only child, but he is tied to helping his brother. But I am not tied by these male bonds of obligation. I have to do something. My Zeba cannot be the sacrifice to save Asif from his fate on the battlefield. I will find the right time to speak to the imam. I will appeal to him to intervene. I will beg him to make Mustaq Khan understand that a sin cannot be committed against this young child because of a father's fears for his son.

When I had finished reading, I wiped away the tears that were streaming down my face. Could I believe this and find a way to forgive my father?

The next day I felt strong enough to read the translation to Aisha during our private counselling session and she advised me to try to understand the significance of what my nannyma had written. Aisha said my dad had acted out of obligation rather than lack of love for me. It was important for me to understand that his love as a parent had always been there, but he had come under immense pressure – the kind that we might never comprehend – to do the bidding of his older brother. In a way my dad had also been oppressed by Taya-ji. It didn't mean that what he'd done was OK, but that things were never as simple as they seemed.

I listened to Aisha calmly, but the words echoed in my mind constantly.

Dad had acted out of obligation rather than lack of love for me.

Dad had acted out of obligation rather than lack of love for me.

Dad had acted out of obligation rather than lack of love for me.

Chapter 32

I felt safe now. My world moved along like clockwork. I studied, I ate and I slept. There was nobody telling me what to do. I could almost say I was my own person. I was independent . . . but I still wasn't happy.

Alice was up at the crack of dawn with me every day. While I moped around the kitchen, Alice would do stretches in preparation for her morning run.

One day she smiled at me and said, 'Why don't you come for a run with me instead of staring at the kitchen wall?'

'I don't think so,' I replied immediately.

'Oh, come on,' she said. 'It will do you the world of good.'

'I'm not sure I really want to.'

'Do you own a pair of trainers?'

'No.'

'Well, I've got a pair you can borrow. You look the same shoe size as me. Five? Yes?'

Alice disappeared out of the kitchen and returned with a pair of running shoes. I stared at her, slightly irritated. Did she not understand the meaning of the word no?

'Put these on,' she said, and when I refused to move, she

shrugged her shoulders and left. I looked down at the trainers lying on the floor. What was the big deal with running? I slipped my feet into the shoes and they fitted perfectly. Maybe it wouldn't hurt to venture out and get some exercise. I went upstairs and found some tracksuit bottoms and a T-shirt that would do to wear.

I did not run that morning. Power walking would've been a better description, but I enjoyed it. I ventured out as far as Tower Bridge, up through the streets to Aldgate, down the Minories and on to the blue bridge that featured on all the postcards.

I gazed at the Tower of London from the bridge. I couldn't believe I was actually looking at it. I'd always been fascinated with Tudor history: King Henry VIII and his wives. What was the rhyme about the fate of his wives again? *Divorced, beheaded, died, divorced, beheaded, survived*. What a psycho. My eyes darted between the towers. I wondered which one had imprisoned Anne Boleyn and Catherine Howard as they'd waited for their executions. I smiled slightly as I imagined Sher Shah in the garb of Henry VIII – two peas in a pod when it came to power and control.

The River Thames ran beneath the bridge. On the one side was the Tower and on the other a twenty-first-century building, City Hall; the London mayor's power house. I marvelled at the contrast between these two buildings – one representing modern democracy, the other a symbol of the feudalism that had prevailed in England for centuries before real democracy had been born. A time of landlords and peasants – much like the village in Sindh.

I thought about Sehar. She had never been to college, but occasionally she exhibited wisdom that far exceeded her age.

I remembered one day at Nannyma's house she had argued that poor people couldn't be elected to a parliamentary seat.

'Pakistan's democracy isn't like Western democracy where anyone can rise to the top,' she had said. 'Power here is concentrated with the super rich and they won't allow their privileges to be watered down.'

'I would have to agree with you.' Nannyma had nodded. 'But how do you think they keep their power?'

'By denying education to the masses,' Sehar had replied. 'People can't ask for rights they don't know about. How many people are illiterate in this country?'

'Too many,' Nannyma had said quietly. 'But landlords like Mohammad Ali Sahib do their best. They serve the people who live on their land. They pay them good wages and set up charity schools for their workers' children. There are good people and bad people in the world. You should know that.'

As I walked back to the hostel I thought about what Nannyma had said: *There are good people and bad people in the world.* Was my father really one of the bad people?

As the days passed I started to run more regularly. I ventured out from the streets of Whitechapel and Aldgate to run along the Embankment beside the Thames. Running made me forget everything. I just focused on putting one foot in front of the other and pushing my body further and further.

'Don't you get lonely running by yourself?' Surjit asked.

'No,' I replied honestly. 'I don't feel lonely. I feel free. My mind only thinks about what it is doing right there and then.' I didn't add that I found it liberating not to have to think of my past, present or future.

*

Ramadan began and I was determined to stick to it, which meant no food or drink between sunrise and sunset. I had observed the fasts since I was thirteen and just because I wasn't at home didn't mean I could ignore my faith. It was a little hard to get up pre-dawn for the *sehri* meal. At home Mum would prepare a breakfast of potato pancakes and masala tea. I'd never given much thought to how she'd worked hard at laying the breakfast table for me and Dad. She must have got up much earlier to get the food prepared. I felt a pang of guilt when I realized that I'd never appreciated or thanked her. My own preparations for *sehri* consisted of a few dates I'd bought from one of the many Bangladeshi stalls in the market, and a glass of cold milk. It wasn't much but it got me through the day.

I could have done with sharing Ramadan with another Muslim, but Nasreen had been moved to another part of the country for her own safety just as it began. Yet again we knew nothing of the details, but I was slowly learning that life was going to be like that in the hostel. Not everyone wanted to, or could, share their experiences. I never did manage to exchange any words with her, but she'd hugged me tightly on the day she'd left, her eyes wide and fearful. I hoped that wherever she was going she was safe from the people who wanted to harm her.

One Monday during Ramadan I was returning from college and my stomach was protesting loudly at the lack of food, making me feel lethargic. I couldn't wait to get to my room and have a lie-down for a couple of hours. The back streets I walked through were quiet at this time of day. The bustling crowd and noise from the high street was only a few blocks away, but these streets were deserted. Walking back from college on some days, my overactive imagination had wandered back a hundred years to the time when Jack the Ripper had terrorized these very roads and alleys. Then my reverie was shattered.

'Help! Help!' An old Bangladeshi man was yelling.

I looked up. He was about a hundred yards from me, hopping around in panic. What was wrong with him? He didn't look injured. A woman opened her front door and peered out. A toddler was clinging to her legs.

'What's wrong?' she called.

'Someone stabbed! Someone stabbed!' the old man yelled. And he pointed down the road. I could just see a crumpled heap on the ground.

The woman picked up her baby and ran back in her house, slamming the front door.

'Help!' the old man yelled again.

The woman's front door opened again and she ran out, a phone clutched to her ear. 'Ambulance! Ambulance!' she was saying.

More doors opened and people emerged looking curious and concerned. They were all Bangladeshi. I found myself drawn closer to the crowd gathering round the shape on the ground and noticed that their curious expressions had been replaced with horror. Who was it who had been stabbed? It was morbid, I knew that, but I felt the need to see for myself the person who had been stabbed. For a moment I worried that I would know them, that it might be someone from the hostel.

My breath caught in my throat as I stared down at the unconscious man. Blood stained his top and someone was holding a towel to his waist, trying to stem the flow. He couldn't have been more than twenty years old and I stared fascinated at his deathly pale face until someone pushed me back. I kept think-ing of Habib, who came to our counselling sessions. For some reason I imagined him being stalked through the streets by his family and stabbed in broad daylight.

'Let the paramedics through,' a voice yelled, breaking my trance.

I turned and walked away. There was no need for me to hang around, and suddenly I wanted to be inside the safe, secure walls of the hostel more than ever before.

Chapter 33

In the third week of Ramadan, my carefully constructed world turned upside down again.

Nusrat-kala's email popped up on the computer screen in the college library, entitled: *Nannyma*. Worried that something was wrong, I opened it. The message was short.

> Dearest Zeba
>
>   My mom's going over to England for Eid.
>
>   Hope you'll take the time to see her.
>
> Love
>
> NK

My nannyma was coming? Why was she coming? She'd never visited England before.

That evening after breaking my fast, I called Tara and explained my dilemma over Nannyma. She told me not to worry and to take my time over my decision. But no matter how hard I tried to, it was impossible. My nannyma was one of the few family members I would gladly have seen.

When the Eid festival to mark the end of Ramadan arrived,

I got dressed in my specially chosen new clothes and walked to the enormous East London mosque to offer my prayers. Groups of women, many with children, smiled and welcomed me with '*salaam*'. I smiled back and went to take my position in the line of prayer. We prayed as one, following the lead of the imam from the men's section, and then it ended and everybody was hugging each other and exchanging joyous '*Eid Mubaraks*'.

My thoughts flew to the Eids of my childhood. My dad had always insisted on hugging everyone outside the small mosque in our town. It was the one occasion when my famously reserved mum reached out to tentatively pat the shoulders of other women.

Somebody hugged me and moved on and I stood there, consciously looking around at these people who all seemed to know each other. A few minutes later it was over and women and girls swarmed out of the mosque to head for homes filled with families and feasts. I remained behind on my own. I had nowhere to go. I sat down to absorb the tranquillity of the mosque and tried to blank out the fact that, despite everything, I missed my mum and dad. It didn't work; the empty space between the four walls just emphasized how alone I felt. Craving company instead, I walked out of the mosque and into the crowds still mingling outside. I crossed the road to head back to the hostel when someone called out my name. It was Habib.

I had got to know him at the weekly meetings and we had become quite friendly. Habib was one of those people who could charm anyone, and even Aisha was extremely fond of him despite his constant badgering at her to do more to help young men who were also being forced to marry.

'*Eid Mubarak*,' he said, walking up to me.

'And to you,' I replied shyly.

'Where are you heading?'

'Back to the hostel.'

He nodded and then asked, 'Do you want to grab a bite to eat? I mean Eid's about having a feast, ain't it? It'll be my treat, kiddo.'

I hesitated. Go for a meal with a boy? Years of being told that I must never be seen out alone with a boy made me think twice and it didn't matter that I was hundreds of miles away from home. The busybody aunties were not here to see me and pass judgement, but still I hesitated and Habib guessed my reaction.

'Chill, girl,' he said with a smile. 'I'm not taking you out on a date. We're just two lost, abandoned souls looking for a friend to share an Eid meal.'

Habib was right and I nodded my head in agreement. We fell into step and headed for Brick Lane, otherwise known as London's Curry Mile.

'You look kinda sad,' Habib observed, when we were seated at our table in a small restaurant.

I managed a forced smile. 'Do I?'

'Yeah, you do. What is it? You missing home or something?'

I wanted to deny it in order to look strong and independent, but my quivering lips gave me away.

'Hey,' Habib said in a concerned voice. 'Don't be down. It's Eid.' He laughed. 'You're commanded to be happy today by God.'

I shrugged my shoulders feebly. 'Yes, I do miss home. I actually miss my mum and dad.'

'That's natural,' Habib reassured me. 'Course it is. You wouldn't be normal if you didn't miss your parents. Do you know I read somewhere that most suicides are committed during Christmas?'

I stared at Habib. Was this his way of trying to cheer me up? I think he noted my startled expression because he quickly rushed to justify what he had said.

'What I mean . . . right . . . is that Eid is like that. It's about family and you're missing them and that's quite normal and . . .' He trailed off and I burst out laughing. 'I'm not doing a very good job of explaining my point, am I?' he said, grinning.

Our food arrived and we picked up our forks to dig in.

'Anyway, listen, kiddo,' Habib said through a mouthful of rice. 'Tell me everything. I've got a good pair of ears. Maybe I can advise you.'

I sighed. It was about time I told someone the whole story, and I actually felt like I could do it without bursting into tears. So I didn't hold back and told Habib everything – from what happened to Sehar to how I was feeling today. It was a huge weight off my shoulders, like confiding in an older brother.

'So basically,' Habib said, now devouring a huge bowl of ice cream, 'you wanna go home and yet you feel like you need to punish your parents for not putting you first.'

I couldn't believe his bluntness. 'Well, I . . . I . . .'

'Do you know something,' he continued. 'A saying just occurred to me. There are those who cut off their nose to spite their own face. It applies to you, innit. You have no idea how lucky you are. You get to go home on your own terms; unlike some of us whose parents would rather we were dead because we ran away.'

'Your mum wants you dead?' I repeated.

Habib put down his spoon and sat back in his chair. 'Yeah,' he said in a voice tinged with sadness. 'When Ramadan started, I felt this urge to call her . . . to hear her voice. I dunno why I did it, but it felt right. I went to the sermon on the first Friday fast and the imam's sermon was all about how the best Muslim is the one who is a good person and who forgives others. I wanted to forgive my mum for being mean to me, and for trying to force me . . . and . . .'

'So you rang?' I asked, when he fell silent.

'Yeah, I rang,' he shrugged. 'But she was brief with me, innit. Said I was dead to her and if I wanted to make amends I would have to marry her niece, who is still looking for a husband. She said it was the only way she could regain her honour with her family back in Pakistan.'

'Oh,' was all I could manage.

'It's all right,' Habib said, picking up his spoon. 'I was upset at first, but you know I got my friends . . . and, well, I'm happier now than I would be if I'd married my cousin . . .'

I just stared at Habib as he trailed off again. I felt sorry for him for him, and yet I knew he was happier here alone than he would be with his mum and a forced wife. I thought about what he had said to me about cutting off my nose to spite my face. Was it true? Did it apply to me? The two people I trusted most in the world, Nannyma and Nusrat-kala, were advising me that my parents wanted me back, yet I was caught in a self-inflicted bubble that kept them at bay.

Suddenly I found myself sobbing, tears streaming down my face. Sitting there in the restaurant, I finally accepted that I needed to go home.

Two days after Eid, Tara and I walked into the cafe and sat down. Nannyma had arrived in England a few days before and celebrated with my parents up north.

Now, my parents and Nannyma walked in slowly. I stared at them and they returned the scrutiny. My nannyma looked the same; serene with silver hair scraped back in a bun and a shawl arranged on her head to frame her face. My mum looked thinner than I remembered with dark circles under her eyes. And my father . . . Dad looked like he'd aged ten years since I'd last seen him. Deep lines zigzagged all over his face. Had my disappearance done that to him?

'*As salaam alaikum*, my dear Zeba,' Nannyma said.

I whispered a response, unable to raise my voice. My parents didn't utter a word.

'Why don't you take a seat,' Tara offered.

They sat down and silence followed until it was broken by Nannyma.

'How are you, my child?' she asked.

'Better than I was in Pakistan,' I replied.

My dad flinched and Nannyma said, 'We are here to take you home, my *beti*. But first your parents must convince you that they have changed. They want you to know that you come first in their lives.'

I nodded slowly. What should I say? Who was going to go first? I thought about the questions I had written down last night. What were they again? I couldn't remember a single one. My fingers touched the paper in my pocket. Perhaps I should just take it out and read aloud the questions? But I didn't get the chance because my dad spoke up.

'Zeba, things have changed. We just want you with us where you belong.'

'I'm not getting married to Asif,' I blurted out.

'We don't want you to either,' my dad replied.

'I don't want to get married for a long while yet, and, when I do, I want it to be someone I choose. Someone from this country if I want . . . a Muslim . . . but maybe British . . . Just whoever I fall in love with.'

My dad nodded and I stared at him doubtfully because this all seemed too easy.

'How do I know you won't back down on your promise?' I asked.

'You have to trust us.' My mum spoke for the first time.

I looked her directly in the eyes. 'What if I can't trust you? What if I don't believe you?'

'We lost you once, Zeba *beti*,' my dad said. 'We won't risk losing you again.'

One of the questions from my list popped into my head and I blurted it out before I forgot. 'People from the community will have talked about me, gossiped about me. If I come home, they will gossip even more. Can you deal with that?'

The question was directed at Mum, but it was Dad who answered.

'You think I care what people say? Maybe I would have cared before . . . before I knew what it was like to wake up every day and not know if I would ever see you again. I wouldn't wish that on any father . . .' There was a pause and then: 'And you think I care what people will say?'

I listened to Dad, but my eyes never left Mum. I needed her to confirm what Dad was saying. Nannyma and Dad were silent as they waited for Mum to speak. She finally did.

'You are my child. You need to be safe at home with me. That is all that matters.'

I believed her because that was what my dad wanted and my mum always wanted what he wanted. She was his shadow, to agree always and to never contradict. It struck me then that I believed my dad. How had I persuaded myself so suddenly? At what stage had I convinced myself that he would put my happiness first? Perhaps it was my nannyma's presence that did it. After all, she had been witness to everything that had happened and I didn't think she would have sat calmly, waiting for me to agree to go home, had she not believed that my parents had changed.

'I've started my A levels already,' I said. Why did I say that? I wasn't sure.

'You can transfer to the college at home,' Dad said. 'It has only been a few weeks. You are a clever girl and you will have no problems making the switch. I'm sure they teach the same courses all over the country.'

I nodded. So what now?

My nannyma spoke, her eyes looking clearly into mine: 'Are you coming home, Zeba?'

I glanced at Tara beside me. She gave me a reassuring look as if to say 'up to you'. I felt ready. I wanted to go home.

'OK,' I replied.

Chapter 34

I said goodbye to my friends at the refuge and they all wished me well. Habib was not around to say bye so I left him a thank-you note.

I hugged Surjit and Alice, and I saved Tara for last. I hugged her tightly because I wanted her to know how grateful I was for everything she had done for me. I knew the lump in my throat would prevent me from forming the words, but she seemed to understand. Despite being tearful herself, she told me I was one of the lucky ones. I promised to keep in touch with her; she was one of my saviours just like Sehar, Nannyma, Nusrat-kala, Saima and Damian.

The journey home was a little tense; Dad tried telling jokes, but kept messing up the punchlines so nobody knew when to laugh. Nannyma kept smiling and Mum kept turning round in the car to look at me every few minutes all the way home to Yorkshire. Months had passed since I had left with my innocent belief that I would return within a few weeks. It felt strange to think I would see my old home again after feeling that I would never be able to return.

When the car pulled into our driveway, I gazed at the house.

Nothing about it looked different and I decided there and then that I would not look for changes either.

We entered the house and Susan ran in through the front door before Dad had a chance to close it. She grabbed me in a fierce hug and began crying.

'I thought I was never going to see you again,' she wailed.

It was weird but Susan's sobs triggered something in my dad and he broke down in tears right there in our hallway. For the first time in my life I saw my dad cry. He cried quite unashamedly as my mum joined him by dabbing delicately at her eyes with a handkerchief. My nannyma just looked on, her serene face giving the impression that this was necessary.

My dad's emotional waterfall succeeded in quieting Susan; she stopped crying and stepped aside as if she was intruding on a private moment. I took a step towards Dad and he enveloped me in his arms.

He cried and I cried too and he said sorry over and over again. I knew then that we, as a family, had turned a corner.

Nannyma stayed with us for three weeks before insisting on returning home. The summer months were long over and the cold had returned to Yorkshire. Nannyma spent most of her time huddled in an armchair in front of the gas fire or cocooned in her bed with the electric blanket on. She promised to return, but for now she longed for her swing on the veranda.

I think if she were worried for me then Nannyma would have braved the cold for my sake. But there really was no need. Things really did seem to be normal. Dad was busy with his shop and Mum and Nannyma spent the days together. Their relationship wasn't as close as Nannyma and Nusrat-kala's, but it was now as close as they could be while my mum refused to shed her reserve. Nannyma seemed content.

I joined the local college to continue my A levels. Susan was studying there too. She had also done well in her GCSEs and in the daytime she and I were inseparable again. Every lunchtime we made our way to the town centre to munch our way through Mrs Smith's chips, just like old times.

There had been some change in Susan's life. She now had a boyfriend. James was a year older than us and training as an apprentice at a local car garage. She'd met him at a music festival while I had been in Pakistan. James had been very keen to meet me and I'd liked him in return. Barely five minutes had passed since our introduction and he'd launched into a tale of how Susan had been beside herself when she'd received my scary email. He had gone with her to meet our old headmistress, Miss Neptune, who had dismissed my claims as the result of an overactive imagination.

'You should have seen her,' said James, nodding his head towards Susan. 'She went nuts saying how you wouldn't play games like that. In the end they made us leave.'

Susan shrugged at the memory. 'I believed you,' was all she said, and I squeezed her hand.

When I'd mentioned this to Tara in one of my emails, she had immediately sent the headmistress a large envelope of literature about forced marriages, and a charming letter about the need to educate head teachers on 'very real child-protection issues', which made me smile.

My biggest fear had been the local community, but my parents shielded me from the gossipy aunties. Even when they came to bid farewell to Nannyma on the eve of her flight, nobody gave me a second look. It was as if the Pakistan summer trip and everything after it had never happened.

At the airport when Nannyma said her goodbyes, I promised to visit her soon, but I knew in my heart that I would not set foot in that country for a long time. There were just too many bad memories. I think my nannyma knew that my words were empty because she kissed my forehead and said she would come to visit me in the summer.

'Perhaps the pair of us might travel together to America to visit Nusrat-kala?' she suggested with a twinkle in her eye. 'Her baby will have arrived by then.'

That was the first I'd heard about Nusrat-kala's pregnancy. I nodded with excitement at the prospect, and gave her one final hug.

A few weeks after Nannyma returned to Pakistan, Asif married an army general's daughter from Islamabad.

My dad told me over dinner one evening, but didn't really bother with the details. He'd been cut off from his own family and although sometimes I caught him staring into space with a thoughtful expression, his eyes lit up whenever he saw me.

Mum told me later as we were washing up that Imran-chacha had passed the news to Dad. The old retired soldier had returned to Pakistan to attend the wedding. I didn't bother to mention that I already knew all this through Farhat.

My friend still popped in to see Nannyma and Husna-bhaji on the veranda and I called every so often to speak with them using an international phone card. The last time we spoke, Farhat told me that Asif's wife, Samia, was both very beautiful and modern – she didn't cover her hair in front of older men.

I could tell Farhat was in awe of this girl, and not because she was from a rich family in Islamabad, but due to the fact that she'd been educated at a London university and owned a flat behind the famous shop Harrod's.

'Samia want to move to London,' said Farhat. 'Taya-ji and Mariam-chachi, they like this idea, but not Asif. They having many arguments.'

I felt sorry for Taya-ji and Mariam-chachi, as well as Samia. All they wanted to do was protect Asif, but I knew that they would not succeed. All Asif wanted to do was serve the country he loved, and he would probably die trying.

To my sadness that day arrived sooner than we expected, just a few weeks after I'd heard about his marriage. We got the call from Nannyma one morning. A bomb had exploded outside an army barracks in the NWFP. A handful of civilians and over thirty soldiers were killed. Asif was one of them. Taya-ji and Mariam-chachi's nightmare had come true. The violence in their country had claimed their son's life.

Nannyma told Dad that Taya-ji had left immediately to claim Asif's body. Mariam-chachi had been sedated by a doctor because she couldn't stop screaming. The whole village was in mourning. The army son who had promised to guard them all had met an early death.

Dad asked if he should travel to Pakistan for the funeral, but Nannyma advised him against it.

'You will not be welcome,' she said. 'Grief looks for someone to blame and you will become the scapegoat.' Even she had been refused entry to Taya-ji's house for helping me escape.

When Dad hung up the phone, he collapsed into a chair and buried his head in his hands. My mum patted his arm awkwardly as I stood frozen on the spot. The guilt seeped slowly into my veins like ice as my mind screamed: *Would this have happened if I had married Asif? Did my dad believe this too?*

But he didn't. He looked up at me from his chair and said in a determined voice, 'I am mourning the death of my nephew and you should mourn him as your cousin. But I don't want you to feel guilty. None of us will feel guilty about his death. Even if you had married him and convinced him to move here, he would have returned there in the end. Just as you insist this country is yours, so Pakistan was his. The death of all living creatures is written. Fate would have dragged him back to the spot where he was killed because it was his destiny.'

I ran to my dad and we cried together, both for what we had lost, and what we had gained.

Twelve months later I found myself writing a Facebook message to Farhat in English on my BlackBerry. Nusrat-kala had sent a laptop for Nannyma from Chicago as soon as her baby son had been born. She'd also arranged for an engineer from Karachi to set up an internet connection as Nusrat-kala wanted to share all her photos and updates on baby Umair. Sher Shah's house was now no longer the only place in the village that had a computer and internet connection. Farhat was still a regular visitor to Nannyma and together they were Facebook addicts, pouring over photos and messages on Nannyma's account. Nannyma also told me that the water women insist on seeing all of baby Umair's photos every time they are posted online. Farhat was of course still illiterate, but Nannyma acted as the translator between us friends.

Hey Fatty

Guess what. I've just been to see Sehar's son! Thanks for finding out Shabana's parents' phone number. They passed on Sehar's mum's contact details to me. I have to admit I didn't think Sehar's mum would agree to my request to see Ishfaq. But she did! She looked sad when she invited me and my parents to sit in her living room. Actually she kept staring at me and saying, 'I'm so glad Sehar made a friend in Pakistan.' I think she's still grieving for her daughter, but baby Ishfaq keeps her busy.

Fatty, he is gorgeous. Did you see the pictures I've posted of him? Don't you think he looks just like his mum? Even got that expression that she had when she disliked something – you know when she used to wrinkle her nose and pull her forehead down. And I can't wait to see pictures of your baby when he or she is born. You must be fat and round by now. Make sure you get Abdullah to take plenty of photos. Remember to ask my nannyma for Nusrat-kala's camera. It's digital. She won't mind you borrowing it. Once you've taken the pictures, give the camera to Nannyma and she will upload them on to Facebook.

Oh, and great news about Husna-bhaji marrying the widower in Sahib Mohammad's village. Ambreen-bhaji told me on the phone that Husna-bhaji's really happy. She deserves a happy ending.

I'll write again soon. Feel a bit nauseous writing while Dad is driving.

Love you.

Zeba xx

I sat back in my dad's car and felt content. My parents and I were on our way home on the motorway. I should have really been at home revising for my winter exams, but the opportunity to see Ishfaq could not be missed. I still missed Sehar. One day I will tell Ishfaq what a wonderful person his mum was. I will describe her as the lifebelt that kept me afloat. He should know that about the mother he never had the opportunity to meet. I think I owe her that much.

Author's Note

A **forced marriage** is one in which an individual, or both individuals, do not wish to marry the other. The Universal Declaration of Human Rights states that: *Marriage shall be entered into only with the free and full consent of the intending spouses.* A forced marriage is forbidden in all religions and is illegal in many countries.

An **arranged marriage** is one in which the two people are introduced to each other through traditional methods, and is a marriage that both individuals enter willingly. The tradition of arranged marriages has operated successfully within many communities and countries for a very long time.

Acknowledgements

I would like to thank the Forced Marriage Unit at the Foreign Office for all their feedback and guidance. Anyone wishing to find out more about the wonderful and much needed service of the FMU can go to their website: www.fco.gov.uk/forcedmarriage

Thank you Abu Fatima, Sabiha Chohan, Zainub Chohan and Anisa Patel for agreeing to read the early drafts and for sticking to that promise. You all contributed to the development of the story in your own unique ways, and for that I am grateful. A mention also to Irfan Akram, Soriya Siddique and Irfan Shah.

And, lastly, thank you to my editor, Shannon Park, for the invaluable advice from the beginning to the end.

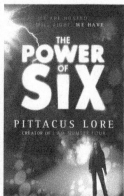
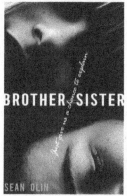

Bright and shiny and sizzling with fun stuff . . .

puffin.co.uk

WEB CHAT

Discover something new
EVERY month – books, competitions
and treats galore

WEB NEWS

The **Puffin Blog** is packed with posts and photos from
Puffin HQ and special guest bloggers. You can also sign up
to our monthly newsletter **Puffin Beak Speak**

WEB FUN

Take a sneaky peek around your favourite **author's studio**,
tune in to the **podcast, download activities** and much more

WEBBED FEET

(Puffins have funny little feet and
brightly coloured beaks)

PUFFIN MODERN CLASSICS
THE BEST WRITING FOR CHILDREN

The best books grow old gracefully. They retain their importance and affect each new generation as powerfully as the one before. These are the titles selected for Puffin Modern Classics. Don't miss them.

Julia Eccleshare

NINA BAWDEN

CARRIE'S *War*

PUFFIN MODERN CLASSICS
Everyone's favourite stories

A poignant wartime story in which Carrie and Nick are evacuated to the Welsh countryside to live with the very strict Mr Evans.

Everyone's favourite stories

MILDRED D. TAYLOR

Roll of
THUNDER,
Hear My Cry

An unforgettable classic about growing up in Mississippi in the 1930s.

PUFFIN MODERN CLASSICS
Everyone's favourite stories

It all started with a Scarecrow.

Puffin is seventy years old.
Sounds ancient, doesn't it? But Puffin has never been
so lively. We're always on the lookout for the next big
idea, which is how it began all those years ago.

Penguin Books was a big idea from the mind of
a man called Allen Lane, who in 1935 invented
the quality paperback and changed the world.
**And from great Penguins, great Puffins grew,
changing the face of children's books forever.**

The first four Puffin Picture Books were hatched in 1940 and the
first Puffin story book featured a man with broomstick arms called
Worzel Gummidge. In 1967 Kaye Webb, Puffin Editor, started the
Puffin Club, promising to **'make children into readers'**.
She kept that promise and over 200,000 children became
devoted Puffineers through their quarterly instalments of
Puffin Post, which is now back for a new generation.

Many years from now, we hope you'll look back and
remember Puffin with a smile. **No matter what your age
or what you're into, there's a Puffin for everyone.**
The possibilities are endless, but one thing is for sure:
whether it's a picture book or a paperback, a sticker book
or a hardback, **if it's got that little Puffin
on it – it's bound to be good.**